THE
SPECTRAL
ISLAND

THE SPECTRAL ISLAND

STEPHEN DE BURGES

Matador
Unit E2 Airfield Business Park,
Harrison Road, Market Harborough,
Leicestershire. LE16 7UL
Tel: 0116 2792299
Email: books@troubador.co.uk
Web: www.troubador.co.uk/matador
Twitter: @matadorbooks

ISBN 978 1800463 868

British Library Cataloguing in Publication Data.
A catalogue record for this book is available from the British Library.

Printed and bound in Great Britain by 4edge Limited
Typeset in 11pt Adobe Caslon Pro by Troubador Publishing Ltd, Leicester, UK

Matador is an imprint of Troubador Publishing Ltd

CONTENTS

PART ONE
LEADLINE OUT

ARM-TWIST

Late Friday morning, and the rain was an unrelenting drum roll. One could imagine being in the tropics were it not for the temperature, which was hovering a whisker above zero.

'Telephone!' Martha shouted through from the hall.

He closed his eyes. 'Can't you deal with it?' he muttered, then aloud, 'coming, dear. One sec.' He put the camera lens he was cleaning gently down, convex surface upwards, and went out into the hallway.

'Who?' He mouthed the word. He always liked that half-second to prepare himself.

She already had her hand over the mouthpiece; he was so predictable. 'How on earth should *I* know? He won't tell me who he is. It sounds very much like one of your funnies to me, and he's pressing. Just remember, nowhere until after Christmas.'

'I know, dear. I know. The phone... thank you. Yes? Christopher Jamieson. Can I help you?'

'Good morning, Dr Jamieson. George here.' The voice was lugubrious and slightly nasalised. 'I don't believe we've met. I'm a member of the Security Services Liaison Committee. There's a little survey job we'd like done out in Ziaŵala. I'm ringing to ask you to take it on for us.'

'Ziaŵala? I've been there before… Yes, I might be interested. It depends on when.'

'Has to be before Christmas, but it's only a four- or five-day thing. Our problem is that we—'

'Sorry to interrupt, George. Stop there. Before Christmas is out, I'm afraid. I've endless family commitments.'

'Ahhh! I understand. Me, too. The festive season is always difficult. Look, can you give me a moment? I'd just like to consult my colleagues here. There may be a solution.'

'Of course.'

Chris pressed his face against the window. He could feel the cold and was certain he could smell the rain. He peered out at the trees along the edge of the patio. They were constantly shifting their shapes through the rivulets of water running down the glass. The patio itself was a bubbling, broiling grey expanse. He pushed the receiver up against his ear and could hear voices in the background, mixed male and female. They sounded quite animated. He couldn't make out what was being said.

Then George was back. 'Dr Jamieson, it's me. We think it should be possible to change the timing. We also want you to know that the Director of GCHQ himself made a particular point in our liaison meeting earlier today of identifying you for the job.'

'Director? You mean, James Burnett?'

'Exactly so. It seems you have the right skills. He also said to tell you that this one is very important, and that you'd find it particularly interesting.'

'I see. Well, if you can reschedule, then you had better tell me what this thing is about.'

'Ahhh! Right, and I wish I *could* tell you. But to be honest, at this stage we don't know much about it ourselves. We do have a meeting of our small working party on Monday, though. We'll definitely know more then. Perhaps you could come and join us.'

•

The meeting was in an annexe to a faceless building, just back from The Mall. At the desk, a bored-looking, middle-aged man glanced at Chris's passport, checked the meetings list, grunted and passed him a name tag. Further along the desk, a heavily built woman, who'd been watching proceedings through half-closed eyes, heaved herself to her feet and came over. She took his backpack from him, plunged a gloved hand into it, rummaged around, and then passed it back to him as he came through the turnstile. She flicked her head to the right and led him along a carpeted corridor and through a security gate into an alcove at the far end, where she deposited him outside 12a. She pointed at the door and, without saying a word, turned and wandered back along the corridor.

He shrugged… *must be the job*, he thought. He knocked on the door. It was a restrained, deferential knock. He wanted to put whoever was in there on the back foot. There was no response, though. He eased the door open a little and peered through the gap. He could see three people on the far side of the room, two men and a woman, their backs towards him. They were standing round a desk pushed up against a wall below a tall, Georgian window framed by red velvet curtains. He coughed, and again, this time louder.

One of the men swivelled around. 'Ahh! Yes, our Dr Jamieson. Good morning. Please come in. Sorry. We didn't hear you.' The man creaked across the room on the polished floorboards and thrust a warm, damp hand at him. 'I'm George. We spoke on the phone. Come on over... meet Freddy, here; he's from Century House. And this is Mavis; she and I are GCHQ. Coffee's on the way, but before we sit down and talk, perhaps you could have a quick look at these satellite thingies.'

He pointed at three A3 satellite photographs on the desk. One appeared to be of an island, elongated and hourglass-shaped, with a narrow isthmus about a third of the way up. The other two were close-ups of building sites.

'Mavis, perhaps you could start us off,' George continued.

Chris noticed the woman's finely sculpted fingers twitch into life and a faint smile flick across her face.

'Of course. First, can I start with an apology, Dr Jamieson? I'll have to be very brief. I have to slip out in a moment or two. I have a scheduled video-conferencing session with Cheltenham, so just a brief word. These are satellite photos taken last week by our Indian Ocean communications satellite. This first is of one of the larger offshore islands of Ziaŵala and these others are close-ups of two construction sites on the place... one in the north, here, and the other in the south, here. As you can see, each site has some half-built stuff and a single, large building. It looks like it's aeroplane-hangar size. Both sites started life as a secondary boarding school project funded by some Arab Islamic charitable organisation. We're told the money ran out and the project had to be abandoned. That was May last. A few weeks ago, though, things started happening there that we don't understand.' She glanced at her watch. 'Ooops! I must stop and leave you in the capable hands of my colleagues. George, Freddy, over to you now. We'll speak later, Dr Jamieson.'

•

Over the years, Chris Jamieson had dealt with many security agency people, with their superior, faintly mocking half-smiles. Usually, they'd be reclining behind big desks in oak-panelled offices, the Queen on the wall to their backs seemingly bestowing trust on them and lending weight and veracity to their stories. From experience, though, he knew they actually spent much of their time making bland assertions, which were either empty-headed exaggerations, or genuine lies. These two, he'd already sensed, would be no different. They'd be neither morally nor professionally constrained by issues of truth and honesty – that, after all, was their training – and any information they gave him would be liberally laced with concealment and sleight-of-hand. It would be flying-pigs stuff, something Chris Jamieson had long been resigned to in the work he did.

George made the first move. 'Freddy, I'm rather closer to this business than you. I suggest I take the lead. Of course, if I start screwing up, just chip in and get me back onto the straight and narrow. Anyway, where do we start? July, I suppose.'

In July, a note from the embassy in Beijing had surfaced in the FCO. A Chinese informant had told his embassy controller that China's Central Committee had learned that a small group of Middle Eastern men was conducting a covert assessment of gold deposits on an island in the Indian Ocean. It seems that the Committee became concerned that there might be politically motivated flooding of the world gold-market, with serious consequences for the yuan and the US dollar.

At first, the FCO hadn't thought much of it and the Indian Ocean desk officer had parked the matter and dropped the embassy note into the Africa FiU, the Forget-it-Unless, tray.

It wasn't there for long. A week later, the British Embassy in Yemen acquired photographs of four men arriving at Sana'a airport on the same day, one from Damascus, one from Basra, two from Tehran. The men had disappeared into the city and two days later surfaced as a group in Mukalla, where they boarded a powered dhow and travelled to Socotra, off the Yemeni coast, and then south to the island of Ivundé. They'd settled into the island's only hotel and the next day had crossed to the mainland and presented their documents at the Ministry of Foreign Relations. Their papers stated they were technical aid staff assigned to the task of reviving the schools project on Ivundé.

An examination of the Sana'a airport photographs revealed that while the Iraqi, the Syrian and one of the Iranians were not known to the British Security Services, the other Iranian was. He was identified as Mohd Reza Mahil, a one-time colonel in Iran's Revolutionary Guard.

At this point in the narrative, George stopped and with a dramatic sweep of a hand flicked open a plain manilla folder lying on the coffee table. He slid out four quarter-A4, full-face photographs, three of lightly bearded youngish men and the fourth of an older man with an untidy stubble. 'There you go! Look a tricky lot, don't they? Wouldn't trust them further than I could throw them, especially, this one. He's the Colonel, the boss man. He's tried to disguise himself. You know, it's so funny. We're used to people growing beards to disguise themselves; but this chappie decided to have it chopped off. In any event, when these photos surfaced, it all hit the fan and an urgent request went out for satellite pics of the island. And that, Dr Jamieson, is where we are now, and that's really all we know.'

Freddy looked up. 'George... the death of the informant?'

'Him? That's no longer relevant, Freddy. Didn't your people tell you? Embassy report came through late Friday. The Beijing diplomatic police are certain it was just a bit of local skulduggery – a wrong place, wrong time thingy, a coincidence. Nothing to worry about there, Dr Jamieson.'

Chris pursed his lips. 'I see.' He wasn't a great believer in coincidence, and George had sounded just a bit too dismissive for his liking. 'And that's the informant you mentioned earlier?' he asked.

'That's right. Just didn't want to waste your time on it. It's a non-issue.'

'I see. OK. So, what is it you want me to do on this island place?'

9

'Ahhh! Yes, and to be honest, we're not exactly sure, but Mavis has the TORs. She'll go over that.'

'And the timing?'

'That's Mavis, as well… good at logistics. And, in fact, I believe she may well be back in her office now… Room 3, far end. I'll tell her you're on your way, and please, ignore that security gate out there; it's not worked for months. Just walk through.'

She was waiting for him in the doorway. 'Hello, again. Come in.' She smiled. 'How did you get on with those two?'

He smiled back. 'Good question. George is a great storyteller.'

She looked at him quizzically. She let it pass. 'Is there anything you feel I can add?'

'Not really, though there was one thing I was going to ask them about but decided against it. You might have an answer. It's that small, pixelated area on the northern site satellite image. I was puzzled by it.'

'Yes, I noticed that, as well. I thought maybe it was just a bit of atmospheric interference.'

'I doubt that. Looks man-made to me. Not to worry. I'll find out for myself – that is, if I take this thing on. Anyway, what is it you want me to do, exactly?'

'I must apologise. I don't have a written set of TORs. The Director said not to bother and that he didn't want to tie you down.' She laughed nervously. 'In fact, he said it would be a waste of time trying to. But, as *I* understand it, what we want you to do is simply to find out what's going on in the place.'

Chris smiled: here was at last a bit of honesty. 'OK. So, let me guess: some high-definition photographs of the construction sites, word-on-the-street stuff, and what those four Middle Eastern characters are up to.'

She nodded slowly. 'That sounds pretty good to me.'

'And the timing problem?'

'And there, I'm afraid I must apologise yet again. I did check back, and it seems critical that we get this thing done *before* Christmas. The Director does have a proposal, though. He suggests you travel overnight to the mainland this coming Thursday and take the ferry across to the island on Friday. You then do whatever you need to do and be back here by the following weekend. That'd be well before Christmas.'

He knew he should have expected it. 'I'd hardly call that *well before* and I'm not at all sure that it solves my problem. If I *am* to go ahead, I'll need to do quite a bit of difficult manoeuvring back home.'

'So, are you saying yes or no?'

'Neither. I'm saying it might, or might not, be possible. I'll need to call you in the morning to let you know the position.'

'I can't stress too much how desperate we are on this one,' she continued. 'So please do your best. Oh, and when you do phone in the morning – and the Director feels certain you'll confirm – could you come up with a communication authentication code? We have an informant on the island – a covert – who can't do your job but may be able to help. Burnett wants an off-the-wall job code. He says you're good at those.'

Chris shrugged. 'I'll give you one now if you want. It's something I used in Khartoum recently with a link who was a back-street dentist. It's simply successive days on the ground paired with the initials of a UK fungi list, reversed on alternate days. It's sixteenth-century Francis Walsingham stuff. I particularly like the congruence… Elizabeth then, and Elizabeth now.'

'Right. And that sounds definitely off-the-wall. If we can get the list together now, I'll be able to send it off to Control in the embassy tomorrow. They can get it to the informant. And perhaps I should mention that the communication process has to be a one-way them-to-you arrangement. You wouldn't initiate.'

'I see,' though he didn't. He could never see the logic or practical value of one-way communication coding. 'Anyway, codes and informants aside, if I went ahead, who would I actually be working for? This looks like an external business. What's Cheltenham got to do with it… or am I missing something?'

'You're not, and I've asked the Director that very thing. He just mumbled something about risk containment. He thinks that anyone developing an interest in this business from the outside won't end up watching GCHQ. They'd be down nosing around Century House.'

•

He made his way through the early afternoon crowd in Paddington to a flower stall at the back of the station.

'Afternoon, Eddy. How's business?'

'Lordy! It's Mr Chris! Long time, sir. Not so good without you. Been away again?'

'No. Just in town at a meeting full of idiots… Sorry, Eddy. I shouldn't talk about colleagues that way. I *am* off shortly, though.'

'It's all right, sir. I understand. I know those types. And, yes, the missus. You're going away, so it's an orange, white, and yellow mix, with a bit of green to set them off.'

'You've got a good memory.'

'Not really, Mr Chris. Those are the exact same mix mine likes. It's a woman thing. I'll just nip round the back. Got some nice fresh stuff there.'

A minute later he was back. 'Tricky foreign climes?'

'That's right.'

'Well, keep your head down, and watch out for that foreign grub!'

•

Remarkably, the mid-afternoon train to the south-west left on time. He settled into a half-empty first-class coach and put the flowers he'd bought in Paddington down on the opposite seat to deter anyone wanting to sit and chat. He took a sheet of A4 from his backpack and from memory drew an outline of the island. He marked the position of the building sites with a circle and added dotted lines for the access tracks. It seemed unlikely that internet maps would show such recent developments.

Satisfied he had it about as right as he could get it, he sat back and let his mind drift through his strategy for dealing with Martha: flowers first, a bit of inconsequential chat, and then the money thing. That should make it work. The key thing was to make sure his story held together. At least, then, she could pretend to believe it.

•

'Such beautiful flowers, dear. Just the right colour mix.' Martha slipped the door chain into place behind him. 'Very thoughtful. And what've you let yourself in for this time? I hope it's not one of *those* jobs.'

'Goodness, no. Nothing of the sort. It's just a small thing in Ziaẁala surveying a couple of building sites to see whether they can be turned into schools. Money's really good.'

'So, what's the catch?'

'Well, I'm afraid it's got to be later this week,' he hurried on, 'but I'll only be away four… five days, max. I'll be back before you even notice I've gone.' He didn't dare look at her, but he could already sense from her breathing it wasn't going to wash.

'I just don't believe it, Christopher! You promised faithfully! I need you here! The children will be expecting you to be around. Why can't it be done later?'

'I know. I know and, believe me, I pressed so hard to get it pushed into next year, but they've got a real problem. It has to be squeezed out of this year's development budget… and you know how important education is to the well-being of people in those places.'

•

'You're incorrigible,' she said, later in the evening. 'I despair sometimes. I really don't know why you put yourself through these things. Just make sure they insure you properly this time. And the money's good, you say? It had better be. I want to get back some of that two thousand odd you shelled out for that camera thing. It left a big hole in my Christmas budget. Right, so how can I help you get ready?'

2
MADAME

Chairman Mulamuezini Airport was chaotic, much more so than on his earlier visit, and he was amused to find himself facing the same furious-looking immigration officer that he'd had back then. There was that same glare and grinding of teeth as the man examined his visa. Even his guttural grunt was the same as he stamped the passport… and, then it came, that dismissive flick of a thumb to direct him through to the right.

Neither of the carousels was functioning in the baggage arrival hall and the narrow space between them was rapidly filling with luggage as a line of sweating porters dragged suitcases, bags and bundles out from beyond a screen and flung them unceremoniously onto the growing pile. He saw his rucksack and suitcase come though and receive the same treatment. He took a deep breath and plunged into the seething mêlée of passengers and porters to retrieve them, praying as he did so that none of his photographic equipment had been damaged.

There were no customs' officers this time round, and the mob streamed randomly through both green and red channels. He chose red; he liked the idea, and he joined the flow out into the general concourse, where he stopped a moment, seeking the inner strength he knew he'd need to plunge into the gesticulating, shouting mob to find whoever it was had been sent to meet him.

His problem was quickly resolved. A youngish white woman detached herself from the crowd and made her way over to him. She came up alongside him and grasped his elbow.

'Dr Jamieson?' She had to shout to be heard.

He nodded.

'Hello. Sorry. Always like this… absolute bedlam! I'm Sybil, the ambassador's PA. I won't ask you if you had a good flight. Sir William has asked me to take you to the embassy for a courtesy visit and then down to the harbour for the ten o'clock ferry – except it's twelve today! I've got you into the first-class cabin. You might be able to find somewhere to sit in there; I stress the *might*. Out on the deck it'll be survival breathing space only. God willing, you should hit the island terminal – literally, and I mean that – around five. Then it's hardly two minutes up the road to the Mirabilé. No taxis, I'm afraid. Anyway, let's get out of this madhouse. Limo's outside.'

•

An hour later, he was wedged with three island officials into the first-class cabin. He had hoped to rest during the seventy-odd miles to the island, but that proved impossible.

His travelling companions, cheerful to a man, insisted on chatting to him endlessly in English with bits of French and Swahili thrown in.

'Who are you?

Ahh, nice name. Where from?

England! Ayee! You must like football and support Liverpool. Oh! And MU!

Mke?

Nom?

Maratha. Yes, very good name! Watoto ngapi?

Wawili only! Oh dear, not enough. Noms?

A boy and a girl. Wonderful!

You are staying where?

Oui. Naturellement, Le Mirabilé. Excellent hotel. You will meet Madame… a very fine lady. She will look after you well.

And how many days you staying?

No! Not long enough! What you going to do on the island?

Will you travel to the north? Up there, a too beautiful place.

You must visit our homes in town for food. You must meet our wives, our beautiful children. Promise… ahidi, ahidi.

We will be in touch. Do not doubt it.'

Their chatter only ended when the ferry struck the island landing stage side-on, shuddered, and slid with a deafening screech along a row of tractor tyres. It jerked to a stop as the prow buried itself into the grass bank. The three men fell forward off their bench and laughed.

'Oh! Mwendo umekuisha. Nous arrivé. Go well.'

They shook his hand vigorously, grabbed hold of their bags, and levered their way out into the mob of disembarking passengers.

He felt quite exhausted. He got up slowly from his cramped position, stretched and moved to the open doorway of the cabin. Scattered across the now half-empty deck there were various passengers, obviously holding back. They were mostly women with babies on their backs. They stood silently, watching intently as the mass of people pushed, elbowed, and jostled their way down the gangplank, off the ferry and onto the wooden landing jetty. Then, when the right time came, the watchers all began to move. He followed and joined in the long winding tail of the queue.

Up ahead on the bank he could see the island immigration officer. The man was dressed in a black and white check T-shirt hanging a long way down over grass-green Bermudas. He was reclining in a pink plastic armchair under a multi-coloured parasol. His arrivals desk comprised three upturned wooden crates adorned with weather-worn travel labels.

The man's right hand was resting, palm down, on one of the crates, his left on an ample stomach. Chris noticed, as he got closer, that the man flicked his right-hand index finger back to signal people through one-by-one, some to his left, some to his right. Now and then, he'd jab his hand in the air to stop the line, as a policeman might to hold up a line of traffic, and he would chat briefly, perhaps to an acquaintance or a neighbour.

When Chris arrived at the boxes, the man's hand went up and he smiled broadly at him. He leant forward and peered at the visa in the passport, nodded, checked the mainland entry stamp, nodded again, and then with a flourish added his own local version. 'Welcome, Mr Christopher,' he said. 'We are expecting your arrival. The ferry made it today, and here you are! That is a good start for your stay on our island, a good omen. Sometimes, one might not be so lucky.'

He leaned forward; his tone softened. He said in a half whisper, 'While you are here, you will need help. I know it; our island has its little problems. I'm Idris, first-floor government offices, next to the clinic. Come, visit, any time.' He sat back up and his cheery manner returned. 'And now, Mr Christopher, you should go around the outside of the Customs shed… and did you hear that, the rest of you?' he shouted at the final trickle of arrivals. 'Don't go *through*! It is crowded and airless in there. Anyway, no customs' officers today… off at weddings!'

Chris made his way around the side of the shed to a football pitch sized parking area of finely ground-up volcanic rock sloping gently upwards away from the water. Over to his left were a dozen or so trucks and, at the very end of the line, a newish, light-cream Land Rover, WHO emblazoned on its door and bonnet.

Immediately to his right were two reddish-grey dust-covered Tata buses, surrounded by a mob of people, mostly women and children. The younger, more agile of the women, their brightly flowered wraparounds hitched up to their knees, were clambering up the ladders on the backs of the vehicles and onto the roof racks, pushing screaming children ahead of them and dragging behind woven reed baskets of squawking, trussed-up chickens.

He swung his rucksack up across his shoulders and grasped the strap of his suitcase. Then, along with a gaggle of men and women, bundles on heads, babies on backs and young children running along behind, he made his way up through the car park and onto the road. Once there, he abandoned any hope of pulling his suitcase along; the corrugations made that impossible. He'd carry it. And so, with his rucksack balanced on his back, he made his way along the deeply rutted footpath at the side of the road.

To his right, a bank of enormous granite boulders reached down into the ocean, disappearing beneath a mirror-like surface, now glowing grey-green in the light of a red evening sun. To his left, there was a continuous line of small rectangular plots, some with stands of plantains and willowy papaya trees, coconut palms and mango trees. Here and there, perspiring women, some with babies bouncing up and down on their backs, were breaking up the dry, dusty ground with hoes in preparation for the planting of maize and the onset of the rains.

Up ahead, the off-white and pastel pink Mirabilé gradually slid into view and within a couple of minutes he was making his way through the car park down towards the hotel entrance.

A fine-looking woman – he guessed in her mid-fifties – came bustling out to meet him. 'Dr Jamieson, I presume,' she said, smiling broadly. 'Welcome. I am Madame Lemessurier, proprietor of this fine establishment, Le Mirabilé. Please come into reception. You are my only guest on today's ferry and I 'ave allotted to you my very best room, Room B16. It 'as fine views of my gardens and the ocean.'

She opened the guest registration book on the counter. 'Please fill in your passport information. Nowadays, no-one checks, of course; it's a never-happen-just-in-case. Use the space below that scrawl. That belongs to the Russian Ambassador from the mainland – would you believe it – plus companion. They come often. She never puts 'er name in and 'e can't write properly! They're on your floor, far end, but worry not, they will not bother you... too busy with other matters! 'Now, domestics: we 'ave a lady called Bibi. She comes Mondays and Thursdays to clean rooms and change linen. And, if you need anything special, I am always at your service, either in reception or in Room 1, B Wing. And talking about special, we 'ave tonight a local delicacy on the menu, fruit bat curry. Please come. I hope also to tempt some special guests I have... ahhh, yes, and I must tell you, our telephones are not good and the island's system is 'orrible... never works. One day, maybe, there'll be a miracle.'

CONTACT 3

The view over the hotel gardens towards the ocean was magnificent in the evening light. This had to be so much better than all that pre-Christmas build-up nonsense; the dreary visits to town in the cold and the wet, being cajoled around by Martha from shop to shop, the endless rummaging through the mountains of consumerist junk. He supposed he should feel guilty. However, she was more than capable of dealing with all that nonsense, and anyway, he was sure she'd secretly welcome not having to drag him round, complaining about everything.

Something caught his eye; there was a slight movement over to his left. He leant forward on the balcony rail, steadied himself, and refocussed. A pink-tipped nose had appeared in a gap between broken concrete slabs lying at angles to each other across the drainage ditch running along the back of the hotel. Whiskers and a dark brown head followed, with bloodshot eyes reflecting the dying light. He watched, fascinated, as a rat heaved its grotesquely large, panting body out onto the grey, pitted surface. It scurried forward and stopped immediately below him. Its head tilted to the right, and it gave a high-pitched hiss and bared its teeth.

The moment passed, and the rat waddled on in the direction of the hotel kitchen – left-right, left-right – into the gathering gloom, its passage marked by a line of faintly glistening saliva.

Beyond the gardens and a now indistinct sea wall, the ocean surface was a deep grey-brown, the horizon a vibrant slice of golden yellow, changing – even as he watched – to green... to blue... to a silken purple. Within moments it would disappear altogether, to be replaced instantaneously by a uniform darkness, relieved only by the stars switching on above in their tens of thousands. He found it quite magical.

Then, there was a voice; he was sure of it. It was barely audible. It came to him on the sea breeze. Out in the darkness over to his right, a light flickered on. It picked out the side of a tree and next to it a low stone wall, before disappearing for a moment, only to reappear further to the left. This time, it jiggled across the tops of bushes for a second or two and was gone again. He waited, his eyes fixed on the spot in the blackness, but that was it. Whoever was out there had switched their torch off and become one with the night.

From a mosque somewhere in the town to the front of the hotel, the fine tenor voice of a muezzin started up, calling the faithful to prayer. The sound was repetitive and hypnotic, crescendo following crescendo, rising and falling, as though mirroring the sea breeze, which was pushing in caressing waves at the bougainvillea clinging to the trellis-work alongside his balcony, and bringing with it the fragrance of frangipani.

Mosquitoes floating up from the breeding pools cupped in the plantain leaves below were beginning to settle on his exposed ankles. He kicked at them – a futile gesture, he knew – and he stepped smartly back into his room and slid the balcony door shut. He'd use the ceiling fan overnight. That had to be preferable to a claustrophobic mosquito net. In any event, open balcony doors would be an invitation to the cockroaches, that were sure to emerge in the dark from the drains and ditches below. They wouldn't be the tiny black variety he used to chase around the kitchen floor at home in the years after the war; these would be shiny, brown, tentacled monsters, armoured and inches long. They'd fly in and crash around like demented whirligigs. He shivered at the thought. Rats he could tolerate; they were sort of stripped-down humans. You could look them in the eye, and you could both agree that mutual respect and retreat was the best answer. But tropical cockroaches were something else altogether. There was nothing about them that was remotely human. They were alien life forms that would crawl out from the ruins of nuclear Armageddon with renewed vigour to inherit the Earth. To him, they were the stuff of nightmares.

He switched on the main light. He'd do a quick security check; they'd advised that in London. Then it would be down to the restaurant to try the promised special offer. With a bit of luck, he might even get a first glimpse of his quarry down there.

He moved to the bed, leant across and looked behind the washed-out seascape above the headboard. Next, he examined the light and fan fittings, and unscrewed, checked and replaced both ends of the telephone. Nothing. He got up on a chair and using his Swiss Army special he unscrewed the cover to the air duct above the door and peered in. Again, nothing, just pristine layers of dust laced with desiccated flies and mosquitoes.

And, at that point, he decided, enough was enough. He couldn't take seriously the idea that someone in such a remote place was capable of setting up a surveillance system, let alone be bothered to do so. He was puzzled, nonetheless. After all, GCHQ would not have organised a costly divert of the UK Indian Ocean satellite from its normal tracking to overfly the place if there wasn't something of real interest going on.

•

The restaurant was poorly lit. Its marble-flagstaffed floor was chipped and pitted, and the takamaka tables and teak uprights were scratched and stained. He guessed they'd been tested close to destruction by the colonial brigade in the years before Independence.

Suspended from the dark-brown painted, wood-panelled ceiling, two enormous fans, their wooden blades creaking round and visibly bending under years of dust and neglect. Along the low outside wall, bamboo split-cane matting had been rolled down to ward off the myriad flying insects.

At first, when he walked in, he thought the place deserted. Then, in the far corner, he saw a shape at a table, inert and bent forward over a book. His impression was of a thinnish white woman of indeterminate age, darkish hair pinned up, rimless glasses, and a flowered top over a white blouse, arms fully covered. He caught her eye as she glanced up. He sensed a smile – or maybe it was consternation, even a warning – as she returned to her book.

The waiter, who, as he discovered later, was also the cook and the hotel handyman, meandered across to his table, thrust a single-item menu at him and stood back, hunched up, without word or smile. Chris stared at the menu for a moment and closed his eyes. He wouldn't disappoint the proprietor; after all, he'd probably need her assistance before long. He took a deep breath and nodded. The waiter wandered off towards the kitchen.

•

Sleep didn't come easily, and after six hours or so twisting and turning, and with his head throbbing furiously, he gave up. His mouth was dry, the air was motionless, heavy, and scarcely breathable. Sweat was flowing from every part of his body, soaking the sheet beneath him. The fan was silent, and it was pitch black. The ambassador's PA had warned him on the way down to the ferry that power cuts were a regular occurrence on the island. She'd added that the hotel generator would kick in within seconds, and so he lay still, waiting.

After a few minutes of increasing discomfort, he rolled off the bed and edged along the wall hand-over-hand until he located his rucksack. He felt for his torch in a side pocket and made his way to the bathroom. It was as he pushed open the door that the fan started up behind him and the light came on in the corridor outside his room, producing a bright line below the door to his room. Half-way along, the line was broken. He bent down, picked up a folded piece of paper and switched on the bathroom light. In capitals on a page neatly cut from the previous year's diary was a single line of writing:

06.30: *CORNER RESTAURANT WALL. AD*

AD... Amethyst Deceiver. He nodded. The note must have been slipped under the door before midnight. It was a simple system check; things were up and running. He tore the diary page in half, and half again, and flushed the pieces down the toilet.

THE 4 MINDER

As far out as the eye could see, the ocean was jumping and glittering in the early morning light, myriad shards of light splintering off in every direction. Close in, a group of noddies, wings outstretched, tips quivering, hovered high above the surface. Every now and then, one would thrust back its wings and drop arrow-like into the water, its silvery target with no chance of evading the oncoming needle-sharp beak.

The pathways through the gardens below, their edges marked out with misshapen chunks of bleached brain coral, were now much clearer than the evening before, and from his balcony he could trace the main path as it twisted and turned away from the building and in and out of rampant bougainvillea. At many points, it would disappear into sprawling red poinsettia and grey and white frangipani, only to reappear many yards further on.

Scattered across the gardens were clumps of plantains, mature mango trees, casuarina and takamaka and in the middle distance up against the sea wall was an ancient baobab, its grey, stunted, root-like branches hanging out over the water. The bushes around its base had been beaten down and dozens of yellow weaver birds were scratching around in the crushed foliage.

•

Three of the men were in the restaurant when he arrived, one slumped forward at a table in the corner up against the low outside wall, the other two at the buffet counter chatting in Arabic. By the time Chris had chosen a table further along the wall, he'd worked out their nationalities: the buffet pair were the Syrian and the Iraqi; the lone man at the table was the younger Iranian.

The older Iranian was missing. He found that surprising. The Colonel had to be the minder of the group, and it was axiomatic that minders never let their people off the leash, free to chit-chat inconsequentially in a public place.

The Colonel was, however, very near, and yet very far away. He was half-asleep, half awake.

Hamad hears his mother calling. Her voice is loud, and higher than usual; she sounds on edge, but then she often does.

'Mo. Come quickly. Food. Wash your hands.'

'Yes, Mama.'

His father must still be at the mosque. Otherwise, she'd never take the risk of calling to him in English. She'd get a beating for that; and for listening he'd get a worse one. He wouldn't cry or shout out no matter how bad the pain. He never did. He'd take it in silence, but later he'd sob into his bedroll on the flat roof, where he slept. He and his mother would carry on using English whenever they could. It was their secret. It was to be his passport from the violence and degradation of the back streets of Isfahan, she'd say, and from the anger and hate that ran in equal measure through the community.

He'll be back soon... I'll go to my extra religious classes, this afternoon. That will please him, and I will tell him I missed the English class...

The water rolls up across the Colonel's face as he begins to sink. It washes through the stubble on his chin and rolls up his nostrils, choking him. Instinctively, he moves his hands furiously below the surface of the water, and floats back up. He wonders how long he's been there and looks across to where his trusted lieutenant is sitting at the table. But the others? He's being remiss. He must check.

The young Iranian at the table raised his head and looked over to his left. Chris saw the movement and stretched over to the right. He could now see that the sea wall turned sharply in just beyond the end of the restaurant and disappeared into multiple, folded layers of dark volcanic rock enclosing a small bay. At the landward end, a set of narrow concrete steps emerged from the still, black surface and led up to gardens at the far side of the hotel.

And there, twenty yards or so out in the water, was the older Iranian. He was on his back, waving his hands up and down just below the surface, creating mini-whirlpools on either side of his body. His white underpants were ballooning up onto the surface. He had his head raised from the water and he was calling in Farsi to his colleague at the table, his voice high and husky.

A commotion started up at the entrance to the restaurant, distracting Chris, as an Arabic-speaking family of four came in from B Wing. He straightened up and watched while the two children, a boy about nine and a girl perhaps twelve, argued, banged and scraped their way into position around a table near the entrance, before rushing for the buffet. The parents seemed not to notice their offspring's behaviour, or if they did, were obviously not bothered by it.

•

At eight exactly, the three men got up and wandered out of the restaurant. Chris picked up his coffee and followed behind into reception. He waited until their voices had died away and then slipped around behind the desk. He pulled the guest register out from under the counter, opened it, and flicked back four pages. There they were. The Colonel's name was in full – *Mohd Reza Mahil*. He was in A Wing, Room 15. Listed below his fine, copperplate writing were three other entries – for Rooms 13, 14 and 16. Each had a single name in neat lower-case print: *goliath, abdel, idrissa*. He returned the register and retreated to the seating area in reception with his coffee and book to await their departure from the hotel.

•

An hour later nothing had happened, and he was about to abandon his vigil when the woman he'd seen the previous evening came into reception from A Wing. She went behind the counter into the office, reappearing a second or two later wheeling an old-style sit-up-and-beg bicycle.

He was already up and moving towards her. 'Good morning, I wonder if you could help me. There doesn't seem to be anyone here.'

She smiled. 'Hello. Came in yesterday, didn't you? How are you settling in? I'm Anna, by the way, and rule one in this place is never to expect to find anyone in reception, except when the ferry comes in. If you have to ferret Madame out, you'll find her. She's always around somewhere... just not here.'

'I'm Chris. My apologies. I see you're off somewhere. It's just a quick query. I need to get around a bit – it's for a book I'm writing – and was going to ask the proprietor. Then I saw you with the bike and thought something like that might be useful, at least for round town.'

'This thing? Not mine. I hired it from Wallimohamed's Emporium, just up the road. They'll have another one squirrelled away somewhere, probably just like this one, a pre-twenty-first century job... Look. I have to go up there tomorrow. Why don't you come along? I'm a regular there, and a personal introduction from me should be worth a few special deals.'

'That sounds a very good idea. Thank you, but don't let me hold you up just now. I need to get out into the hotel gardens, anyway, before the sun gets too high.'

'Well, good luck with that one! Just be careful. It's a dreadful maze. I've never been able to get more than a few yards into it, myself. The pathways just appear and then disappear into impenetrable tangles of bushes and thorns. Madame claims there's an easy way through to the sea wall, though I'm not too sure I believe her.'

A few minutes later, as he watched Anna make her way out of the car park, he decided there were rather more pressing things to do than fight his way through the tangled undergrowth of the hotel gardens. He turned and headed along the ground floor of A Wing to the concrete stairway at the end, next to the emergency exit, and made his way up the steps to the first floor.

At the top he could hear muffled voices, one a commanding voice and with that distinctive timbre he'd heard already earlier that morning, bouncing across the water. They were speaking in English. For a moment this threw him, but then he realised it was probably the only language the four of them had in common.

He moved to the outside wall and could see the fifth door along was open. He edged along the wall until he was opposite Room 14. The words coming from 15 were now distinct.

'Abdel and I will go north after mosque… back by dawn, Insha'Allah. These materials are needed there. Goliath, you and Mohammad will prepare for the arrivals.'

'Yes, Colonel, but I was thinking—'

'Thinking! Not good for you. That *is* what will happen. Questions? None? Good. Now, go to your rooms. Rest.'

Chris froze. They were about to appear a few yards ahead of him. He could carry on along the corridor as though he were exploring the hotel, as any new guest would, or he could turn and run. He chose the latter. He swivelled round and ran to the top of the stairwell and down the steps two at a time. At the bottom, he pushed out through the emergency exit door, which slammed shut behind him with a clang. Cursing under his breath, he ran along the path at the front of the hotel, in through the main entrance and into a deserted reception area. He slipped around the counter and into the tiny office, where he propped himself up on the back wall, breathing heavily.

He listened. There was no sign of pursuit. Surely, they *must* have heard him. What he wasn't to know at the time, though, was that at the end of each meeting of his team the Colonel would intone a prayer and each of his juniors would touch him on the right shoulder as they left his presence. It was a ceremony signifying and blessing both his seniority, and the indissolubility of their joint purpose.

There'd been more than enough time for him to get safely away.

DEMI-JOHNS 5

The call to evening prayers woke him. He rolled off the bed, pulled on his mosquito boots, and made his way down to the car park to check they'd gone. He figured he had an hour at most.

He headed to the top floor of A Wing and along to 15. He knelt and examined the lock. It was the simplest sort of old-style West Midlands lever lock. He took out his jeweller's screwdrivers and selected a size four and a size seven. He inserted the four above and the seven below and whispered his way through the routine he was well-acquainted with: *Left... Press... Twist... Up... Across... Twist... Down...* There was that expected, satisfying click. He stood up, listened for a moment, and then gently pushed down on the handle and stepped into the room.

He closed the door and pressed his back against it while he waited for his eyes to adjust to the darkness. Within a second or two, the room gradually coalesced into dark shapes. He took six measured steps to the curtains, pushed his right hand through the join and gently slid open one side of the balcony door. That would be his escape route, albeit with a dangerous drop into the bougainvillea below.

Next the light; he took two steps to the bed and felt around for a pillow. Back at the door, he dropped it along the gap at the bottom and switched on the ceiling light. He took a strip of tightly rolled paper from his pocket and inserted one end into the keyhole to block access to a key. The other end he bent down at right angles to seal in the light.

He crossed to the wardrobe, which was tight up against the far-left corner. It was empty. The dressing-table had been pushed up along the right-hand side of the bed. He checked the drawers. Nothing. In the oblong space which the dressing table would normally have occupied were two large, open-framed wooden containers, each containing a demi-john-sized, purple-tinted flask sealed with a wired-down rubber bung. The bottles were labelled in Arabic and simplified Chinese characters. He photographed the containers and labels.

He got down on his knees and opened a black suitcase wedged up against the end of the bed. It contained layers of neatly arranged clothing. He slid his hand systematically through the various layers. Again, nothing. He reached into the pockets on both sides of the suitcase and recoiled as his hands came into contact with the coldness of metal. He eased out two fully loaded cobalt-blue pistol magazines. A glance at the lettering on them was sufficient. They were for an Iranian PC-9 ZOAF semi-automatic, a pirated version of a German handgun. He laid them on the bed, photographed them, returned them to the side pockets, and closed the suitcase.

On top of the bedside cupboard there was a hand-held Geiger counter, clearly visible through a protective covering of bubble wrap. He photographed it and then looked in the drawers. They contained the regulation Bible and Koran.

There appeared to be nothing else of interest in the room, so he moved silently to the door, unplugged the keyhole, retrieved the pillow and switched off the light. He waited a moment or two, and then walked back across the room. He dropped the pillow onto the bed, slid the balcony door shut, recrossed the room, and stepped out into the corridor, pulling the door firmly to behind him. He stood motionless, listening. All he could hear were a few amorous cicadas clicking away in the trees over to the left of the car park, and somewhere up in town a squawking two-stroke.

•

Scarcely half an hour after he'd left his room, he was back, lying on his bed under the ceiling fan. A large quantity of some unknown liquid, magazines for a German look-alike pistol, and a Geiger counter made up an altogether frustrating haul. He'd found nothing he could relate to the building of schools, or anything else for that matter.

THE FREE-THINKERS

6

They walked up into the town inside a line of red dust-covered concrete breeze blocks, which marked off a pedestrian area from what was once a bituminised road, but was now a mosaic of corrugations, and patches of tyre-shredding broken-up asphalt.

Set well back on their right was a line of shops: first, a miniscule, corrugated-sheet duka, every inch taken up with a mishmash of cooking pots, sacks of maize, sweet potatoes, beans, onions, mangoes; then two larger adjoining concrete-block places, each bedecked in roll after roll of brightly coloured cloth piled higgledy-piggledy one on the other. Women in light headscarves and brightly coloured wraps were manoeuvring this way and that through the merchandise, stroking everything they passed.

Next was Frankies. 'Well worth a visit,' Anna said. 'There's a garden at the back, where you can sit in comfort away from the noise and this dreadful dust. Food's good and coffee's not bad, and always on tap. I'm told the owner visited the US once... caught the bug.'

'Right. You've obviously been here a while.'

'Too long! I'm doing research on a local language that's on its way out – only a few hundred speakers left. It's a bit of a long-haul job for a PhD in Auckland. Ooops! Look... up ahead, by the blue truck. We've been spotted.'

Meera, in a bright yellow salwar and flowered top, her black hair flowing and flashing out behind in the sunlight, had appeared from behind the truck and was now standing, hands on ample hips, looking down towards them. Anna waved and, as though she had received a pre-arranged signal, Meera jumped into action and, like a released spring, came bouncing down towards them.

'Angelina. Oh, it's you! What a wonderful surprise! Our very best customer. It's so nice to see you again.'

'You've got to believe this, Chris,' Anna said out of the corner of her mouth. 'I was here less than twenty-four hours ago.'

'And who's this, your handsome friend?' Meera continued as she reached them. 'But we will find out. Come along, both of you, into the Emporium. Wallimohamed is out back doing his whatnots. I shall summon him. You both need Darjeeling. I can tell. In addition, today, I happen to have my latest samosa invention. It is an eternal mystery: no fish, no vegetables, no meat. There is a prize if you can guess what. Hah! And I think you will not win it.'

She stopped to breathe. Anna moved in fast.

'Hello, Meera. Yes. Thank you, and this is Dr Chris Jamieson. He—'

She got no further.

'Ah! Jamieson!' Meera pushed open the door into the double-fronted shop. 'Come in. Come in. Oh, a so famous name, great African explorer, and from a fine malt whisky-making family, the finest whisky ever, Pater used to say. He always had a case at hand, another in the capacious boot of his Renault Roho, and his triple-star, eighteen-year-old bottle behind the bar in his golf club.'

A substantial Valli came in from the back. 'I believe I hear voices. Come, Meera, my dear. Bring them through to your parlour. I am sure they would wish to be seated in comfort. Close the shop just now and we can all have a good old chinwag. If anyone is desperate plus, you know they will knock, and anyway our takings always go up when we are closed.'

He turned to the visitors. 'Anna, welcome. And this, I know, is Dr Jamieson. A little bird told me of your arrival, sir. This place is full of loquacious birds, rumours and leaky grapevines. That is the nature of small communities. But, enough of philosophy and social observation, welcome to our Emporium. You must call me, Valli, and my good wife, Meera. And you?'

'He's called *Chris!*' said Meera, 'but I like the *doctor* bit – like our Mina, dear. But now I prepare a Darjeeling and a samosa mid-morning delight.' She disappeared into the kitchen, her voice trailing after her, and getting ever louder as she went.

'Excellent!' said Valli. '*Chris*, it shall be. Yes, I heard from Madame that you were safely ensconced in the Mirabilé – a quality hotel, we are told. But the food – diabolical in extremis, my daughter calls it, instant death for the unwary traveller. It's that cook and chief bottle-washer. Madame's too, too loyal to him. Meera would have him out on his ear in less than an instant, but Madame fears his family of many will go hungry. And, yes, when we reflect, we know she is right. It's a dilemma, you would agree?'

Chris Jamieson nodded. 'Yes. That sort of thing is always a great problem.'

'Anyway,' Valli continued, 'I have been told you like to photograph nature. That's interesting. You see, I, too, like to photograph nature. I have an extensive collection of visuals and I am sure I will be able to help you.'

The next hour was filled with a one-way mélange of historical and biographical events:

The family business had been started up in Kampala in the days of Empire. Then, Wallimohamed's grandfather was thrown out by Idi Amin.

'He was an idiot, a maniac, numbskull!' Valli added.

The family had moved down to Dar-es-Salaam, where Valli's father – now an old man – still runs a small amenity store from a little hotel he owns on Oyster Bay.

'Now, that is a fine hotel,' Meera enthused. 'Blessed by sweet salt ocean air and excellent health-giving food, with none of that curry and rice junk, which is so bad for the complexion, to say nothing of one's social interaction!'

A young Wallimohamed, seeking pastures new, had moved to Ziawala, and then to the island. They had two children, a daughter, Mina, a qualified doctor, and a son, Johan.

'Studying to be a great businessman at a fine university in England,' Meera added. 'And Valli, you must not forget our Bess... so like a daughter, also.'

When Mina was a one-year-old, they'd taken on a well-

educated Anglo-Indian Christian girl recommended to them by a diplomat in the British High Commission in New Delhi to help bring Mina up.

'Named, she was, after our glorious Queen Elizabeth,' said Valli. 'And so, we call her Bess. That's not her real name, you understand. One day, I think she may feel able to tell us about herself.'

And, while their story was full of interesting snippets of family history, recounted with great vigour and drama, it wasn't long before Chis began to wilt. He looked across at Anna. She'd surely have an answer; she'd know a way out. Her glazed eyes, however, told him he was on his own.

Then, rescue came. Above the talk, and the rattle and creak of the ceiling fan, there was a growing swell of chanting voices from somewhere to the front of the building.

Meera leapt to her feet. 'Sssss! It's that lot again!' She rushed out to the front of the shop, where she frantically pushed the night-bolts into place.

Valli waved his hand gently. 'Relax, you two. Worry not. Those nincompoops have been doing this for many Fridays now. They will soon run out of fuel and go home to cool off. Meera just likes to be quadruple sure – always bolts the door – and perhaps she is right; a wise thing it is to be careful. Who knows what drives the mob? Let me explain. There is a small group of silly whatnots demanding special Islam for our island. They have their civil law. Now they want the whole thing, lock, stock and barrel. They march up and down the main road every Friday after mosque carrying banners in the national language and English, and what horrendous English it is, too.'

'That's very interesting and you'll forgive me,' Chris

said, 'if I ask you about religion… I thought, maybe with your names…'

'Yes, yes,' said Valli. 'And no problem… easy mistake to make, Chris, and you are a person who does not make mistakes easily. I can tell. It's a story with a long tail. You see, we are free-thinkers. We like to be free to choose the bits we like!' He guffawed. 'That is one of my father's best jokes. It started when Grandpa and Meera's family were ejected willy-nilly from Uganda by that Idi Amin.'

Meera was nodding furiously. Valli continued, 'And two years later, like a coward in the night, and under the cover of dark, that Idi Amin skedaddled from Uganda to Saudi Arabia, the home of that great religion, and the guardians, there, took him in. Why? Who knows? They even afforded him all his needs: a fully furnished, many-bedroomed house, money aplenty, many meals a day and ladies galore, on call 24/7… my apologies, Meera, dear. And, when my grandpa and pa heard about those things, they wondered how it could be. They decided there and then to become free-thinkers.'

Meera chipped in. 'Yes! But, of course, we are very low profile, heads down, free-thinkers and everyone accepts us… except for those nitwits out there.'

'I think I hear them on their way now,' said Valli.

'And good riddance, till next week!' Meera added with real vehemence.

'Where are they off to?' Chris asked.

'First, the town centre, and then it's a sharp right towards our Mina and Bess!' Valli laughed. 'Ahh! But those two girls are so clever. They squeeze the customers in, Fridays a.m., bolt the doors of the clinic at one o'clock on the dot and carry on in their fortress until the whatnots have given up and gone home to boast to their wives of their heroic deeds.'

It was Anna who was first to see the opportunity. 'Yes. And Valli, Meera, you'll forgive us, but we really must get going, ourselves. Like Mina and Bess in the clinic, we need to get on with our business, otherwise neither of us will have anything to boast about – to anyone!'

REFLECTION 7

Anna joined him in the restaurant the next morning.

'That was quite something, yesterday. Thank you for taking me,' Chris said.

She laughed. 'Yes. They're not exactly normal, though, even for this place.'

'Normal? Maybe not, but who *is*? I abandoned the notion of normality years ago; it's meaningless, and damages people. We're all odd in some way. It'd be a pretty boring world if it were otherwise. Incidentally, what do you make of that mid-east group? I see there are four of them here this morning. They're in the corner behind you.'

'Is it safe to talk?'

He glanced over her shoulder. 'Mmmm. Should be OK.'

She leant forward conspiratorially. 'Well, they *are* definitely more than average odd. Madame says they're building primary schools. All I know is that they're off every evening, regular as clockwork, and not back till some ungodly hour the next morning. How on earth do you build schools in the dark?'

'With some difficulty, I'd say. You ever speak to them?'

'Not really. The small, roundish one'll smile when he's by himself; he might even comment on the weather. The others just look away when I pass them.'

'A cultural thing, I guess. Anyway, time for me to run. Wallimohamed mentioned I'd find the hills south-west of the town good photographic territory. I want to get going before the sun gets too high.'

'OK. Well, be careful out there. Nisreen – she's one of my research informants – tells me there're hyenas and leopards around the edges of the town right now. It's the end of the dry season and they're hungry; lots of local cats disappearing.'

•

About a mile along the vehicle track to the south of the town, he came to high double gates with a heavy-duty chain-link fence stretching away into the bush on either side. At knee height, running parallel to the main fence, and a foot or so in from it, was a three-wire electric-fence system with regularly spaced, white porcelain insulators sparkling in the morning sun. Along the top of both the steel gates and fence were parallel strips of barbed wire on yard-long steel mounts angled outwards. He took it all in at a glance. It was obvious he couldn't just cycle into the place claiming to be looking for rare flora and fauna to photograph.

And then, in the shade of a mature mango tree over to the right of the gates, he saw an elderly Ivundéan. He was obviously the watchman. The man was lying back on a flimsy green plastic chair, his spindly legs splaying outwards from ragged khaki shorts. As Chris dismounted, the man's eyes flicked open. He straightened up, pulled himself to his feet and meandered over, a broad smile creasing his wrinkled face. He grasped Chris's hand, shook it vigorously and explained in a mixture of disconnected English words and phrases that no-one could go onto the building site – it was forbidden, and anyway, he didn't have a key to the lock on the gate.

They shook hands again and Chris thanked him and turned back along the track. A modified Plan B was needed. Once out of sight of the gates, he stopped and pushed his bike up the slope and into a cluster of umbrella acacia, where he laid it on its side.

Further up the hill there was an expanse of mixed primary and secondary forest which fell away on his right down towards the construction site. He made his way to the trees and up through them until he came to a clear area of yellow-lichen-covered scree jutting from the hillside. Over to his left he could now see other hills and, to his right, headland after headland pushing out into the ocean, and beyond them, an unbroken line of white foam, where the swell fell forward over itself and smashed onto the edge of the reef hidden below. And there, immediately ahead down a steep rock-strewn slope, was the madrassa site.

He eased his camera out of his backpack and systematically moved it round in a controlled swing taking photograph after photograph, focussing on anything that might be of relevance: the gate, the security fence, the locks on the main door of the hangar building, the security cameras and lighting around the edge of the corrugated iron roof, the half-built concrete block walls of the school buildings.

Figuring that was everything of interest, and in growing discomfort from the heat, he decided to retreat. He bent to pick up his backpack and, as he did so, he registered a flicker of light over to his left coming from the upper slopes of a hill perhaps six or seven hundred yards away. Still bent, he waited, and there it was again, distinct against dark green forest foliage. He straightened up and turned his camera, which was dangling at his waist, in the direction of the hill. He rapidly adjusted the focus and switched to automatic video.

After a minute or so, and no further flashes, he decided that what he'd seen was probably a trick of the light, or the reflection from some metallic mineral on the surface amongst the trees. He switched his camera off, picked up his backpack and began making his way down through the trees.

•

Meera was busy tidying the shelves when he walked in.

'Doctor! Welcome. Good timing. I'm just closing up for an hour. Come through to the parlour. It's lunch time, plus or minus, and you must stay.'

'No. Please don't go to any trouble, Meera. I just wanted a quick word with Dr Mina.'

'Ah! My Mina… still at the clinic with Bess, I'm afraid. They work too hard, those two. But no matter, you *must* stay. It is big trouble if you don't… and here comes Valli.

He likes his lunches, and he says they taste so much better when there is company!'

'The word is that you were out with your camera earlier,' Valli said, as he came through to the parlour and settled into his armchair. 'No doubt you got some interesting snaps. Now, I was doing my daily thinking earlier, during our yoga session, and I thought it would be very wise for you to go north. It is wonderful up there, with floras and faunas you will not see anywhere else in the world. I know; I have seen them... Please... just one moment.'

He heaved himself to his feet and disappeared into an adjoining room, reappearing moments later carrying a bulging manila folder. 'Many photographs here. Please take them. They may help. I can have them back later. But, right now, the question is how to travel up north. There is the Tata, of course. Ah! But that will break your bones. It takes ten hours or more to get to the coast. Sometimes, even, it never arrives. In the rain, it always breaks down or goes for a bumpy slide into the bush. No. Tata, out. Better to walk. Then, there is my Toyota, but that is only fit to deliver to villages, max. half-way up. If it went all the way to the north, I know it could never limp back again. You would be left there, lost forever. The answer I believe is to arrange something with the aid people, and so I will talk to our Mina. She knows people; she has connections.'

'Yes, and she's so smart,' added Meera. 'Amazing! How can Valli be her father? Impossible, I always say... I joke, dear!'

'I'm sure,' Valli said dryly. 'So, Chris, our Mina will be in touch. That may be soon. And when you go, my business will donate utensils and some lamps with oil for the villagers up there. Be sure not to forget to take your best camera with you and keep your binoculars always at the ready. You never know what you might see.'

EMMELINE

Emmeline Freemont was in her ancient Beetle, weaving her way through the traffic on Edgware Road heading to her Saturday morning judo session. She was humming tunelessly to a Villa-Lobos piece. It was music steeped in the colours, sounds and movement of Brazil, a country she'd fallen in love with, and where she'd found true love for the first time, or so she thought. Like her, he'd been temporarily attached to the Rio Embassy consular office, replacing a career Foreign Office official on home leave. But then, one night and without warning, he'd disappeared into a steamy jungle retreat somewhere up the Amazon with Mercedes, a well-known, buxom Brazilian dancer. It was then she decided her mother was right, that she should forget men and concentrate on making a difference in the world.

Her office-link phone rang. 'Bugger off!' she shouted at the phone. It echoed round the car. 'My weekends are sacrosanct!' Then she relented and switched to hands-free. 'Yes? Who is it? What now?'

A woman's voice came through, slightly distorted by the two-way code-conversion process. 'Emmeline, it's Edith Reed-Robertson. I'm sorry to bother you on a Saturday morning, but there's a meeting in Cheltenham with the Director at nine tomorrow. I'm calling to let you know your attendance is required.'

'Apologies, Edith. You got me at a bad moment. I thought it was that lot in the London office being indecisive again. You know what they're like. What's the meeting about?'

'I believe it's that island business.'

'Right. Well, I'll have to use the office limo, I'm afraid. Train's impossible on Sunday, and I can't trust my VW. I can go over and pick it up now if that's OK.'

'Yes. Please go ahead. I'm sure the Director will approve.'

•

Judo and lunch were a washout. Chris Jamieson was preying on her mind. What had she drawn him into? She could have pressed the Director's PA for more information, but she knew that would have been a waste of time and effort. The old B would just prevaricate, and even lie, and claim she knew nothing, when in fact, she always knew everything, and revealed only what she felt inclined to. She was the Director's gatekeeper, a power she guarded with great tenacity.

The p.m. traffic from the office back to her flat was light, which was as well. Migraine had taken hold and she found herself driving through an aura of flashing reds, yellows and blues, and the odd dancing black-and-white zebra. She was an old migraine hand and had a tried and tested technique in such situations. She leant forward over the steering wheel, staring ahead at the road, and mumbled a meaningless sequence of words in an endless loop around her head, as though to corral the pain, which she swore was exactly what it did.

•

Next morning, she was away by half-six, and at the Communications Complex in Cheltenham just after nine. Her headache had now been whittled down to a dull aching spot behind her right eye.

At ten minutes past the hour, she was led into a meetings' suite, where she was joined by a researcher, a technician, and a Deputy Director from MI6, calling himself Leon. They all signed the need-to-know list. At fifteen minutes past, James Burnett, Director of GCHQ, and a junior Minister of State from the FCO, came through from an adjoining office.

'Apologies for dragging you all out on a Sunday,' Burnett said. 'Unfortunately, this island business has been scaled up to an orange-red.' He turned to his head of research. 'Harry… a run-down, brief, and in English, please.'

'Do my best, Director,' Harry replied. He nodded to the technician.

Three hand-written phrases appeared on a screen behind him:

Beijing Informant: demise of
Sat. Imagery of the island/radio transmissions
Iranian sub.

Harry continued, 'We've received a note from the

ambassador in Beijing with further information about the death of the embassy covert. It now appears it wasn't the straightforward murder that we were first led to believe. The man was choked with his own scarf and his head was smashed in and forced through the railings at the back of the embassy compound, ripping off both ears in the process... apologies for the detail. What the baddies *didn't* do, it seems, was rob him – and he had over a thousand US dollars on him. The ambassador now suggests that the idea of local skulduggery is no longer viable and his view is that it's a warning to the embassy from somewhere quite high up the political food chain.'

Harry looked over at the Director and the Minister. 'The ambassador's notes?'

The Minister nodded. 'Of course.'

'Thank you. The ambassador added two footnotes.' Harry retrieved a sheet of A4 from the table. 'Note one – I'll read, if I may: *The nature of the crime is such that we now think it is more than likely linked to the gold business and suggests the gold story may be genuine.* And note two: *The Americans are thick on the ground here. They have a number of embedded informants and are certain to have heard about the gold business. They may be prepared to help but I would need clearance if I'm to follow that one up.'*

The Minister joined in, 'And I will add, we *are* now talking to the US. Thank you, Harry. The second item please.'

Harry continued, 'Late last week, we rescheduled our Indian Ocean satellite to overfly the island at night. And, around Friday midnight – local – we got this.' He nodded to the technician.

Two ghostly green images came up on the screen alongside each other. 'These are the two building sites on the island,' he continued. 'The one on the left with this distinctly bright oblong – that's the hangar building – is the northern site. This other, the dullish grey-green image, is the southern site. I'll interpret. This brightness is a heat signature: it shows that oodles of energy are being churned out in the building. Also, you will notice this small, super-bright patch... here. That's an open door, and you can just make out two figures. It's anyone's guess whether they are male or female. There's nothing on this other site... dead as they come.' He glanced over at the Minister; eyebrows raised.

'Yes, Harry, go on.'

'Right. We also picked up radio signals from this lit-up place. The building contains what we believe is a high-power transmitter sending out signals in the form of complex modulations and an artificially generated female voice repeating long sequences of English alphabet letters. This suggests the building is operating as a traditional numbers station, very much an old-fashioned thing now, but still pretty effective. And, at present, as far as we can tell, the output is gibberish. If that's correct, what we're looking at is a systems testing process underway. We can't be entirely sure, though. It may be generating meaningful data.'

'Excellent, Harry. Now complete the circle,' the Director said.

'OK – and this is the third item. Right now, fifty miles east of the island there's a stationary Iranian submarine, an intermediate size Qaaem. It's normally deployed in the Arabian Gulf and round to Oman. It happens to be a vessel we're well-acquainted with.' He stopped and looked up. 'Director?'

Burnett had a whispered conversation with the Minister and then turned to the group. 'We all need to be very clear about *how* we know our intelligence on this is correct. We cannot afford to open ourselves, or our masters, to any accusation of misrepresentation. So, Harry, please go ahead.'

'Here's the thing. This sub's an old friend, you might say. Two years back we acquired a mark one quantum accelerometer particle transmitter for testing. Arrangements were made to covertly insert this device – it's a very small unit – into the core structure of this very vessel early on during its construction in an Iranian dockyard. It works, and we can now tell exactly where the submarine is, and at what depth. Each hour, the accelerometer sends a single particle pulse – like a tiny radio wave – for a micro-second. We normally pick the signal up using our high orbit satellite, though for a week now there's been an American UAV from Djibouti over-flying the island a few hours each day, and the US has allowed us to piggy-back on that. It's been picking up the signal loud and clear. And so, for example, I can tell you that as of our latest check – moments before this meeting began – the submarine was motionless fifty-one feet down and forty-nine nautical miles to the yard, due east just south of the mid-point of the island.'

'That's enough, Harry. Thank you.'

The Director turned to the group. 'And I will now confirm that we a have two-way radio flow between the hangar and that submarine... gibberish both ways, or so it seems. Right. Tea. Coffee.'

•

'We got anyone on the island, James?' Leon asked the Director quietly as they converged on the coffee table. 'I'm not as up-to-date about this one as I should be.'

'I suspect, Leon, that's more our fault than yours. Anyway, to answer your question, we were instructed to send someone reliable out last week to do some simple footwork, and so we sent this chap, Christopher Jamieson. He's a low-key ex-academic, who's done a fair bit of contract work for us over the years... Look, there's a lot more to this business, and I think you and I need a much fuller discussion, particularly as your people will probably have to take over at some point. My lot are only temporarily running the show. I'm told that's because of the communications angle. I don't buy that, by the way. I think it's more that GCHQ is off the radar on this one. Anyway, let's talk later. I'd like to push the meeting along so everyone can get home.'

James Burnett moved back to the front of the room. 'Right. Can we reconvene, please?'

Thank you. Let me summarise. It seems we have a jigsaw with God knows how many pieces: gold deposits, a done-to-death Chinese informant, an Iranian colonel with form, plus three unknowns. We've two construction sites, one with a numbers station linking it to an Iranian submarine, and in the middle of all this a sleepy backwater of an island. It's a disturbing witches' brew, and we've no idea how near the boil it is. Right now, we'd welcome any ideas any of you have on how to move forward on this thing.'

The Minister spoke first. 'A bit of information: I think

you all know we have a Dr Jamieson on the island doing some preliminary work, getting photographs and the like. We heard earlier today that Dr Jamieson is fine, and we're told he's getting lots of photographs.'

'Thank you, Minister,' the Director said. 'Em, you have something?'

'Well, *lots of photographs* sounds interesting. Couldn't we get hold of what Dr Jamieson's got so far? And perhaps we could ask him to try to get onto that northern site.'

James Burnett hesitated for a moment. 'The photographs, yes, certainly, but we'd be crossing our civilian ethical code on the site incursion thing. We will give it some thought, though. Leon, you have something?'

'The Russians, Director, why not talk to them? Any way you look at this business, it's in their interest to help, and they've informants galore in Beijing.'

'A good idea, Leon, and we happen to know that the Russian Ambassador to Ziaŵala is a regular visitor to the island. We've assumed it's for personal reasons, but who knows? Yes, Harry?'

'I was wondering, Director, whether we need to get someone else – a professional – onto the island to work with Dr Jamieson?'

'And we are actively looking at that one. Thanks.'

'Anyone else? Right. Enough for now. Keep thinking. The Minister and I will look at your suggestions, plus one or two other things we already have ideas about. Thank you again, and remember to sign the forget-everything list on the way out.'

•

Em headed off to her obligatory Sunday afternoon tea at her mother's place just outside St Albans. She wouldn't phone ahead. She didn't want an earful on the phone about being late, and the same again when she arrived; one working-over per visit was more than enough.

As she was manoeuvring the office limo into the parking space alongside the house, her mother came striding round from the back garden, loppers in hand.

'Emmeline, you're late again! I hope you didn't scrape my wall. Anyway, why are you driving that thing? That's for chauffeurs!'

'Sorry, Mother. I had some office work I had to catch up on. I can't afford to go into a new week with a backlog of stuff, and my VW's got problems.'

'Tttt! That wreck. You need to buy a decent modern car, an electric one. Save the world! And that stupid office – you working for those spineless men. Tell them to do their own filing and typing. You shouldn't be running around after them. You're better than all of them put together. *You* should be in charge and ordering *them* around.'

'Yes, Mother… maybe, but they're not *that* bad.'

'Not *that* bad! They certainly *are* – even *worse*! I saw them when I picked you up from that office Christmas party – you remember, a couple of years ago. They're just wimps. I can tell; they're just like your father was.'

Em had never known her father. He'd disappeared before she was born, something she'd since realised had been inevitable. He'd looked at his options, was frightened by what he saw, and scooted off in the dead of night – if her mother was to be believed. From time-to-time, she wondered whether he was still alive and, if so, what he was like. She liked to think there was still hope for her and that she wasn't destined to end up like her mother. "God forbid that!" she muttered, as the thought struck her yet again.

'What was that?' her mother called from the kitchen. 'You say something?'

'No, Mother. Just breathing heavily.'

'Breathing heavily, you say? It's that dog, gives you a bad chest. Silly little yappy thing it is, and that stupid name – Cedric! They wouldn't give you two pence for such a scrawny creature in a Taiwan back-street market, and—'

'It's two *Pee,* mother! Anyway, what do *you* know about Taiwan back-street markets?'

'Yes, and pee is about all it does – all over my garden. I'm sure the damp patches in my garage are caused by that, and I know a lot about Taiwan. I've read all about that place. Now come and help me bring this into the dining room, and no picking!'

Thank God! Food, at last, Em thought. This was her salvation. Her mother always became more human when she started eating. She'd mellow, slow down, and become marginally approachable. It was always a good time – indeed, the only possible time – to raise anything contentious.

'Mother, you've not mentioned my father for some time, but you did just now, and I often wonder whether you ever tried to find out where he went to in those early years, so you could claim support.'

Her mother leaned forward and focussed on cutting into a fine Victoria sponge. 'You know, dear, the WI really like a good Victoria. I take one to the meetings every week. You should join, you know. They could do with a bit of organising. I'm sure you could do that very well. And you can cook... well, more or less. Yes, indeed. And, when you were very young, I used to make and sell lots of cakes, pies, tarts – that sort of thing. We got by quite well really. Then, I started teaching again. But eat up. You're far too thin; you need to put some weight on. I made some other things earlier that you can take back with you. They're for you, of course, not that dog!'

THE INVITATION

The Toyota truck juddered to halt in a squeal and a cloud of red dust. The driver came running in and thrust an envelope at him. 'Dr Jamieson, for you, sah!' He gave a big smile, saluted and left.

Inside was a note:

> *Sunday, 0900.*
>
> *Dear Dr Jamieson,*
>
> *I'm leaving for the North this morning with the UNICEF Land Rover. It would be very nice to have your company. We will need to stay overnight up there in an old government rest house, half an hour from the north coast. It's a bit run-down, no water, no power, but there's lots of space. Coming back next day, p.m. Father says there's interesting stuff to photograph nearby and as you might guess he's a bit insistent. Meera even more so!*
>
> *I'll be at the Mirabilé at about 11.15 this a.m.*

and really hope you can make it. (Otherwise they'll disown me!)

Very kindest regards,

Mina (Dr)

P.S. The hotel may have a sleeping bag but we can improvise if not. Don't worry about food. Meera has ensured we will have more than enough.

Just after eleven, he was back down in reception. The place was deserted. He left notes on the desk for Madame and Anna and sat down with his book. At 11.15, the UNICEF hard-top arrived and Mina hopped out. She was an unmistakably younger version of her mother and an obviously bright, vivacious individual. She introduced herself and her driver-companion, Thierry, a French WHO official.

'Roads are terrible this year,' Thierry said, as they drove up out of the hotel car park. 'As usual, we'll need to push the PWD to get the grader out of its cocoon. They'll have all sorts of excuses and will guarantee without fail to do it within days. They won't, of course, so we'll pester them again and again, till they get so fed up with us, they'll actually do something about it.'

'And you may think these corrugations are bad, Chris,' Mina added, 'but wait till we come to the bridges. Crossing those things is life-threatening. They're all one-way twin concrete strip affairs, each hardly a wheel's width across. First one coming up, in fact. Hang on!'

The corrugations became closer, sharper and more pronounced as the vehicle approached the bridge, and it began surfing at an angle along the tops of them. Thierry pushed down furiously on the accelerator and aimed for the concrete strips. Then, as the Land Rover slammed back onto the dirt at the other end of the bridge, he switched back to surfing mode, and with each successive sideways judder slowly regained control.

Passing the few other vehicles they met on the road, was a test of nerve and skill. Each driver had to abandon the marginally drivable part of the road – the middle – and charge past the other vehicle, desperately trying to control the rear of their own, which was intent on sliding into the ditch on their side of the road. It was an each-man-for-himself manoeuvre, a triumph of faith over physics.

These heart-pounding death-defying bits of the journey were complemented by long periods of physical discomfort, when the Land-Rover had to twist and turn through the deep, back-jarring potholes in the stretches of broken asphalt that remained from colonial times, when there'd been a tarred road to the top of the island.

•

It was around three when the Land Rover rumbled into a west coast village of twenty or so wooden, corrugated-iron-roofed huts hugging a sandy bay. Through the gaps between the huts, they could see two fishing boats at the water's edge being prepared for the evening's fishing. And, up above the high-water line, marked out by ragged strips of dried seaweed, they caught sight of five or six women sitting on split bamboo mats laid on thorny undergrowth. Here and there, they glimpsed children chasing around on the sand.

Perhaps fifty yards past the last hut in the village, they

came to the rest house. On the left of the entrance to the overgrown driveway was a huge black boulder on which someone had painted a large outline smiley face in white. Underneath, they'd scrawled the word 'SMILE' in untidy capitals. Weather-worn paint streaks were running down from each letter.

'That face has been there since before Independence,' Mina said. 'It gets fainter with each passing year, and the tears get longer. I swear it's crying for these poor people. Father says the paint in those days was real, not like the rubbishy, watery stuff they have today. Anyway, here we are; this is the government rest house. Looking it now, you wouldn't believe it used to incredibly busy, with magistrates, the island doctors, district commissioners, hut-tax collectors, water-engineers coming and going There was even the occasional, adventurous tourist, intent on reaching the north coast. The place provided lots of local employment, but now these poor people have to survive on what the men can catch and what the women can grow or gather in between taking care of their babies. Many of the poor little things don't survive past six months. It's quite awful.'

'And we tell them they should move to the north coast every time we pass through,' Thierry added. 'Water off a duck's back. They just nod, smile politely and ignore us. Anyway, Chris, when we've unloaded our overnight stuff, why don't you take your camera and head up that hill across the road? There'll be some interesting specimens there.'

'And some real nasties,' Mina added, 'that come out of the undergrowth towards evening, so I wouldn't go too far if I were you, and it gets dark quickly here. The sun just drops out of the sky like a stone into the ocean.'

•

Chris made his way out of the rest house, past the smiley face, and turned left up the road. Perhaps a quarter of a mile along he came to the vehicle track that led to the school building site. He took the sketch map he'd made from memory on the train back from London out of his camera case. It looked spot on.

•

Back at the rest house later that evening, he casually mentioned that he had heard there was a school being built nearby.

Thierry shrugged his shoulders. 'Yes, and it makes no sense at all, of course. But something's definitely going on there. I drove along the track a couple of weeks ago; it's just up the road. The place now has a huge, new fancy fence around it and there's a watchman sitting outside the gate, although he looked a bit of a dopey character.'

'Yes,' Mina added, 'and Father says it's all a load of tish-tosh. There was furious activity earlier in the year with lots of locals, bussed down from the north, running around earning money beyond their wildest dreams. Then, everything stopped. My father thinks someone ran off with the cash box. Those Middle Eastern types in the Mirabilé are supposed to be doing something about it, but Madame says they sleep most of the time. And that reminds me.' She looked at her watch. 'Nine already. I don't know about you two, but I need to get my head down. Heavy day tomorrow:

endless mothers-to-be with this or that problem, and the kids – jiggers, putsi flies, you name it. We have a first-rate local nurse there, but she's a little too conscientious and is always in a distressed state; so too are her medical supplies. We'll leave her lots of stuff. Then, on Tuesday, I have to make my monthly visit to the general hospital on the mainland to collect our supply of medicines.'

THE RESIDENT

As the footpath dropped away from the lower boundary of the rainforest, the construction site gradually slid into view. Over to his left he could see a wide south-facing ledge which would give him a clear view of the whole site. It was an exposed position, but there was no danger. The Colonel would be in the middle of his morning swim in the bay and his men at breakfast in the Mirabilé restaurant. And a sleepy watchman outside the gate wouldn't be a problem.

He clambered up onto the ledge and set up his tripod. He took photographs of the half-built school and the hangar building and its security systems. He'd seen this all before. He was looking at a site very similar to the one in the south. There were two differences, however: a small excavation area running from behind the school wall down onto the beach, and a security fence which stopped on low cliffs on either side of the site, leaving open access to the ocean. He changed the lens on his camera and took a number of photographs of the excavation area. He then switched to video and recorded the perimeter of the site from one end of what was essentially a giant U shape around to the other end.

Running back from the gate along the access track was a line of blue-gum trees. He recalled reading somewhere that eucalyptus trees growing near gold ore deposits would readily take up and absorb traces of gold ions from deep underground. They'd trap what was a toxic mineral to them in their leaves to prevent damage. It was a long shot, he thought, but if he could get hold of a few leaves, they could be tested for gold using a very simple procedure.

Satisfied there was nothing else of interest, he packed away his gear and turned to make his way down the slope towards the line of eucalyptus trees. As he did so, a metallic screech reverberated around the site below him. He dropped onto all fours and then flat onto the rocky surface. He swivelled round to face the site and dragged his recording binoculars from his backpack.

Within seconds he'd found his target. At the left-hand corner of the hangar building, standing side-on in the shade of a laurel, was a short, round man in knee-length khaki shorts, flip-flops and a white sun hat. His shoulders were hunched forwards as he lit a cigarette.

Chris waited for the man to move and was rewarded with some fine front views as his target turned and looked up the hillside, directly at him, it seemed.

'Heavy... dark-framed glasses... fortyish plus... Chinese, maybe Korean,' he whispered into the camera microphone, as he rapidly took picture after picture, adjusting the focus, light settings and pixel depth from moment to moment. 'Push your hat back further! Hair?' But the man turned and walked back along the front of the building to the half-open, narrow personnel door, and squeezed himself sideways-on back into the building. There was a screech and a thud. Instantly, the site reverted to its former silence.

Chris lay still for a couple of minutes, and deciding the show was over, he got to his feet and headed down the side of the hill and across the vehicle access track, out of sight of the watchman. He picked half a dozen of the grey-green leaves from the nearest blue-gum, dropped them into his backpack, and made his way back towards the rest house.

•

Madame emerged from reception to meet the Land Rover as it squealed to a halt in the Mirabilé car park.

'Allo! Welcome back, you good people. I think, Doctor Chris, you 'ad a nice trip with Thierry and our mini Mina, eh!' She laughed. 'Naughty! And poor Anna, left all by 'erself. I know, I know, the job must be done, n'est-ce pas? You got some good pictures?'

'Yes, indeed, Madame, lots: just what I needed. I'll show you later. Right now, though, I need a shower and then a bit of R and R. I've discovered I'm not as resilient as I once was.'

Under his door, there was a note.

IMPERATIVE. SEND ALL PHOTO DISCS + NOTES TO EMBASSY. TOMORROW'S FERRY. DR MINA MAY BE ABLE TO HELP, OR FERRY CAPTAIN. SECRETARY WILL MEET. FD

•

Early next morning he made his way up to the clinic. Mina was sitting at the dispensing table, looking relaxed. 'Good morning, Mina. Thank you for yesterday. It was really productive. Look, I know you're off on the ferry this morning and don't want to hold you up, but I was wondering if you could do me a favour.'

'Of course,' she replied. 'I'm organised for once, ready to go. How can I help?'

'A secretary in the embassy is liaising with my publishers in London. I'd promised to send some material just about now, and wonder if you can take it across for me. It's just an envelope with a photo disc and a few leaves that need identifying. She'll probably be waiting for it off the ferry but, if not, perhaps you could call the embassy from the hospital. I'm sure they'll send someone to collect it.'

'Of course. And while you're here, come on through and meet Bess. She's the busy one today, getting ready for the pre-natal clinic.'

Bess, a neat, slim woman, dark hair tied back in a bun, had bright, alert eyes which smiled as she spoke. 'Ah! This has to be our Dr Jamieson. Meera now owns you, of course, and has been telling me about you – at length! Welcome to our clinic.'

'Good to meet you, Bess, but please don't let me hold you up. I just dropped by to ask Mina a favour.'

'Of course, and things *are* a bit hectic. Look, why don't you go off and have some tea with Mina? You can then make sure she goes off to catch that ferry. The immigration officer will bless you for that. He usually has to send someone up for her, last minute.'

ROSALIE AND HER COWBOY

'You mentioned earlier you were working with informants,' he said to Anna at breakfast the next morning.

'Yep. Two of them – Nisreen in town, and Rosalie up the coast a bit. In fact, I was wondering how your stamina's holding out. It's just that I've had a note from Meera saying their driver is taking a load of free itsy-bitsies – cooking utensils and the like – to a small settlement up the coast a bit later this morning; it's part of the Wallimohamed family humanitarian campaign. She says I should visit Rosalie – the truck passes her place – and that Valli is double-plus insistent that you must go along with me. I'm sure he's thinking of a bay on the east coast that's close to Rosalie's place. It's ideal for sea-life photography. I hope you'll come. In fact, it's an offer you can't refuse. If you do, you'll put your sanity – and mine – at risk! If you put your bike in the back of the truck, you can use it while you're up there.'

•

Rosalie's place was set back from the road down a gravel and beach-pebble driveway. It was a sprawling, double-fronted, white-painted, concrete-block bungalow with a red corrugated iron roof. On one side was a flower garden surrounding a well, on the other, rows of custard apples and purple granadillas trailing over wooden frames set parallel to the front wall of the building. Parked alongside the house, in an area marked out by two neat lines of halved coconut shells, was a newish-looking Land Rover.

Rosalie appeared from around the side of the house. Chris judged her, initially, to be a thirty-something Mauritian, or possibly Seychellois, but quickly realised neither was likely. Anna would have to use a native Chizumbe speaker and a local islander as her language informant.

'Rosalie, really sorry to turn up without warning,' Anna said. 'Valli's truck was coming up, and I took up the offer of a lift, and I've brought Dr Jamieson – Chris – with me. He's working on a fauna and flora publishing thingy and would love to go over to the bay with his camera. I told him about the wonderful bird life over there.'

'It's not at all a problem, Anna. I love visitors, but sad to say they hardly ever turn up. And Chris, it's really nice to meet you. Welcome. Come in. Daniel is out back. I'll get him in.

Danny! Visitors!' she called, as they walked into the living room.

Danny appeared from the kitchen, and while Chris had been mildly surprised to see the Land Rover, he was now astonished. Danny was white, six feet something, broad-shouldered, and his accent immediately marked him out as a mid-western American.

With the introductions over and coffee served, Chris couldn't resist it. 'Forgive me for saying this, but the last thing I expected to find out here was—'

Danny cut in, 'And I know what you're going to say. We get it every time a new aid agency official visits on the way up the coast. The answer's simple. Rosalie's mother was an island woman and her father the British District Commissioner for Central Region on the mainland. For some reason, which is impossible to understand, the colonial government included the island as part of his patch. He used to say it was because they were both as remote from civilisation as one can get, and that made them equally difficult, and easy, to manage! Anyway, they sent Rosalie off to school in the UK and then to the US, to Iowa State. We met in Canyon City, I think it was, got hitched shortly afterwards. We decided the modern with-it life wasn't us, decamped and came here… for the simple life.'

'Be careful, Daniel!' Rosalie said. 'That's a fine expression of our sentiments, but it's definitely over the top! We have lots of modern weaknesses: our coffee, our own beer – grow the maize out back – and technology we definitely have. Danny couldn't survive without his daily country and western fix from Diego Garcia Forces Radio. Then, there's our generator, cooker, paraffin fridge, and the Land Rover out there. We'd be totally lost without that. No technology! Danny's just a romantic.'

'OK, Rosie, enough!'

But she was on a roll. She wasn't going to stop. 'And, to prove guilt beyond all reasonable doubt, Danny, I dare you to take Chris out the back and show him what you're working on. Go on. Anna and I have some work to do.'

•

In a bamboo and thatch lean-to attached to the back of the house, resting in a heavily padded launching cradle, was an eighteen foot, dark grey, rigid-keel inflatable. On the transom were two 60hp outboards.

'Good Lord, Danny! This is something I wouldn't have expected to see on this island.'

'And in a way you're right, Chris. There isn't another remotely like it anywhere. It's my only *real* personal indulgence, except for my Rosie, of course. It reminds me of my time in the Marines. Rosie and I use it for fishing, and it's also the unofficial lifeboat around here. Locals appreciate that; it gives us leverage, something we wouldn't survive here without.'

'Where do you get fuel for it– and the Land Rover for that matter – living out here must make that a real headache.'

'Sure. And it really *would* be if we had to use the road you came up on. However, there's a forestry track. It starts just a few yards down the road to the bay. You'll pass it later when you go over there. In colonial times, there was a small lumber industry. It was made for that. It's mostly flat and as straight as an arrow down to the town – no tar patches or corrugations. It comes out onto the jacaranda tree road up beyond the government offices and the clinic.'

'Sounds like everyone should be using it.'

'You'd think so. The thing is, though, it's a narrow, single track, and runs through some real, isolated territory. If you break down in there, it's life-threatening. Far worse for the locals are the endless evil spirits they believe infest the place. They claim witches are buried there. A load of twaddle, of course, but we don't complain. It means it's almost our own private road, and we're always well-prepared: overnight supplies, nets, tools, tyre chains, high-lift jacks – the lot.'

An hour later and they were still talking pros and cons when Rosalie appeared. 'Lunch, you two! And Chris, I know you want to go off with your camera, but there's plenty of time. It's hardly a mile to the bay, and if you have one or two of our specials, you'll be there before you know it.'

•

He cycled off along what started almost as a road, but which rapidly turned into a sandy track. This came to a stop at the lip of a wide, sweeping bay. He could see that a vehicle of some sort had recently gone over it, down the slope a few yards and then, with obvious difficulty in the loose sand, had reversed back up.

He left his bicycle on its side and wandered along the top edge of the slope. The tide was close to full-in, and the upper reaches of the bay formed a band of pristine grey-yellow sand stretching in an almost geometrically perfect curve around to the north. He could see immediately why Valli had insisted he should visit the place; it was idyllic, with bird life galore. He found a spot at the base of a coconut tree, where he was able to sit in some comfort and take photographs, protected from the worst of the mid-afternoon sun. After a while, he dozed off, and it took the sound of Anna's repeated calling to wake him.

He made his way back along the beach to where she was waiting and up over the rise. His bicycle had already been stowed in the back of the truck.

'Well, what do you think?' she asked.

'Astonishing! There can't be many places like it left on Earth: deserted, peaceful and untainted.'

And yet, he sensed that wasn't exactly true.

PART TWO
REACHING

12 ENIGMA

On Tuesday evening, James Burnett's secure-line phone rang at home. He was almost expecting it.

'The island?'

'Yes, Director,' said the overnight duty officer. 'Came in a few minutes ago. Section's seen it, and says he thinks you'll want to as well... asap, and he says we'll probably need access to Delta.'

Burnett had full confidence in his African and Indian Ocean liaison chief. He was reliable to a fault and his intuitive intelligence was second to none. If he felt there was something he should come in for, then so be it. 'Right. Give me an hour. Alert Century House: they may want to get someone over and ask Section to get a team together to do a primary on the stuff. We'll use the comm. suite next to my office.'

'Will do.' And with that, the link was cut.

Burnett picked up his mobile. 'Ralph, can you bring the car round, please?'

He'd just got his raincoat on and was opening the door

when he heard the distinctive click from his dark green Jaguar outside on the drive as the handbrake went on.

'That was quick, Ralph.'

'Not really. I was already in the garage getting my things together. Where're we off to?'

'Thank you. No. That's kind of you. You get on home. It's only the office, and there won't be much traffic around in this weather. I'll return the car to the garage when I get back and switch on the security.'

'I really don't mind taking you over there, Director, but if you're sure, thank you.'

•

The world never stops; and so, neither can GCHQ. It never sleeps; there's no down-time. People come and go, day… night, and always in a low key, seemingly calm, unhurried sort of way. From the outside, one wouldn't think much of import was going on.

But, late on that Tuesday evening, external appearance belied reality. In the communications suite next to the Director's outer office, Section Head, two researchers and a technician were frantically trawling though dozens of photographic images and pairing them up with Chris Jamieson's spoken notes, which were being electronically transcribed into text. They then grouped and prepared the materials for projection, enlarging and removing any unnecessary and distracting background noise and visual content. On a separate desk was a single sheet of A4 containing the copy of an e-mail – two short paragraphs – from the British Ambassador in Ziaŵala.

When Burnett arrived, the team were as ready as they were ever going to be.

'Evening, everyone. Sorry about this. Harry, could you call the canteen? Coffee for everyone – my account. Now, what've we got?'

Section Head nodded across at the technical officer, and four rows of images instantly appeared on the screen. 'These are the guests in the hotel on the island. This top row is the Middle East lot. You'll recognise the Colonel, and we now have personal names for the other three. This one, here, is the second-in-command. He's called Goliath – sounds a bit like a circus act! Then, we have Abdel and Idrissa. In row two we have the Russian Ambassador and a secretary from their embassy on the mainland. It seems this is their third short visit together in the last couple of months. This woman at three is Anna something or other. She's a PhD student from Auckland, doing research. We've already checked with NZ on that one. It's OK. And this final row is a family group. Jamieson notes they use Arabic and says there's something odd about them – just feels it! But I'll come back to that one, if I may.'

Burnett nodded. 'OK. Go back to the Middle East group. What's Jamieson say about them?'

'There's a transcript on your desk. I'll summarise: first, they speak English when they're together; second, they sleep during the daytime, and are out at night; he doesn't know where they go; he says he's working on it. And third, and this is interesting, it seems he got into the Colonel's room one evening and photographed some bottles of chemicals and other bits and pieces. He says they're for use on the northern site... don't know how he knows that.' He nodded to the technician. 'This is the stuff. He also found a couple of pistol magazines – top left – no weapon. He says they're for a PC-9 ZOAF. We haven't checked.'

'It'll be right,' said the Director. 'That instrument, bottom left, a mini-GC?'

'He says so. Tech'll check in the morning.'

'No. Don't bother. What about the labels on those flasks?'

'No idea. We've a few Arabists on site overnight – that Morocco thing. We could track them down and get someone in late for the Chinese. It looks like that simplified stuff.'

'No. That can wait till morning. Go back to the Arab family.'

'Well, our good Doctor was up a hill taking photographs of the southern site – the one near the town – and noticed a flash on a neighbouring hillside. He pointed his camera in the general direction and took a stretch of video. We've managed to isolate a single frame with something on it. He was being watched, and his observer turns out to be none other than our Arab family man from the hotel – at least, we think so; it's a bit grainy. See what you think.'

Burnett looked at the two images that came up on the screen next to each other. 'Yep. Same person. OK. Next: any good images of the construction sites?'

'Lots. We've been selective. We've chosen four.'

James Burnett studied the images. 'Good Lord! Talk about security. That's quite something for a school-building site in a place where we are told nobody ever steals anything.'

'But there's also something else… something rather juicy.'

'I thought there might be, Harry. I noticed you were twitching. Go on.'

Harry signalled to the technician. Three photos slid onto the screen, alongside each other: the first a full-body view of a man, the second a side view, the third a close-up, full-face view.

'What have we got here?'

'Jamieson says this character appears to be living on the northern site. The man came out of the hangar building for a ciggy when Jamieson was up a hill taking photographs.'

'Chinese?'

'Can't be sure, but it looks like it. Jamieson also suggests possibly Korean. He's certainly not Middle Eastern.'

'Well, now that *is* interesting.' The Director pursed his lips. 'OK. Get Delta powered up; I'll authorise. Let's see if we can track down this chap and also the Arab stalker. Now, the ambassador's note?'

'Doesn't say a lot. Jamieson sent across some eucalyptus leaves to the embassy with instructions to test for a crystalline deposit in the veins. It seems that would indicate the presence of gold ore nearby, underground. He said it was a long shot and only a positive result would mean anything. The ambassador simply notes the test was negative. We've no idea what all that means.'

'I've heard of that one. It's a trick some mining companies get up to when they want to do some exploratory prospecting and don't want to be seen digging holes in the ground. Right, Harry. Let's get Delta going.'

•

By two in the morning, they had the identity of one of the two men, but they could find no record – written or visual – of the other, the fifth member of the Colonel's team.

The Director left instructions with the duty officer to set up an advisory meeting in the FCO first thing in the morning during the Minister's priority items' consultation hour. He then left for home, and for the four hours' sleep he'd get before he'd have to be back on the road again.

•

The Director's P.A. was waiting for Em as she came out of the lift.

'You're late again. You'd better get in there fast! He's got his desperate look, and it's plus a late night. He's even got your coffee organised. That's a first for him. Good luck.' She opened the door to the inner office and pushed Em in.

James Burnett was sitting at a side table. 'Come over, Em. Coffee's here. I'm afraid it's that island thing.'

He summarised Chris Jamieson's material and informed her that the NSA in Virginia had been asked to assist in identifying the Asian man living on the northern building site. Overnight, they'd come up with the answer.

'And,' he continued, 'as a result, what was a mere question mark on a small island – a minor crisis if anything – has suddenly become a full-blown, code-red one. So much so, it's now been decided that we meet with the US in Djibouti this coming weekend to map out a joint course of action. I want you out there to represent us.'

'Djibouti! You're not serious, Director! You *do* realise who'll be left in London, with me out of the office?' Em said.

'Of course, but he can't do all *that* much damage.'

'Don't you believe it! Remember, the Service put him out to pasture down in London because of the chaos he was causing here.'

'I know, Em... OK, I'll get personnel to send another pair of hands down to hold the fort. In the meantime, get in there tomorrow and tell the idiot not to do anything about anything without first referring it up to my P.A. Right now, though, I want you to stay here and update yourself on various matters. I've briefed Edith. She'll point you in the right direction. She's waiting for you in her office.'

•

The Director's P.A., Edith Reed-Robinson, pointed at a desk at the far side of her office. 'You can use that, Dr Freemont.' She passed Em a list of routines and protocols. 'And please observe those,' she added. 'Your first task is to prepare a message for the embassy in Ziawala to the effect that Dr Jamieson is needed in Djibouti at the weekend. I'll send it off for you. After that you need to access Dr Jamieson's restricted file; it's on the computer. Single click the BCB.1x on the desktop – top right. This afternoon, you and I will work on the Djibouti travel arrangements.'

Em skimmed through Chris Jamieson's file, and as far as she could recall, the only addition to the information they already held on him in London was the inclusion of an additional section headed *Service Consultancy Activities.* This identified sixteen overseas projects he'd led on behalf of various agencies of the British Government. Only four of them – in Costa Rica, Sudan, Tanzania and Peru – were spelt out in any detail, with ten or so pages on each, along with links to his personal reports. The other twelve were simply the name of a country, a project title, a date, and a reference number.

'Sorry to bother you, Edith,' she called over to the Director's PA. 'There're a number of projects here with just a title and a reference number. How do I get access to them?'

'Ah, those. My apologies. I should've told you. They need higher authorisation than this office.'

'Higher? You mean the Chair of the Intelligence Committee or the Minister?'

'Sorry, I really wouldn't know about anything like that. It's just that *we* don't have access.'

'I see. Thanks.'... '*For nothing*,' she added under her breath.

Following the list of restricted project reference numbers, was a brief addendum headed *Personal Observations*. It listed a couple of pages of non-attributed verbatim comments from people who'd apparently worked with Chris Jamieson over the years. Em skimmed through them. Most were general and anodyne, but there were three that caught her eye. She read and reread them:

A stubborn man! He delivers, nonetheless. I found his methods and solutions somewhat unconventional.

Never discount his instincts.

Ignorance he accommodates willingly, but foolishness he definitely does not tolerate gladly! (And didn't I half suffer for it!). You've been warned!

She smiled. In her one brief meeting with the man, he'd already more than amply demonstrated those very characteristics.

13 CONVERGENCE

'Ah! Dr Chris, bon jour. Ça va, this fine morning? I 'ave been waiting for you to finish your breakfast. I 'ave an envelope for you. It was left behind the counter at – 'ow you call it in English – an ungodly hour? I 'aven't peeped.'

'Thank you, Madame. Did you happen to see who brought it?'

'Non, mon chéri. It was just there... maybe a secret girlfriend, or magic, per'aps! Inside, it may say, n'est-ce pas? Then again, it may not.'

Chris took the folded diary page out of the envelope.

PRESENCE ESSENTIAL DJIBOUTI SATURDAY.
TRAVEL TO THE MAINLAND A.M. FERRY.
MET. AIR TO DJIBOUTI ARRANGED. NEED A
COVER STORY. HR

He read and reread the message. Perhaps this was a way out for him, the next throw of the dice in a game that he was increasingly uncomfortable playing.

Madam was watching him closely 'You look troubled, Dr Chris. I see distress. There is a problem. Can I 'elp?'

'Thank you, madame. It's a small matter, really. It's some information for my work here. It's just that I'm puzzled why the message should be delivered in the middle of the night by some unknown person.'

'Strange things 'appen 'ere, Dr Chris. It is a place full of mystery. My 'ubby is always telling me that.'

•

Half an hour later, Chris walked into the clinic compound. Bess came out to meet him.

'My apologies for bothering you, Bess,' he said. 'You must be busy, with Mina off on the mainland. It's just that I woke up this morning with a slight problem and I've been wondering whether I should do something about it.'

'What is it exactly?'

'I was up at Rosalie and Danny's place yesterday, and cycled over to a bay on the east coast. I felt fine. Then, this morning I woke with this sharpish pain in my left shoulder. It's settled down a bit now, but I think maybe I should go over to the hospital to get it checked out. Mina mentioned that they're quite well kitted out for this sort of thing.'

'Yes, oddly, they are, and, unfortunately, we're not. Our equipment just isn't up to it. I'm sure Mina would insist you do exactly what you're suggesting. Let me get you something to help you rest, and I'll get one of the aid people upstairs to drop you back down at the Mirabilé in the Land Rover. In the morning, you'll need to make sure you get on the ferry. It's early tomorrow.'

'Thank you, Bess. When Mina gets back this evening, could you let her know what's happened, but don't let her come rushing down to see me. I'll be fine.'

•

It was a bitterly cold, wet Thursday evening at Stansted. Emmeline Freemont, bent forward against the driving rain, hurried across a deserted apron and onto an American Airlines Constellation. She was given a double seat up against the bulkhead at the front of economy class. Further back there was a rowdy group of twenty or so other passengers, all of them look-a-like, bronzed young men.

Settled in, she was soon half-asleep, eyes closed, head resting against the window. She felt someone flop down beside her, and was instantly alert, and shocked. 'Good Lord, Director! What on earth are *you* doing here?'

'Hi, Em. Sorry if I made you jump. I'm coming, too… last-minute directive from the P.M.'s office. I got on up front just as they were closing the doors. You wouldn't have seen me.'

'Where're you sitting?'

'First class, by myself, and I've got my own hostess – a privilege of position, I guess. Come up and join me. We can run over the arrangements for the meeting, and the food will be a lot better. You might even get some rest. This lot back here are going to be at it all night.'

•

Next morning, Em was woken by clapping and cheering from the main cabin as the Constellation banged down through a red, dust-laden dawn onto the runway of Ambouli International.

A blacked-out Humvee was parked nearby, waiting for them. It took them to the left, between a line of F15 Predator drones and past a couple of C130 transports. It slowed down at a security gate, and they were waved through into the military base.

'We're meeting in here somewhere, no idea where; it's a big, faceless sprawl of a place,' James Burnett said, as their vehicle headed towards the exit gates at the far end of the base. 'It seems they can't – or won't – provide suitable civilian accommodation on site, so we're booked into the Djibouti Princess in town. It's not a bad place. I was there a month or so back. One of its virtues is a great fitness suite with an Olympic-size swimming pool.'

This was Em's first visit to Djibouti and now, as she looked out of the air-conditioned limo across the flat, arid plain to a low dusty plateau in the distance, she sensed it wasn't going to be an easy one. If she could manage it, though, a bit of swimming, sauna, massage and some quality R and R might just about make the weekend tolerable, and there was the added advantage that she'd get a recovery day off back home. She'd be able to get over to her mother's place and rescue poor Cedric from her clutches.

•

Just before midday on the Friday, Megan Prytherch, First Secretary at the British Embassy in Ziaŵala, met Chris Jamieson at the mainland ferry terminal. After a mediocre lunch at the Ngwazi, belying its reputation as the best restaurant along Freedom Avenue, they were taken in the embassy limo to the airport, in through the emergency gates and straight onto the tarmac, to a waiting Z60 Learjet.

It was only when the plane had levelled out and was heading due north that Chris felt it appropriate to broach the issue of their visit to Djibouti. 'Any idea what this is about, Megan?'

She shrugged. 'I'm pretty much in the dark. The ambassador was scheduled to come, but his wife's at a critical stage in one of her recurrent bouts of malaria and he didn't want to leave her. I'm a last-minute infill. He's prepared briefing notes for me, though I've not had a chance to look at them yet. I think it's something to do with liaising with the Americans about gold deposits up in the north of the island.'

'I've heard that as well,' Chris replied, 'but Americans? I didn't know they were involved. Either way, I'm surprised that they should bother getting us to Djibouti just for a meeting. It seems a bit like overkill to me.'

She shrugged. 'I'm puzzled about all the kerfuffle, too… could be done with a bit of video-conferencing, or a few simple telephone calls. The ambassador did let slip, though, that the Americans are deadly keen that we have a face-to-face on it. It seems they think that's the only way of coming up with a satisfactory solution to the problem – that is, if there is actually a problem.'

•

Two hours later, as they made their way across the marble-floored concourse of the Djibouti Princess, Chris Jamieson was surprised to see Mavis heading towards them, hand outstretched.

'Dr Jamieson, how nice to meet you again,' she said. 'You'll remember me – Emmeline Freemont – London.'

His hesitation was momentary only. He smiled. 'Emmeline. Yes, of course. Nice to meet you again.'

'*Em*, please… and First Secretary, Megan,' she continued smoothly. 'It's great to see you, Meg. Congratulations on your promotion. The last time we worked together was, I think, Rio?'

'Hello, Em. Yes. Quite an adventure, that one! It's good to see you looking so well. That Jake chap, by the way, did you ever come across him again?'

'Him! Thank God, no. I daresay he's still lost in the jungle with his brunette. At least, I hope so; it's the best place for him! Anyway, you two, you're going to find tomorrow really exhilarating. It starts with a short breakfast briefing with Director Burnett at 06.30. At 07.30, we leave for the US base, where we'll be sequestered somewhere until we all resolve what it is we have to resolve. And before you ask, I've no idea what that is. Personally, I'm hoping everything can be tied up tomorrow and I can get back home on Sunday. I've got a desperate mother and dog problem.'

As she said it, Em knew she was tempting fate. Things never turned out as expected when her Director got involved. He had a way of opening doors one never knew were there, and he seemed to take pleasure in levering people through them.

DJIBOUTI DANCE

'Remember, we co-operate fully with our American colleagues,' James Burnett said. 'We need them; they know a lot more than we do; they've got resources. Just follow my lead and whatever you do, don't volunteer things. One last thing; we're being joined by an MI6 colleague, Ida something or other. She's coming in on an overnight commercial flight and should be landing about now. She'll come straight to the meeting. Em, when you can you, please brief her. And that's about it. We're off to the base in half an hour. In the meantime, Chris... a quick word?'

•

Just after eight, they were settling into the palatial base conference suite, everyone bemoaning the waste of a good weekend. Chris Jamieson sat down quietly at the back, wondering where the whole thing was heading. The business had now become altogether too complex and unpredictable for his liking. He was being well and truly levered out of his comfort zone.

His train of thought was interrupted by approaching voices from the corridor behind him. He instantly latched onto one of them; he'd heard it before, and quite recently. It had a distinctive timbre. Frustratingly – and most unusually for him – he could put neither a name nor a face to it. And so, when the new arrivals entered the room, he was both prepared and unprepared. Amongst the group was the Arab family man he'd last seen three days earlier in the Mirabilé with a wife and two unruly children. And now he was here, conversing in fluent east-coast American English.

The Djibouti US base commander, who led the group in, introduced himself, the American Ambassador to Ziaŵala, and the man from the Mirabilé, a Major Alphonse Stryker of the National Security Agency in Maryland. Burnett introduced the British group.

'Couple of others from Diego Garcia just landed,' added the Commander, 'and I'm also told an MI6 colleague is on the base somewhere and will be joining us shortly. While we wait, I suggest coffee. Over there.'

Jamieson joined his recent Mirabilé fellow guest. 'Hello. You get around a bit.' There was genuine humour in his voice, though, try as he might, he couldn't suppress a slight tinge of sarcasm.

'Don't do too badly yourself, Dr Jamieson. Great photography by the way; Lord knows how you got me on film. Either you're brilliant or I'm losing my touch. It could be both, of course!'

Chris smiled. 'Wife and children here with you?' He meant it as a joke, though from the response he wasn't sure it was taken as such.

'What a thought! God, no!' It was said with real vehemence. 'No wife or children. That stuff wouldn't work with my life. No. That was a cousin and her kids. They've gone off to Amman to visit family members before going back to the States. Kids were brilliant; they resisted the temptation to use English, well most of the time. They were insufferable, though, ill-behaved, spoilt brats!'

The arrival of Ida and the US and UK representatives of the Diego Garcia base brought their discussion to a halt and was the signal for the Djibouti commander to bring the meeting to order.

'OK. Our meeting will continue until we get this thing tied down, and that means into this evening and then tomorrow, if necessary. I suggest that anyone who's got plans for the weekend should put them on hold.' He paused. 'My assistant, Brenda, has just come in – behind you – along with Freddo, our Comtec guy. Between them they'll build up a visual record, and Brenda will also ensure that each agency's lead representative gets a full electronic record. And now, I'd like to invite Director Burnett to take over.'

James Burnett moved to the front of the room and perched on the corner of a table. 'Thank you, Commander. Good morning, everyone. Our agenda is simple: to produce proposals for taking this island matter forward. Our two governments will then allocate responsibility for any action that's required and will let us know *before* we leave Djibouti. Right. I suggest we start by trying to make sense of this character who seems to be living on the northern madrassa site. There he is, up on the screen. He's Zhou Leong Hai, a Chinese scientist. A couple of years back, he was accused of embezzlement and bribery by his work unit manager. The intelligence we have suggests it was a trumped-up charge to protect a senior party official. Anyway, one night, before they could pick him up, he disappeared across the Yalu river into North Korea with his wife and child. Our guess is he figured the authorities would never think he'd do that. Who in their right mind would? Anyway, Chinese security spent months looking for him in his home area of north-east China and to the south in and around Hong Kong and Macau.

Once across the Yalu he ended up in the hands of the Propaganda and Agitation Department of the Workers' Party of Korea and they put him to work in a weapons production facility somewhere in Pyongyang. The next time he appears on the radar is when he gets off a plane in Sanaa, and now he's on the island... Ambassador Shaw, something to add?'

The US Ambassador nodded. 'Yes. Our embassy in Beijing was recently approached by one of Zhou's cousins. He said he'd had a message from Zhou about what had happened to him. The gold info, but *not* the Zhou link, was then leaked to someone in the Chinese Central Committee, and that's when it hit the fan. There may be no connection, but I can add that there's recently been a marked increase in development aid to the Ziawala Government via a back street Shanghai bank.'

'Thank you, Ambassador. That's helpful.' James Burnett now looked across at Chris Jamieson and smiled apologetically. 'Sorry, Chris, but with the Zhou issue clear, can I now ask you to lead? I know I was uncertain about this earlier, but I suspect we might all benefit from some academic rigour.'

Chris had earlier agreed, very reluctantly, to consider managing the meeting – after all, it was sucking him in further – and now, as he made his way to the front, he wondered just how poisoned the chalice was he'd been handed.

It was Megan Prytherch who started the ball rolling. 'Chris, how about we begin by listing our assets?'

And so, *Assets* became the first of the mind map's legs on the screen. That blossomed in various directions and sub-directions: *People... Embassies... Djib/DG facilities... Security Agencies.* Other legs emerged: *Difficulties/ Challenges... Communications... Action... Threats.*

Chris found it a real challenge keeping the levels of generality and specificity in some semblance of order in the minds of the participants and, at many points during the flow back and forth, it struck him how awful it would be to have these people as students. Their creative but diverse and sometimes chaotic thinking processes would drive him mad. However, he stuck to a tried and tested strategy: he'd agree with everyone; he'd systematically massage the various egos; he'd gradually wear down everyone's emotional and intellectual resistance up to the point where everyone was exhausted, and a workable compromise could be reached.

•

And so, by 1830 hours exactly, and with the threat of an evening session looming over the gathering, six recommendations to be sent back to Washington and London were finally agreed.

The proposals were brief and suitably devoid of any detail:

1. *Set up a single US/UK activity communication point in Ziaŵala*
2. *Gain access to the construction sites on the island*
3. *Deploy UAVs to continuously monitor the sites and the Qaaem submarine*
4. *Monitor the activity of the Middle East group living in the hotel*
5. *Establish a UK/US embassy liaison committee in Ziaŵala*
6. *Prepare a detailed inventory of Chinese aid to Ziaŵala.*

'And that's it,' Chris said wearily as the last recommendation went up on the screen. 'The devil, of course, is now most definitely in the detail!'

There was a spontaneous outburst of applause. Whether this signified relief that their immediate ordeal was over, or a compliment to his stamina, was unclear to him. Later, on reflection, he decided it was probably because he'd managed to push everything up the line to the politicians, their masters, and save everyone from a dreary Sunday.

IMPLEMENTATION

Zhou Leong... Leong Zhou... Hai Zhou Leong... And there he was. He'd tracked him down along with his research papers. They were all in English. Their focus was broad, cutting across ionisation, laser design, and meta-materials.

Em appeared in the doorway. 'Chris. Sorry. We've been summoned... conference suite down the corridor, and it's now! Meg and Ida are already there. I've been sent to get *you*.'

He was surprised. 'Me, as well? I've done my bit. Tell him I'm printing out Zhou's academic papers; it's important, and there are lots of them.'

'Please, Chris, don't put me through this. To be fair to him, he did tell me to ask you nicely. He never stops... drives me mad sometimes. He can be worse than my mother and that's saying something! Please. You've got to come.'

He shrugged. 'OK, if I must. What's it about, anyway?'

'God knows! Anything's possible, but whatever it is, none of us is going to like it.'

'Make yourselves comfortable,' Burnett said, as they joined the others in the conference room. 'We've got a fair bit to get through. The US Ambassador and I have been talking to our governments and we've managed to establish common ground on most of the contentious stuff. The single co-ordination point issue took a lot of back and forth, but it's now been agreed.' He stopped and looked across at Megan Prytherch. 'And I'm afraid, Megan, it's got to be our covert on the island.'

Her intake of breath hurried him on.

'I know, and *I'm* not happy with it, either, but nothing else makes sense. In any event, that *is* the decision. Linked to that, the Americans have agreed in principle to give us a couple of their Mark IV particle transmitters, one for the embassy, the other for the co-ordinator... Chris, you're looking puzzled?'

'Not puzzled, just surprised that the US would actually hand over a Mark IV transmitter to some unknown person on a backward little island in the Indian Ocean. What's the *in principle* thing?'

'It seems the US Secretary of State has yet to approve.'

'What if our covert refuses to take the job on?' Megan asked. 'And there's the training issue.'

'We believe refusal's unlikely, Megan, and I doubt training will be an issue.' He looked over at Chris Jamieson. 'And, Chris, I guess you know what's coming next.'

'I'm *sure* I do.'

'But look, there's no obligation,' Burnett continued. 'This is now way beyond what you signed up for.'

'I understand, but I don't like half-finished jobs; that's not me.'

'Al Stryker did say he'd give it a go; he's going back to the island anyway, but his photography skills are crap – I quote him – and his ability to manipulate bits of wire in locks about the same. And, Em, you're aware of the duty-of-care issue around putting a non-services person into a potentially hazardous situation.' He hesitated to let the point sink in. 'And my apologies for this, but I'd like you to go to the island with Chris.'

He hurried on. 'Ida, I'm sorry if this *isn't* what you want to hear, but I'd like you in my office to co-ordinate our end. Your Director mightn't agree, of course, but that seems unlikely. After all, we're taking the pressure off him. This business is something your people would normally have to deal with.'

Ida sighed inwardly. She would have relished the prospect of a bit of action or inaction, as the case might be, on a remote Indian Ocean island, but she knew it made sense for Em to do it. And anyway, an attachment to Cheltenham for a week or so – out of Century House and away from that horrendous paperwork – was an excellent consolation prize. She smiled. 'He'll agree. I'll make sure he does.'

'Megan,' Burnett continued, 'I've talked to the ambassador, and he confirms you'll be available to lead the co-ordination in Ziaŵala. A protocol group needs setting up to conduct a Chinese activity monitoring operation. You personally will continue your liaison with our island covert. OK. I think that's about it. Any questions, anyone?'

Chris looked up. 'More an observation than a question, Director. It strikes me we left something out today in our discussion earlier. Em, you'll remember I asked about that pixelated patch on the satellite image of the northern site. No-one picked it up. I'm wondering whether we might have missed a trick.'

Burnett nodded. 'You're right. That one did slip through. I can't see it would have changed our conclusion. Nothing we can do about it now. Anything else?'

'I have a personal problem, Director,' Em said. 'It's my mother. You know what she's like, *and* she's got my poor dog! Two days together is their max. After that, they're as likely as not to kill each other.'

Burnett was aware of the saga of Cedric and Em's mother. They were something of a legend in Cheltenham and had kept the family liaison department entertained for years. He smiled. 'I'm back in the office at 08.00 on Monday, Em. I'll send someone down first thing to see her and let her know your return has been delayed a day or two, and we'll arrange for Cedric to be put into kennels. That place next to the canal?'

'That's the one. Thank you. I just don't want her in some cop-shop accused of attempting to murder a noisy canine. Oh, and can you make sure it's a woman who goes down to see her?'

'Of course. Now, that leaves one matter,' Burnett continued. 'UAV aerial surveillance starts Tuesday. Djibouti and DG will between them provide round-the-clock visual and communications monitoring over the island. Right. Anything I've missed?'

'Just the next twenty-four hours!' said Megan.

'Apologies, Megan, I often fail to see the trees for the wood. It would be helpful if you could be back in the embassy tomorrow getting Em's consular status documentation together. Em, Chris, you'll stay here tomorrow. The base commander has some useful equipment. You'll need to familiarise yourselves with it. Monday, you'll travel back to Ziaŵala on the Lear and onto the embassy and then over to the island on the Tuesday ferry. Ida and I will return to the UK tomorrow after breakfast. That's it. Done! Bed!'

•

Em locked her door and flung herself onto the bed, kicking her shoes off as she did so. She felt physically and mentally exhausted.

The phone rang. 'Bloody hell! I don't believe it,' she shouted. 'Doesn't he *ever* stop?'

'Em. Could you come over for a minute? There're a couple more things.'

'All right, Director. Give me a sec. Need to reconstitute myself.'

She pushed open his door.

'Come in. Help yourself to a malt. Got a good age.' He was alert and cheerful; she found it intensely annoying.

'Am I going to need it?'

'Depends how you see these things. First you need to know that there's a Chinese naval group – three warships – in the Indian Ocean, heading in the general direction of Ziaŵala on an official show-the-flag visit. The Chinese informed us about it a couple of months back, well before the gold story started circulating. We don't think that one's a problem. There's something else that is, though. The US has lost track of an Iranian Kilo sub they were following… a 2000-ton ex-Soviet monster. It surfaced briefly in Socotra a week ago, and then disappeared. We picked up some radio chatter early on, which indicated it was heading due south, and as you know there's already an Iranian Qaaem sub right now sitting on the sea bed a few miles to the east of the island.'

'Lord! Shouldn't we let Chris know?'

'I've thought about that one, and my ethical self says we *should* tell him, but I've decided to be a coward on this one and leave that decision and the timing to you.'

'Well, thank you for that!' Her annoyance was obvious, but it was mixed with more than a bit of pleasure. She was being empowered; he was letting her off the leash.

'I'm not being as cavalier – or generous – as may appear, Em,' he continued. 'It really *is* about timing. Right now is a touch premature. In any event, it would make not one iota of difference to his decision to help. In fact, it would just reinforce it. I know him.'

•

After breakfast, Burnett joined her by the pool.

'Em, a quick word. You'll need to sign for any equipment you take with you from the base here. They won't expect it back; it's just an accounting thing. Make sure, though, that you take it in *your* luggage when you travel back. Your consular accreditation will get you through unscathed. They might just search Chris.'

'Understood. There's one other thing, Director – and my apologies for asking – but I was wondering whether you could hand-write a Weapon's Release Authorisation for me? I'm told the base commander's got a Sauer he'll let me borrow.'

James Burnett pursed his lips. Weapon authorisations were something he seldom provided – for *any* of his people. The fit-for-purpose rules were rigorous. Circumstances had to be extraordinary, and in his Service there was little need for it. However, sending this woman into an unknown situation, and one that was completely beyond his control, fitted that bill. She would have to operate autonomously and at the same time be responsible for Jamieson, a civilian consultant. In any event, if there was anyone in his organisation whose judgement he trusted, it was Emmeline Freemont: she knew the constraints; and she was cautious and meticulous.

'OK, I'll do that just now, but remember…'

'I know. I know.'

THE RETURN

'You're good with that thing, Em,' Chris said.

'Been better. I need practice. I trained on one of these with the Ministry of Defence police. I was good then – second in the class. The men didn't like that. Anyway, it's coming with us, only as a persuader… You never know.'

He wasn't reassured. He'd long accepted that in some circumstances a firearm was necessary, but he found such weapons distasteful; he'd had too many pointed at him over the years to feel otherwise. He'd seen gun-pointing persuasion morph into action more than once, when initial reticence had become blind determination.

The other equipment the base commander made available was much more to his liking, though. The radio-communication units and the night-vision gear made real sense. They opened up options, whilst a firearm just closed them down.

•

'I was wondering, Em, how we get through mainland customs with our gear,' he said later that day. 'It's unlikely anyone will bother searching us, but you never know.'

'Not a problem, Chris. Megan has already faxed through my diplomatic accreditation letter. I'll take all the stuff in. It'll be OK. They'll just smile or grunt, depending on which side of the bed they got out of that morning, and wave me through. Megan says it always happens like that, though she did say the island can be less predictable. It seems they don't understand the rules. She suggests we travel over on the ferry separately. I can always wriggle out of a problem. It'd be a lot harder for you.'

•

The next morning, Megan Prytherch picked Em up from the Mao Luxuriant Palace on Freedom Avenue and took her down to the harbour to catch the ferry. And, despite Megan's repeated reassurances about the four-hour journey, Em was apprehensive. A sightseeing trip round the protected waters of a local harbour was one thing, a longish sea journey across open ocean was something else altogether. She had a strategy, though, and as soon as she was on board, she rapidly worked her way through the growing mass of passengers to the front of the main deck and found an unoccupied corner. She put one suitcase down, sat on it and dragged the other one up across her knees. She wanted to be as far away from the fumes of the diesel engines as she could get.

Chris Jamieson arrived at the ferry by taxi ten minutes later. He made his way to the first-class cabin, where he squeezed himself in next to two sullen-looking mainland policemen.

This time his journey across to the island turned out to be very different. His travelling companions were totally uncommunicative and spent the journey half-asleep, though occasionally one of them would come to life and make some ribald comment in Swahili about any woman who dared peer into the cabin through the window. Chris smiled to himself and wondered what they would have done had they been aware he was a near-fluent Swahili user and knew much of the rich stock of insult and obscenity the language boasted.

Em, meanwhile, remained resolutely wedged in her corner, head down, eyes closed, and it was only when the ferry turned into the island harbour and then scraped up along the landing stage that she came back to life, cramped but triumphant.

She took Chris's advice and remained where she was, watching as the bulk of the people surged forward, squeezed themselves onto the gangplank and then turned into a bloated snake as they splayed out down onto the wooden jetty. It was only when she saw Chris reach the gangplank that she picked up her suitcases and joined the tail end of the disembarking passengers.

Out in the car park, Mina was waiting for Chris. She was leaning on the open door of Valli's Toyota and waved him over as he appeared. 'Come to pick you up,' she shouted. 'How'd it go?'

'I'm fine, false alarm. However, the heart man did say I should take salt tablets and drink plenty of water for dehydration. It seems a bit contradictory to me, but there you go, and thank you for coming, but you really shouldn't have gone to the trouble. Anyway, how did you know I was going to be on today's ferry?'

'I didn't, but you know my father. He's the source of all knowledge and wisdom, and has his little birds all over the place. He just said, "He's coming," and thrust the keys into my hand.'

As she was talking, Chris caught sight of the tall figure of Em emerging from the customs shed. She had two young men in tow, each carrying one of her suitcases. 'Mina, that woman just coming out with those two lads… I noticed her on the boat. She has to be going to the Mirabilé. Perhaps we could give her a lift? I can sit in the back of the truck.'

'Of course, and I'm sure we can squeeze both of you up front,' said Mina. 'I'll go and get her.'

•

Madame Lemessurier came out of the main entrance. She was smiling broadly. 'Dr Chris, finalement, you 'ave arrived. Wonderful! I see you are well… And, 'oo do you 'ave with you? It must be my new guest? Goodness! And I think she is already another of your fine ladies.'

She turned to Em. 'Come along in, my dear, and excuse me for saying, but I must tell you the competition round 'ere for Dr Chris est très grand. You join a long line. To compensate for this disappointment, 'owever,' and she smiled broadly, 'I am going to give you the best room in my Mirabilé. All my rooms are the best, you understand, but yours is the very best! It is on the ground floor, Wing B. And already I know your name. It came in early this morning – a note from the government offices in town. *Emmeline Freemont*, it said. What a wonderful name! Also, *Dr...* incroyable, n'est-ce pas? So many doctors in this small place.'

17
OMEN

Rosalie Marquand was finally drifting off on that hot and humid night, when a tiny point of light appeared in the far corner of the ceiling. Half-awake, half-asleep, she watched it with one eye. The light grew in size and intensity, and began spreading out and flowing down the walls of the bedroom. The rumble that followed brought her to full consciousness. It was the distinctive noise of a lorry with a beaten-up suspension system banging its way across the tops of the corrugations.

'Danny, Wake up! Wake up!' She poked her husband in the back. He grunted and moved away. She leant across, grabbed him by the shoulders and shook him furiously.

'What? What is it, Rosie? What's wrong?'

'A lorry – just now – going east. How's that possible?'

'It's not! You're dreaming. Go back to sleep. It's the middle of the night for God's sake! We gotta be up at five to catch the tide.' He turned over… and then froze. He, too, could now hear the noise of a vehicle. He sat up. 'Ooops!

Sorry, Rosie; you're right, but that'll be it coming back. The driver's made a mistake. He probably meant to go south. You know what some of those guys are like, half-asleep most of the time. They operate on screwed-up auto-pilot.'

'No, Danny. You're wrong. Listen. That's just a small truck. What I heard was a *lorry*! I know what a lorry sounds like… and I *wasn't* dreaming!'

He watched the light from the truck appear on the far wall of the bedroom, move up onto the ceiling, and around each of the walls as that vehicle, too, turned off onto the east coast road.

'Jeez, this is just ridiculous! Something's not right. I think I'd better go and see what's going on. They may need help. You get back to sleep. I won't be long.'

'No chance! You're not going out there by yourself! I'm coming with you.'

•

Danny manoeuvred the Land Rover off the track and into the bush well back from the lip of the bay. 'We'll go on foot from here, Rosie,' he whispered. 'Something's happening down on the beach; we need to be careful.'

Rosalie retrieved a torch and night-glasses from the glove box, and they made their way back onto the track and towards the bay, ready at a moment's notice to jump into the bushes and conceal themselves. As they came towards the top of the rise, they could hear voices and, at the top, they could see the lights from four or five torches flicking across the cabs and sides of two vehicles – a lorry and a truck – parked directly ahead just above high-water mark. Further down, at the water's edge, two more torches were trained on boxes in a small inflatable. Out on the water, perhaps two hundred yards from the beach, there was a string of bright multi-coloured lights bouncing up and down and swaying from left to right, illuminating a grey metallic surface below in an ever-changing mosaic of light and shadow. Figures – six or seven – were moving in and out of the patches of light.

'Binoculars, Rosie. Quick. Jeez! No,' he muttered, 'I don't believe it. Can't be!'

'What is it?' Rosie hissed. 'Let me see!' She tugged the binoculars out of his hands.

'Impossible!' Danny continued. 'It's a sub, sitting on the surface. We've got to get the hell off this track right now. Move. Up the slope over to the right. No torch!'

'What do you think's going on?' she whispered, as they made their way gingerly around patches of low-lying thorn clinging to the hillside. 'Smugglers?'

'On this island? Not a chance. Anyway, it's a submarine, for God's sake! Can you imagine that? No. This is something else altogether.'

About half-way up the slope, they came to a clear patch of ground. 'This'll do,' Danny whispered.

They lay down on the stony surface and took it in turns to watch the inflatable through their nightglasses as it made its way back and forth between the submarine and the shore. In the light from the torches, they could see boxes of various sizes being offloaded and manhandled up the beach. Some were lifted into the back of the lorry, others into the truck.

It was Danny who first noticed the grey tinge of dawn developing over to their right along the edge of the ocean.

'Put the glasses away, Rosie!' he whispered. 'We need to get out of here.'

•

Back in the house, they sat with coffee, waiting for the return of the vehicles. They didn't have to wait long. First came the rumble and then the engine noise. The lorry turned right and headed up the north road followed by the truck, which turned left, down towards town.

'OK, Rosie, my love. That confirms it. We have a problem,' Danny said as the noise died away. 'The question is what do we do about it.'

'We go to town and report it to someone, of course.'

'I don't disagree, but we'll have to be ultra-cautious. We don't know what's going on or who's involved in this business, whatever it is. We'll start at the Public Works Department. That lorry looked like a PWD vehicle to me.'

•

They drove down the forestry track, past the clinic, and into the PWD compound, where they spoke quietly to a trusted contact.

'A lorry, last night?' He checked the work sheets. 'Nothing here, but that doesn't mean anything. Supervisors often take vehicles for their own private use. They sneak them out and never record it. What you're saying sounds very strange. I don't think I want to know. If I were you, I'd be really careful who I talked to.'

Their next stop was the clinic. Mina came out and joined them in the compound. 'You two look serious. Come in. We've a few minutes before we start. We'll get some Darjeeling organised.'

Over tea, Rosalie recounted the events of the early hours.

'Good Lord! That's pretty disturbing,' said Bess. 'It doesn't sound like our island. No-one smuggles things here, and certainly no-one drives lorries and trucks around in the middle of the night. There must be some official you can report this thing to. I'm not sure who, though. They're all a bit of a funny lot.'

Then it was the Mirabilé. Madame was in full flow when they arrived. She had Chris Jamieson cornered in reception. She looked up as the Land Rover came down into the car park. 'Ooz that? Ahhh, it's our Rosalie and her man, Daniel. I must get that lazy cook of mine to make some fresh coffee…

'Come in, you two. Sit down. I was just telling Dr Chris that I am a person 'oo is a detritus washed up on the shores of empire, or 'owever it goes – so that's why I am 'ere. And I mustn't forget 'ubby. He ended up 'ere too – detritus, like me – and now 'e's under the best bit of white marble in the country next to my baobab. That was his favourite spot… But hold on. I'm talking and you two look worried. You 'ave something to tell us.'

'We have a problem, a big one, Madame,' Rosalie said, 'and need advice.'

She began relating the events of their early morning adventure, but she didn't get far.

'Stop! 'old up!' Madame said, 'Anna and my new guest are just coming back from their walk into town. See them out there. They must join us and listen to this.'

•

Five thousand miles away, James Burnett was driving to work in his wife's VW, hoping to get an early start clearing the backlog. His phone rang. He switched to hands-free.

'Director, code orange and rising. Can I speak?'

'Yes, but circumspect.'

'Critical from treasure island. Major target movement and ongoing. Make sense?'

James Burnett hesitated. 'Just about. Get hold of Ida. Ask her to contact Em, via the embassy. She knows what to say, and copy our Century House liaison in.'

'Everything?'

'Yes.'

BREAK-IN

Rosalie and Danny's story switched to speculation and general expressions of concern. Em glanced across at Chris Jamieson, inclining her head slightly. 'Excuse me,' she said to the group, 'back shortly.'

He joined her in reception a couple of minutes later. She was leaning on the counter, frowning and staring at a neatly cut-out diary page.

'I was going to have a word about what we've just heard, but now this has appeared in my box.' She passed it to him. 'Does it mean what I think it means?'

DR M VITAL BRING FORWARD CLOSE INSPECTION-NORTH, ASAP. URGENT. PP

He stared at it for a moment and nodded. 'It means exactly that: PP is today, and ASAP is tonight.'

'Lord help us, Chris! That's impossible. We can't even get up there, let alone break into the place.'

'True. But if we can solve the first of those problems, we'll have the answer to the second.'

She was irritated. 'For God's sake, speak English!'

'I mean Rosalie and Danny are the solution, and we need to grab them now before they disappear.'

'I'm not sure I understand. But, before we do anything, you need to know something I got from the Director. He said I was to pass it to you at an appropriate time. I think that may be now.'

She summarised the information about Chinese naval activity in the Indian Ocean, and the missing Iranian Kilo submarine.

'Well, your timing's impeccable, Em. That information more than confirms it. This has to be done tonight… and stop shaking your head! Come on; they're moving.'

'Rosalie, Danny, before you go, can we have a quick word? I was on the mainland over the weekend and met the British Ambassador. He mentioned there may be a problem linked to those madrassa building sites and asked if I could look into it as I went about my flora and fauna business. Em, here, came across from the embassy so we could work on it together.' He hesitated. 'We think what you saw last night relates to that matter. The thing is that Em and I now urgently need to get onto that building site up north, and we were wondering if you could help us.'

'Of course!' Rosalie said. 'We can drive you up there, but there's a watchman, and a fence round the place.'

'Yes. Thierry mentioned that the other day. I think, though, there may well be access from the sea.'

'The sea? Well, that's definitely us. When?'

'I hate to say this; you must both be exhausted.' He took a deep breath. 'Tonight?'

Rosalie shrugged. 'Exhausted is something we can catch up on. Danny, your call. Weather? Tide? Launch site? Fuel? Time? Think positive!'

Danny closed his eyes and, after a moment, the faintest of smiles played on his lips.

Rosalie was watching closely. 'Yippee. It can be done, and *I'm* coming!'

Danny now became quite animated. 'There's a small bay a short stretch up the east coast from our place that we sometimes use. We can get to it in the Land Rover with the trailer and boat hitched on. A bit of a bumpy cross-country ride, but then it'll only be an hour and a bit on the water.'

•

That evening, around the dining room table in Danny and Rosalie's house, the plan was agreed. The men would be dropped off at the launch site and take the inflatable up the coast to the madrassa beach. The women would drive on up to the abandoned rest house and onto the site track. They'd conceal the vehicle and make their way up to the vantage point Jamieson had used earlier. From there, they'd be able to view the whole site and warn of any emerging threat.

'We'll need to communicate,' Chris added. 'We'll use these.' He produced three Djibouti base radio-communications units from his backpack.

At this point, Danny and Rosalie looked across at each other. Em noticed their mutual acknowledgement. 'I'm sorry,' she said. 'We've not been entirely honest with you. Perhaps we should explain.'

Rosalie raised her hand. 'No, Dr Em, please. We understand. We don't need to know any more. It's not an issue. And, I think, right now we'd better get going.'

•

With only the rolling shape of the low cliff edge vaguely etched against the stars to guide him, Danny gently manoeuvred the inflatable in towards the shore. He stood at the console, listening to the hiss and slap of the water, and feeling for every movement of the swell under the keel. He knew a surge would soon materialise, seemingly out of nowhere, and the boat would rise up and roll forward on it, gathering speed as it did so. His timing and reaction had to be exact.

And then it came. He throttled back instantly and held the boat as straight as an arrow. A moment or two later, with a quick twist of the accelerator, he forced the boat towards the sand and gravel cove that marked the southern end of the construction site beach. The swell broke under the rigid keel and became a wave, which hissed forward up the slope, taking the boat with it. Danny was ready. He leapt over the side, grabbed the front of the inflatable and held it from being sucked back as Chris Jamieson jumped off onto the sand.

As the next wave began falling back, Danny pushed the boat back out, forcing it sideways on as he did so. He threw himself on board and paddled furiously until the front had come fully round. The boat was now fifteen yards or so out from the bay. He dropped the paddle and threw a small anchor over the front, waited until it held and, as the boat began to swing around, he lowered a second anchor over the stern. Moments later he was on the beach, breathless and wiping the salt water from his face.

'That'll be OK. Tide's dropping. We'll be able to wade out to her when we get back. Right, Chris, across those rocks to the right and we'll be on the open beach. Where to after that?'

'Along to the far end of the beach, up through a small excavation site into some empty half-built stuff. Directly across from that is a hangar-type building. That's where we stop and think. There may be a problem.'

'Like what?'

'The place is bedecked in cameras and movement-sensitive security lighting linked to an alarm system.'

'Wow! So you think maybe the watchman will be a problem?'

'You never know. In any event, we should use these.' He took two sets of night goggles from his backpack. 'And, if a light comes on, just flick the goggles up.'

•

Five minutes later, they were standing in an opening in a shoulder-high concrete block wall looking across at the hangar building. 'OK, Danny, there's a cable linking the security lighting and alarms. It's on the surface over towards the gate. I'm going to have to find it and short it.'

At that moment, three lights directly opposite them on the side of the hangar building came on.

'Too late!' hissed Danny. 'We do that?'

'No. Not possible. We're well out of range. Let's see what happens next.'

The site remained silent: there was no alarm. The lights went off and, at the same time, lights at the front of the building came on.

'What's it mean, Chris?'

'It means, I think, that Lady Luck is with us. It looks like the system's screwed. It could be anything. Calibration, sequencing, positioning, timing, rats, fruit bats, or even spiders. We'll give it another minute or so just to confirm. Then we'll go round the end of the building to the other side. There's a personnel door there, directly in line with one you can see on this side.'

'So why not use this side?'

'See the footpath leading to it?'

'Sure. But there's only the watchman, and he's locked out; he'll be asleep, anyway. We can just walk in.'

'Not exactly. Come on. We need to move. I'll explain later.'

•

Em was propped up against a rocky ledge, its stored-up daytime warmth seeping into her back. She was peering through her night-vision glasses, monitoring the building site. The on-and-off security lighting made concentration difficult, though far worse was the niggling fear that at any moment a snake would emerge from some hidden recess and slither across her legs.

As far back as she could remember, she'd not been able even to look at a picture of anything resembling a snake without shivering in horror. It was a reaction she neither understood nor could control. Her mother called it ophidiophobia, saying it sounded respectable – grand even – and blamed it on an over-imaginative Sunday-school teacher obsessed with the serpent in the Garden of Eden. And now, here she was in exactly the circumstances she'd heard Chris say were ideal for them. It was only the pressure of her immediate task and the threat of a crisis erupting below them that was preventing her turning into a hopeless jelly. She steeled herself and watched as two figures ran across the open ground between the school building walls and the hangar building.

•

'Danny, torch, lock,' Chris whispered, when they reached the personnel door on the far side of the building. 'This won't take long.' He pulled a small crochet hook and a size eight jeweller's screwdriver from a side pocket in his backpack and inserted them in the padlock. Then, with one flicking away above the other, he quickly aligned the heavy levers one by one. There was a satisfying click, more felt than heard. He gently lifted the lock off and passed it back to Danny. 'I need you to hold that, Danny, and wait here for me.' He took one of the radios from his backpack. 'Use this. I've got one and Em and Rosalie have got one. It's live, and we're all linked. Green is *Clear*, Orange, *Caution*, Red, *Crisis*. Press whatever's necessary. It'll override the current state. If you *see* a *Red*, or have to send a *Red*, drop the lock and get the hell out of here and back to the boat. Wait fifteen minutes, then head out. Don't hesitate. Em'll talk you through it on the headset. I'll be back soon... I hope!'

He pulled the metal handle down slowly and evenly and eased the door inward fraction by fraction, his left hand bridging the opening at the base to prevent any sudden movement. Gradually an unimpeded view ahead and to the left emerged. Above, suspended from the arched, metal frame supporting the roof, were a series of low-power fluorescent strips. Ahead there was a high metal partition, which he guessed ran down the length of the building. To his left he could see a low wall of concrete blocks and beyond that a number of stacked oblong containers.

He crawled over the metal doorframe and onto a rough concrete floor. He could now see a passageway running off the central partition. That would lead to the matching personnel door on the other side of the building. To his right there was a further partition cutting across the building. It contained two doors. From the one on his immediate right came the low hiss and crackle of a short-wave radio; that would be the radio room. The other door he knew was almost certainly the problem one.

He looked round for his escape options. He could always run for the opposite personnel door, but that would be seriously problematic; he had no way of knowing whether or not it would be unlocked. Then, there was the main door up at the front, to his left, but again... locked or unlocked? Realistically, there *was* only one escape option, the way he'd come in.

He straightened up and, with his back pressed against the outside wall, moved sideways towards the row of concrete blocks. He stepped over them and in amongst the containers. There were seven groups, some wood, some metal. The group on his immediate right comprised five neatly stacked, dark-green, ridged metal crates. He'd start there. He eased up the heavy, well-greased lid of the top one. It contained a shoulder-held rocket launcher along with four rockets nestling in pairs alongside. It was a short-range missile system. He pulled his camera from his backpack, photographed the contents, and took a step back to photograph the black numbering on the side of the crate. As he did so, he noticed an oblong piece of yellow card attached to one end of the bottom-most crate. On it, in the neatest of black felt-tip capitals, was a simple identification of the contents: RPG-7 (5X4).

He knew that he was going to find an identifying card on each of the groups of boxes. Someone had methodically labelled each stack, and thus done his job for him. All he had to do was photograph each of the cards.

Seconds later, he was on the move again, towards a partly open door in the central partition. Once through that, though, he sensed he'd be trapped. He gently pushed at the door and held his breath. It swung open with a sigh.

He stepped inside, into what was an Aladdin's cave of specialist scientific equipment, and steadied himself against the door frame. He switched to video and moved his camera in an arc to cover the whole room. He then moved warily between two work benches to the far wall, where there was a large wooden storage bin containing fist-sized rocks. To the right of that were two glass filtration tanks, minute bubbles of gas covering the insides of the lids. Next to them was a row of glass containers, some open and some sealed, holding small quantities of a grey-silvery metallic material, each a different shade. He wouldn't get too close. He took a single photograph. That would be more than enough.

He backed out of the laboratory and moved swiftly down to the radio room. He pushed open the door. Facing him was a bench containing an array of military radio equipment. A receiving channel was outputting static.

Later, he'd debate endlessly with himself as to whether he'd become over-confident, or just been plain careless and unable to resist the urge. But he did it: he stepped through the doorway into the room. Instantly, an ear-splitting alarm started up immediately behind him, above the door.

'Damn it!' he shouted in frustration. He took two steps across the room, photographed the equipment and two documents lying alongside it. Then, it was two steps back to the door, and half a dozen more to the side entrance where Danny was waiting.

'An alarm!' Danny exclaimed 'Great!' He sounded distinctly pleased. Here, at last, was a bit of action, albeit without any real threat to accompany it.

'Padlock on *now*,' Jamieson shouted, 'and let's get out of here, and fast!'

'But Chris, no-one here and the watchman's locked out.'

'Yes! No! Explain later. Run! Same route.'

THE FIERCE BIRD

Zhou Leung Hai was a simple man, a quiet man, yet a highly skilled scientist with an endless capacity for work, study and research. One would never think of him as a man of action. He knew nothing more satisfying than to sit in the shade of a tree reading Mandarin literary texts and, when he could get hold of them, scientific research papers. He placed little score by supposed great political ideas. Communist Party mantras, the sayings of the Dear Leader, the rantings of so-called western preachers of democracy, were all just noise to him, and of no value. They all amounted to much the same thing – mere disguises for human avarice and a narcissistic craving for attention and power.

He often reflected on why he was in the mess he was in. His conclusion was always the same: he was one of life's natural victims and there was nothing he could do about it. He'd been sucked in by circumstances. If he'd smiled at the right times, slapped people on the backs, invited people round for quality foreign brandy and shark fin soup, or just given the odd backhander, like some others he knew did, he might well still be at home outside Benxi with his wife and daughter. But no, he'd made the mistake of being too simple, too honest, and had paid dearly for it.

Then the crisis had come, and out of nowhere. He'd been accused by a senior Party official of misusing research funds allocated to his work unit and selling research data to an American CIA agent disguised as a tourist. It was complete and utter nonsense, a fabrication, a subterfuge, and a way of getting rid of him, and the evidence he himself had come across of corruption, but he would never have been able to prove his innocence in the face of declarations by powerful public officials; that was a given. And so, he'd been forced to flee across the North Korean border with his wife and teenage daughter.

When he'd surfaced with his family in the People's Democratic Republic of Korea, penniless and with no way back, he'd been passed to the North Korean National Security Office for processing. They'd quickly recognised his value and had put him to work incognito in a sprawling, scientific military complex near Pyongyang. They allocated him his own one-room flat six floors up in a faceless, grey tower block on the outskirts of the city, well away from the prying eyes of the nouveau riche and the hordes of political cronies who lived a life of relative comfort in inner-city condominiums.

He was ordered never to attempt to contact anyone in China either directly or via one of the many smugglers who daily crossed the river. If he did, he was informed, he and his wife and child would... and he could never bring himself to even think the words, though they were there, burnt into his brain. And so, if he kept quiet and did the bidding of his masters, he and his family were safe and together, at least for the time being.

Or so his reasoning went. Then, in the August, a Security Bureau official came to his workstation and told him he would be leaving within the week for an island in the Indian Ocean to assess gold deposits. He was told to forget about his family. They would stay behind and would be looked after. He knew exactly what that meant.

Even though the risk was immense, he contacted the man who'd smuggled them across the river into the DPRK and paid him to take a message to his brother in Benxi telling him what was happening. In his note he begged his brother to do all he could to get his wife and daughter back into China, if he wasn't back from the island and in touch by Chinese New Year. He knew that if he wasn't back by then his wife would be left with no means of support, thrown out of their flat, and sent to a labour camp. His daughter would be sent away for re-education, or more probably sold for a few dollars as a bride across the river in China to some ill-educated farmer desperate for a wife.

His minder in the factory had told him to forget about any equipment he might require on the island; everything would be provided.

He was put on a flight to Sanaa, where he'd been met by an Iranian, and taken to Socotra by road and dhow. There, he'd been secreted below decks in a second dhow, and three days later taken ashore after dark in a small inflatable and driven to a construction site, where he was met by another Iranian calling himself Goliath. He took him into a hangar-type building and instructed him to set up living quarters in three linked compartments in the corner at one end.

The following day, late in the evening, a Colonel Mohd Reza Mahil had turned up and told him to draw up a list of the equipment and chemicals required for a detailed qualitative and quantitative analysis of the composition of the rocks in the excavation area enclosed within the site, and in the silt on the sea bed running out from the beach.

Then, over the next few weeks, there'd been a flurry of activity – invariably at night. Scientific equipment, generators, air conditioning units, a CCTV system, a radio receiving-transmitting unit, electric fencing cable, and endless other bits and pieces had arrived and been dumped in the building he was in. Within days, it had all been organised and put in place, and he was ordered to begin his work.

It was around this time that the Colonel arrived late one night with a quad bike in the back of a Land Rover. He told Zhou to do his testing and analytical work in the daytime and to patrol the site on the quad bike every evening. At the meeting, the Colonel had handed him a pistol and a shoebox containing six ammunition magazines. 'If any person gets in here, you must shoot him,' he'd said. 'The site is fenced and electrified, and only I, Colonel Mahil, have the key to the gate. Anyone else found here is trespassing and must never be allowed to leave.'

Zhou had nodded dumbly, quite horrified. 'I know nothing about guns,' he'd said. 'I do not even know how to make this work.'

'You are a scientist!' the Colonel had spat at him, dismissively. 'Work it out – and practise. There is much space here. Shoot some bats! Many of those.'

And so, Zhou had been left locked in, not to examine gold ore deposits, but to deal with something much more complicated and technical. He also now had to share his temporary home with a weapon of death. It was a dreadful predicament. But he was under no illusion: the freedom, safety – even lives – of his wife and daughter were now in jeopardy. The ransom to be paid for their safety was the success of the endeavour he was involved in. And the thought that now haunted him, on a daily basis, was that at some point he might have to point a gun at a fellow human being and take his – or her – life. If he didn't, he'd be condemning himself and his family to a dreadful future.

•

And, on that night, as Chris Jamieson was tiptoeing towards the radio room and Danny was hovering at the personnel door, lock in hand, Zhou was enveloped in a comforting dream, a dream of home.

He's wandering through the flower-filled meadow which slopes gently away behind his family home near Benxi. It has all the colours of the rainbow.

He's leaping over a river and soaring like a Jiu, an imperious golden eagle. He's diving, soaring, floating, diving again, again, and again, but never arriving anywhere.

He doesn't want to arrive. It is safe not to arrive. He is part of an eternal cycle of existence... But something goes wrong. As he dives, his path is blocked by a fierce black eagle of monstrous size. He gets closer and closer and sees a single, crimson, bloodshot eye and feels its yellow breath as its giant curved crimson beak opens to seize him.

It squawks and screeches, deafening him. There can be no escape.

And he wakes up screaming, beads of sweat rolling down his face, forming multiple rivulets down his neck. It is fully ten seconds before he realises… *the alarm!*

He cursed 'That incompetent technician!' He'd watched him install the system the previous week and warned him the calibration looked wrong. Even a mouse would set the thing off, but Abdel had simply flicked his fingers at him and told him to go away, and now it had happened and he was going to have to switch it off. He knew that if he didn't, the infernal deafening wail would go on for ever. He rolled off his mat and felt around on the concrete floor for his glasses, torch and flip-flops.

As he got to his feet, he heard, above the wail of the alarm, the clang of the personnel door beyond the radio room. He froze. It wasn't possible. No-one had a key to that door except the Colonel and anyway he knew about the radio room alarm and was not the sort of man to set it off by mistake.

From the top of a cupboard in the corner of his tiny sleeping compartment, he grabbed the pistol the Colonel had forced on him and, in underpants and flip-flops, he stumbled through his shower room, out into the main thoroughfare and over to the radio room. First, he had to switch that damned alarm off. He couldn't think straight with it clanging away, let alone attempt to tackle a possible intruder. He slid his hand frantically along the top of the door frame, grabbed the reset key and thrust it into the keyhole in the plastic box on the wall.

The silence – and relief – were instantaneous, and the return of the annoying radio static almost reassuring. But panic came flooding back. What should he do? Something? Nothing? He checked the personnel door. It had been locked from the outside. He ran back to his room, pulled on his shorts and vest and went out through his own personnel door. Puffing with the exertion, he ran along the side of the building to the main entrance and clambered onto his quad bike. Whoever it was had to have got in through the main gate. They'd probably bribed the watchman.

All the security lights along the side of the building were on but before he got anywhere near the gate, he could see it was still locked. Of course, that stupid watchman didn't even have a key. He *couldn't* have let anyone in.

He brought the quad bike around in a half circle, switched off the engine and stood up, peering into the darkness beyond the lights of the vehicle. He could see nothing, nor sense any movement. Maybe, he'd imagined that door clanging shut.

He waited for a moment, trying to come to terms with his predicament. Should he just go back to bed and forget any of it had happened? After all, the Colonel needn't be told and even if someone had broken into the place, it could only be wayward youths looking for something sellable.

He started up the quad bike and drove it slowly towards the half-built school buildings He'd swing around behind them, and he'd go over the roughest patches of ground. The lights would bounce around and the vehicle would make lots of noise. Surely that would frighten any miscreants off.

But, as he began to think he'd done all that was necessary, the lights of the quad bike caught a side view of two figures dressed in black with backpacks and what looked like goggles mounted on their heads. They were at the upper edge of the excavation site. Instinctively, he braked hard; the vehicle lurched and skidded to a halt. He grabbed his gun from the footwell, stood up, took a deep breath, and pulled the trigger. Once… twice… three times.

•

'Chris. What the hell was that? You OK?'

'Yep, keep moving, Danny! Over to the right a bit, then down!' He switched on his two-way radio. 'Em! We may have a problem. What can you see?'

'Oh, God! He's got a gun. You both OK?'

'Yes. What's he doing?'

'Stopped. Just sitting there, with his head in his hands.'

'OK. Makes sense.'

'What d'you mean?'

'Later.'

'I can't see you! Where are you?'

'Excavation area, moving to the beach. He can't follow us down here; won't try anyway. We'll be OK now. You two need to get moving. We'll see you at the launch site. I'll call on the way in.'

•

Just over an hour later, the Land Rover, with the inflatable bouncing along behind, was heading cross-country back towards the north-south road.

After a whispered consultation with Em, Chris passed his camera up front. He leant forward and gave a carefully worded commentary as Danny went one by one through the photographs he'd taken inside the building. Rosalie was driving. She was hunched forward, her arms and hands gripping the steering wheel, her neck taut and stretched.

THE CAT IS DEAD

There were voices in the kitchen. They were hushed. Chris wandered through.

'Morning,' said Danny. 'Last one up. Em's washing the salt off the trailer. She volunteered. I couldn't say *no* to that.' He grinned. 'Just before you came in, I was saying to Rosie how hard I found it keeping up with you last night.'

Em came in from the back. '*I* heard that, and I wouldn't be impressed, if I were you!' Em said. 'He's just plain stubborn. He just refuses to be beaten.'

'My wife calls it bloody-minded, and if you had my legs and back right now, you'd see things very differently. Which reminds me, Em and I need to apologise. We knew that character on the quad bike would be around. We didn't think he'd be a problem, though.'

'Well, he wasn't until he tried to shoot us!' Danny said, ruefully.

Em looked up. 'Now, that's the funny thing; he didn't. I could see him very clearly. He stopped his quad bike, stood up, and fired – one, two, three – just like that, straight up into the air. Then he sat down again. He was more likely to have downed a passing bat than hit one of you two.'

Rosalie nodded. 'And that's exactly what happened. The thing is, though, Dr Em, this is still a bad business, isn't it?'

'I'm afraid so.'

'And I think it's not going to be good for us here,' Rosalie continued. 'You know, only last week Danny and I were talking about the state of the country, the corruption, and things. Also, there've been men going around the villages getting people on edge, threatening them with eternal damnation and the fires of hell, and telling them to lock up their wives and daughters. They never bothered us, of course. If they *had* come here, we'd have given them what for. Danny's a whizz with words when telling someone to disappear.'

'Corruption is one thing,' Danny added, 'but we couldn't survive here if a bunch of maniacs started running the place. Anyway, what are we going to do now? Obviously, the authorities on the mainland need to know what's going on. I think we should contact the Immigration Officer. He seems to know everything and everyone.'

'Yes, but that might be a problem, wouldn't you say?' Rosalie said.

'Possibly. And I suppose, even if we could trust him, all he'd do is pass it up the line. It'd still disappear into the bureaucratic sludge.'

'There may be a way of cutting through that knot,' Em said, 'a fast track, if you want. Chris and I could probably get a report directly to the British Ambassador on the mainland. He'd be able to contact the President more or less immediately. Chris?'

'Makes sense. We could send something through on the ferry tomorrow. I'm told the captain runs a reliable private courier system. For a few US down payment and a guarantee of more on delivery, it seems he'll go to considerable lengths to get a job done. Of course, what the President will do when he knows is anyone's guess.'

•

Later that morning, as the Land Rover was passing the clinic heading into town, Chris leaned across to Em. 'I've had a thought… that spare radio,' he whispered. He nodded towards Danny, sitting up front.

She shrugged. 'Don't see why not. Can it be locked?'

'Mmmm.'

He leant forward. 'Danny, could you drop us off in the town centre? We need to pick up a few things. We'll walk back down to the Mirabilé. We were wondering whether you'd like to hold onto our spare radio for the time being. There may be more action in that bay, and we need to know if anything else happens. You'll be able to contact one or other of us at any time. We can also lock it so that only you two can use it.'

'Oh, yes!' Rosalie replied quickly. 'We'd like that. What's the locking thing?'

'I can code the start button to your index fingerprints. If anyone else tries to use it, the circuits will fry.'

'You mean like in those films – a sizzle and a bit of smoke?'

'You got it. One other thing: it'd probably be wise not to say anything to anyone about last night. It may be that the cat's not yet out of the bag.'

'But, Chris, that guy who shot at us knows?'

'Didn't shoot *at* you, Danny!' Rosalie said.

'OK. The guy with the gun, then.'

'Somehow, I don't think we need to worry about him,' Chris said. 'I'd bet anything that when we disappeared, he breathed a sigh of relief and went back to bed, desperate to forget it all happened.'

•

The town centre was as it should be; light early evening traffic, men sitting in twos and threes under trees, conspiring, women with babies on backs, bundles on heads, going about their business, and, at the top of the hill inside the concrete blocks, just beyond Valli's Emporium, a group of ragged urchins kicking up dust as they chased a punctured, plastic football around.

'You know, Chris,' Em said, 'if my mother were here, right now – God forbid – and looking at all this, she'd go on and on about how idyllic it all was. She'd pull out her camera and start causing offence all over the place, and if I told her what we'd just been through, she'd huff and puff and say I was suffering from an overactive imagination. To be honest, the prospect of ending up like her terrifies me. She's from a different universe, and not even a parallel one! How about your wife – Martha, isn't it? What would she make of this place?'

'I don't really know. I doubt she'd even be prepared to come here. A while back, I wanted to take her to Peru. All she said was that she spends too much time having to worry about me when I'm away without having to worry about herself as well. Nowadays, I tell her when I'm off again. She just says to make sure my will's up to date. I think she doesn't want to know where I am or what I'm up to… Hang on. Valli's. We need some rope.'

'Rope? What on earth for?'

'We've got to get into the building site outside town and that requires rope. There's a fine takamaka tree well away from the track and next to the security fence. That plus rope and we're in, and it's got to be this evening.'

'This evening! Bloody hell, Chris! Have you lost your marbles? When are we ever going to get some sleep?'

•

Meera emerged from the back of the shop. 'Ah! My two doctors! Best customers, ever. And where is my soon-to-be doctor, Anna? No worry! No worry! Come in. Tea?'

'Hello, Meera,' Chris said. 'Thank you for the kind offer, but I'm afraid we must turn it down. We've just been up beyond the town looking for flower specimens. We've probably got ticks and God knows what else all over us. We need to get back for a shower. We've just dropped in for a few yards of rope – strong, but not too thick or heavy. Do you have such a thing?'

'Rope? Not a problem! Hang on!' She smiled broadly. 'I joke! A moment. I will consult Wallimohamed. Ropes are his department. He knows his ropes! Right now, he's in the engine of the Toyota, swimming in oil. I'll go and pull him out. Ah! He'll be a mess!'

She was soon back. 'Yes! Yes! He apologises. He is very slippery.' She smiled. 'And he says we have just what you need. It's behind the counter, left, first shelf... and, yes, I see it! Here you go. He says it is twenty yards and you must have it for the price of ten – oh! And a ten percent discount; he so likes tens. And you must both come and visit us at ten tomorrow for mid-mornings. You can pay then.'

'Thank you, Meera, and this looks spot on. Mid-morning tomorrow? Yes, we promise. Wouldn't miss it for anything.'

•

'Odd, back there,' he muttered as they walked into the Mirabilé car park.

'What was?'

'It's as though we were expected. It's difficult to tell with those two... I'm probably just imagining things.'

Madame Lemessurier and Anna were leaning on the desk in reception, chatting.

''Allo, 'allo, you two,' Madame said. 'Where you been? No breakfast! Mauvais, n'est-ce pas, Anna? And they look so tired.'

'No, we're fine, Madame,' Chris said. 'We were out before dawn looking for orchids above the town. Dr Em's an orchid fanatic and we heard there's a special type up on the hill. It's called vanille sauvage. I first came across it in the Seychelles.'

Madame was immediately attentive. 'What's its fancy name? I love those names. My 'ubby loves them, too!'

'The Latin? It's *vanilla phalaenopsis*. You've got something similar in your garden. I can see it from my balcony.'

'Oh! Magnifique! You will spell it for me, and I will write it down.'

'And tonight,' Chris continued, his story developing greater fluency with each passing word, 'we're going to go up a hill to the south of the town to see some *Angraecum brongniartianum*. They have pearly white and green flowers, and when it gets dark, the perfume they produce is exquisite. I've just got this rope from Valli's in case we have to negotiate a few slopes.'

'Wonderful! But if you are going up that 'ill tonight, you must be careful: leopards, 'yenas, and those terrible snakes... And, Dr Em, soon-to-be Dr Anna 'ere will, I am sure, let you use 'er bicycle.'

21
BACK-UP

A dying glow suffused the sky behind them as they turned off the track. They concealed their bicycles and began making their way up the slope on foot.

'Chris, was she serious about the snakes thing?'

'Don't worry, Em. They'll pick up our vibrations, way before we get near them, and be off. She likes a bit of drama. We should probably use our torches, though. It's rough underfoot, ankle-twisting stuff.'

When they reached the forested area, they noticed a greenish glow threading its way up through the trees to their left. It grew stronger as they got higher.

'That's the site,' he said, 'screwed-up system like the other place, I shouldn't wonder. Just stay close. We'll be on a flattish patch of rock soon.'

Gradually, the security lights at the far end of the hangar building slid into view, followed by the rest of the site.

He came to an abrupt halt. 'Torch off, Em. We have a problem. Look.'

'Good Lord! The place is crawling with men.'

'Yep. That's our plan out of the window. I think all we can do now is set up the video and audio on my camera for a few minutes. Maybe we can pick up something useful.'

•

'I know it's ridiculous,' Em said later, as they wheeled their bikes down into the car park, 'but she's sure to ask about those Agra-whatever flowers. What's our story?'

'No need for a story. We won't disappoint her. I just happen to have a very fine photo of an Angraecum on the camera card. All you need to remember is that they have a beautiful almond scent.'

'Lord help us! I bet you were a boy scout in your youth!'

'No. I'm just a detail obsessee, or so my wife claims.'

•

Back in the Mirabilé, they sat on the bed, watching the video.

'What's the language? she asked.

'Can't tell; volume's not good enough.' He paused the video and peered at the screen. 'They look Arab to me… early twenties, Middle East bazaar clothes. I think we're looking at a plausibly deniable group of professionals. How many, do you think, Em?'

'Eighteen… nineteen?'

'So, with the Mirabilé four we have at least twenty-three.'

'Yes, and that's really bad news, Chris. It's critical that report goes off on the ferry tomorrow.'

'I agree. Let's get a draft outline together just now. Then I'll finish it off and put it onto a disc. It won't take me more than half an hour. I can get it down to the ferry captain in the morning. You need to rest.'

•

He'd been overly optimistic. As midnight approached, the words on the screen began sliding into each other; the lines kept changing places; gibberish was beginning to fill his head. 'Morning, first thing… ten minutes,' he muttered. He sat on the bed and bent forward to unlace his mosquito boots. He fell sideways and, half-on and half-off the bed; he was instantly oblivious to the world.

PART THREE
SCUDDING

SILENCE AT DAWN

There was an absence. It drew him into semi-consciousness. Something was wrong. He opened one unfocussed eye. The fan was still, the air heavy.

He rolled off the bed onto all fours and pushed himself up onto his feet. He stumbled across the room, pulled back the curtains, slid open the balcony doors and stepped out into the early morning shadow. Over towards the sea wall, he could see the sun beginning to touch the upper tips of the pale branches of the baobab.

There was an omnipresent silence. That morning birdsong was missing from amongst the plantains and the poinsettias. There were no weaver birds cavorting and squabbling in the foliage around the foot of the baobab.

And something else was missing, something even more ominous. At that very moment, the fine tenor of the muezzin should have been echoing out from the mosque, calling the faithful to prayer, and cars and motorbikes rumbling and backfiring their way through the town, as men made their way to their morning devotions. But there was nothing.

He leant over the balcony, straining to hear something – anything – from the floor below, but there was no cook banging around in the kitchen, no clatter of plates, and no Madame singing as she went about laying out the buffet counter.

He closed his eyes in frustration. He'd seen this before. But then – in a very different country – it had been the absence of early morning whistles in the streets, and the shouting of the gangmaster summoning workers out to lorries waiting to take them to the paddies. He knew exactly what the silence meant.

'Sod it!' He needed to hear his own voice. Events had overtaken them; the window had closed and sooner than even *he* had expected.

There was banging on his door. He snapped into focus and stepped back into his room. He hurriedly pushed his laptop and radio under the bed and grabbed at his clothes.

'Hang on! Won't be a second!' The banging stopped, only to be replaced by a panic-stricken voice. 'Dr Chris! It's me. I'm sorry. Oh, Mon Dieu! We need to talk now! 'Urry!'

He opened the door to a very frightened woman.

'Come in. Sit on the bed... deep breathing. What's happened?'

'Dr Chris, there is a big problem... you see, I like to visit my 'ubby early every morning and then I go to my kitchen. But this morning there was no cook. So, I go to the car park and look up the road to 'urry 'im up, but 'e's not there. Instead, there are three men up at the crossroads with big guns. They are pacing. Now it's almost seven – No cook. Everywhere is dead!'

'Anything else happening?' he asked quietly.

'Yes! No electricity, and those four Arab types 'ave gone. I 'eard them drive off in the dark. They 'ave vamoosed, and they 'aven't paid one cent in the last three weeks! I 'ave peeped into Dr Em's room. She's fast asleep. Anna is downstairs keeping guard and Mr Abdullah is not in 'is room, but 'is things are there!'

'Abdullah?'

'You know! 'E was 'ere with 'is family last week – those noisy kids! Came back by 'imself, on yesterday's ferry.'

'Oh, him. Abdullah. Yes, of course.'

'What's 'appening to us?'

'Not sure, Madame. I think, though, that we have to wait and see how things unfold. Why don't we have a mini conference? Dr Em won't mind being woken up. You can blame me, and if you can find Mr Abdullah, he might know something. I'll be down just now.'

'Oui. Oui. Can do that!' And, half-walking, half-running, she disappeared off into the corridor.

He looked round his room. He'd have to conceal his equipment. His radio would go into the bougainvillea alongside his balcony; no-one would willingly push their hand into that stuff in the expectation of finding something hidden there. His recording binoculars would go in the air-conditioning vent above the door and his draft report he'd wipe from his computer. He had it all on microchip. In an emergency he could always swallow it and recover it later. As yet, though, there was no problem. Whoever it was out there would be too preoccupied establishing control over the island to be bothered with the residents of the Mirabilé… but that time would almost certainly come.

•

He found Em in reception, leaning on the counter and staring up towards the road.

'Here we go, Em. What we got?'

'Two under the mango and a third out in the open in the middle of the junction. That report?'

'On micro. No problem, though I'm afraid it's not going anywhere. Madame's panicking and so I suggested she get you up and go and find Abdullah – that's Stryker's local name. It seems he came over on yesterday's ferry; an interesting sense of timing that man's got.'

'Yes. She came whizzing through a few moments ago dragging along a nervous-looking wreck of an Anna. She also said the Colonel's group has cleared off... not surprising, I suppose.'

'Not really.' He looked up towards the mango tree. 'You know, I think I might just wander up there and have a word with those chaps. They might even let me take a few photographs.'

'Lord help us! You serious?'

'Why not? There're probably worst things one could do.'

She shook her head. 'But why on earth would you want to do such a thing?'

'Dunno, really, except I'd like to know what sort of people we're up against. If I ask if I can take a photo and they smile and line up, we'll know they're locals, and not those types we saw last night.'

'Either way, Chris, they're going to be as nervous as hell. It would be dangerous.'

'Maybe. Here's the thing, though. If you were one of those men and a daft-looking, middle-aged white man, looking like a tourist, comes meandering up the road towards you, T-shirt, shorts, hairy knees, sandals, the whole thing – that's me! – what would you do? You might laugh, but I doubt that. You're more likely to develop an instant insecurity complex, take the safety catch off your AK, and tell the idiot to shove off, back where he came from. No... either way, it's as safe as houses. Anyway, I guarantee those guys have been told that shooting anyone is a definite no-no, and bad for business.' He looked pensive for a moment. 'Thinking about it, why don't you tag along?'

She looked at him quizzically. 'But that'd make it worse!'

'Not really. The opposite. There's only *one* thing worse than turning a middle-aged foreigner into a Swiss cheese, and that's doing it to a young, foreign woman! That'd be sort of double haram squared... Come on. Let's do this. It'll get your blood circulating. It'll be fun; I promise you.'

She took a deep breath; he was laughing at her. 'OK. I will, then!' she said. 'But if I end up dead, my mother will blame you, and you really don't want that!'

They walked out of reception and made their way slowly up through the car park and onto the road.

'They're twitching, Chris. I swear it,' she whispered out of the corner of her mouth. 'And what's that guy by the tree up to?'

'Seen him. Relax. He's using a radio, getting instructions from head office. Probably. Just keep smiling... oh! Here we go. We're being cut off. Now, that's interesting.'

'What is?'

'Later. Right now, grit your teeth, think of whatever, and show lots of deference. They're in charge. We're timid suitors and of no strategic interest to them. They don't want anything to do with us.'

The man making his way towards them raised his Kalashnikov. 'Stop! Arrêt! Halti!'

'Hello! Bonjour. Good morning,' Chris said, with as broad a smile as he could muster. 'Please, can you tell us what is happening? The electricity is not working in the hotel. It is very hot in there, and we're short of food.'

He wasn't really expecting an informative response, nor did he get one.

'Back! Back!' The man waved his gun at them, and with a flourish he flicked the safety catch off.

'OK, Em, that's it. Retreat. Don't look back. Hum your favourite piece of music to yourself. We don't want to offend his dignity.'

•

'That really wasn't nice,' she said, back in reception. 'Thank God you didn't try the photo idea. Anyway, what do you make of them? What was the interesting thing?'

'Well, I think they're locals, and not very well-trained ones. Their AKs are still covered in grease, straight out of those crates. You could see it glistening in the light. As a raw recruit, the first thing you learn is to clean your weapon thoroughly and above all never to take the safety catch off a loaded greasy firearm. You're likely as not to shoot yourself in the foot!'

'But that's exactly what that guy did, and he was pointing the gun at us!'

'True. Sorry. I didn't think about that one earlier.'

But she knew he had thought about it; he thought about everything. He'd been playing the odds and using her as a counterweight.

He hurried on. 'I also noticed they have a heavy machine gun in the box by the tree. It's still in bits. My bet is they don't know how to put it together.'

'So, not those types we saw last night.'

'No. And when you think of it, you'd only put foreigners on the streets to run a takeover in the very last resort; it'd be counter-productive. You use locals as the public front, the fall guys. They take the heat, and the blame. The ones we saw last night will be the backstops, ready to move if things threaten to get out of control. That's a standard pattern in these things. Ahhh, and I see Madame and Anna are now in the restaurant. Let's join them.'

•

'What to do, Wallimohamed? What to do?'

'Not sure, my dear. Perhaps we should wait. We are fine for the moment. I believe this isn't the work of those incompetents. Somewhere, there are foreigners. Our people march and shout, but they wouldn't do this. Things may right themselves. I do hope our good Doctor is safe and got the right photographs.'

'I so agree. What about Mina and Bess?'

'They are very sensible. They will be calm. We will talk to them both, and we will help to our fullest.'

'But it is so…'

'Shhh, my dear. I know. You and I will decide what is right. For now, I suggest we observe and remember what we see – and, above all, we wait. As night surrenders to day, the time will come. Of that we can be sure. I trust we have good supplies in. We may yet need them.'

'In that department we are in A1 order. Shall we discuss with the girls now?'

'Yes, my dear, an excellent idea. We can all put our heads together and decide what to do. Let us join them on the roof. We shall take some Darjeeling up.'

'And shall we pray to the Almighty?

'Yes, indeed, my dear… even all of them.'

LOCKDOWN

'No generator. In case!' She was insistent. No-one felt inclined to ask in case, *what*? 'And, Dr Em,' she continued, 'you think those Arab men are part of this? They've scrammed and 'ave not paid me!'

'Could be, Madame. Who knows? Let's not judge too quickly. They might be innocent victims, stuck out there somewhere, hiding, and in fear for their lives... And, of course, we don't know where Mr Abdullah has got to.'

'Oui. But 'is things are still in the room. He is around somewhere, maybe lost in my garden. Those others 'ave taken all their clothes and all that stuff they 'ad there. That is très équivoque, n'est-ce pas?'

'Sounds like it,' Anna said. 'Though there's not a lot we can do about it.'

'That's right,' Chris added. 'We need to wait. There'll have to be a part-curfew at some point and people will be allowed out a few hours a day, probably in ones and twos. When that happens, Em and I will need to be able to get round town. And that gives me an idea. A simple map would be very helpful, just something showing the main streets and buildings. I was wondering, Madame, whether you and Anna could put something together for us.'

'Oui! A good idea… and very sensible. I know this place like the back of the 'and, and I'm sure Anna knows a lot; so come, Anna, we'll use that table. I will get paper.'

•

'That'll keep them busy for a while,' Em said quietly as she and Chris went off along the ground floor corridor of B Wing. 'There'll be endless debate about directions, distances, and spelling, of course.'

'And Madame will win them all. It's a bit more than keeping them occupied, though. A sketch map could have practical value. It would help us, or whoever, figure out the locations of those people out there and how many of them there might actually be.'

Em puffed out her cheeks. 'True, but I can't see why we should bother.'

'Yes. But if we *were* able to contact the mainland, such information would be invaluable.'

'Fair enough, and I can see that working for the town area. What about the rest of the island?'

'That's a bigger problem, Em, but there *are* ways of doing it.'

'Well, if you say so. Anyway, cold shower for me right now. That walk up the road got me all hot and bothered.'

•

As she opened the door to her room, she heard the low, repeating buzz. She got down on her knees and retrieved the radio from under the bed. Button 3 was green.

The response was instantaneous. 'Hello! At last! Dr Chris.' It was a female voice, low but recognisable.

'No. It's me. Em. You and Danny OK?'

'We're fine, but we've three men sitting just up at the junction with guns. They came to the house earlier, hammered on the door and told us not to go out or they'd shoot us. The cheek of it! They even told me to go and get dressed properly, or they'd shoot us, anyway! Would you believe it? I think they didn't like my shorts. Anyway, two of them were local types. The other didn't say anything; he just stared at me. Danny says he looks like an Arab. Since they left, we've been watching them with the binoculars through the minyara hedge. Danny's out there now. We've been wondering whether we should drive into town. We can push the Land Rover down the garden across the road down to the bay, and onto the forestry track. They wouldn't see us.'

'Hang on, Rosalie, slow down! The town's out. Don't even think about it. There're men with guns all over the place. Everyone's indoors. You must stay there. You should also find a secure place for the radio.'

'Like a hidey-hole?'

'You got it. Look, I'd better let Chris know what's happening there. Sit tight. We'll speak later... say, round about nine.'

•

As she showered, her thoughts turned to Chris Jamieson. He was altogether an interesting character and she wondered whether she was even beginning to feel attracted to him. It was ridiculous, of course. She knew that at times of crisis, people could be drawn together. She was also ultra-conscious of the oft-repeated insistence during training that one must never, ever, get involved in any way with colleagues. She'd already made that mistake once. *Think of the negatives, especially the consequences*, the Director would say to newcomers to the Service. That was always an effective line, and in Chris Jamieson's case, there certainly *were* negatives: he was married, older, and had endless infuriating characteristics. He knew the answer to virtually everything, but he always let others think *they'd* thought of it first. Again, if only he could be a bit more contrary. The only time she'd seen him annoyed was at the briefing in Marlborough House. But then, George and that Freddy were such fools, albeit clever ones, one would have to be a saint not to be riled by them.

'I'm being bloody ridiculous!' she muttered. And, as she said it, she could hear her mother's voice loud and clear. *He's just another man! Men are a feeble, untrustworthy breed. You don't need them. Avoid them.*

•

The afternoon was intensely humid, the air still and heavy. It was as though the weather was conspiring with the enemy to add to their discomfort. Madame Lemessurier, who around that time would normally have retired to her room, with both ceiling and table fans on full blast, pushing hurricane-strength winds across her substantial frame, was beginning to lose resolve. And, towards evening, as they sat in the restaurant trying to keep cool in the merest sensation of a breeze trickling in from the sea, she finally cracked. 'That's it! we've *got* to 'ave that generator working, n'est-ce pas? Dr Chris, you think it OK to use it?'

'I'm sure it's OK,' he replied, relieved she was at last coming to terms with their predicament. 'Those fellows up the road won't even be awake. I doubt they'd *hear* it anyway. Let me crank the thing up, and then we can get the fans going, make some ice, cool down with some of Em's double malt to celebrate!'

'Celebrate what?' asked Anna.

'So many things. One moment… I'll be back.'

THE VISITOR IN THE NIGHT

Em joined him in his room just before nine. 'Time,' she said. 'They'll be getting worried.'

It was Danny who replied. 'Hi, Chris. Four men now – two locals and two of the others. You OK? What's it like down there?'

'We're fine. There's not a lot happening. Look, Danny, we need some help with a map I've got here.' He reached under the bed and pulled out the sketch map of the island he'd made on the train on the way home from the London meeting. 'There are a few things we want to add to it.'

For the next ten minutes, Danny rattled on, prompted by Rosalie, while Chris marked the positions of all the accessible beaches and the main footpaths, vehicle tracks and settlements on the island.

'That's about it,' Danny said. 'Can't think of anything else, and Rosie's nodding, so it must be right.'

'Thank you for that. It's really helpful. Em and I now

need to work on what we've got here. We'll speak again in the morning. There're sure to be more queries.'

He switched off his radio and sat back.

'I didn't know you had that map. Where on earth did it come from?' Em asked.

'You'll remember, your George – or maybe it was that other twit – told me I couldn't take photos of those satellite pics or even make a sketch of the island. Well, I drew this from memory on the way back home from the meeting, and it's just as well. I discovered later that all the internet satellite maps of the island have been pixelated out, but I guess you knew that.'

She nodded. 'Look, can I ask you about something you said the other day. You hinted this business wasn't about gold.'

'That's right. I'd suggest there's everything else on God's earth on the island, *except* gold – Madame's wedding ring and all those bangles the women wear, aside.'

'So, it really *is* a religious extremist thing?'

'That remains a real possibility. It's just there's a fly in that particular ointment – our Chinese scientist. A few weeks ago, he was in a munitions factory, in North Korea. Now he's here, along with a sophisticated laboratory, on a building site, working with rocks. That doesn't square with the religious extremism thing.'

'So, that leaves us where?'

He hesitated. 'I *could* make an educated guess, Em, but I don't want to. Things remain too unclear, and uncertainty can be dangerous. As you well know, it's led to wars in the past. To get anywhere close to certainty, we'd need what that guy's got in his laboratory – all his chemistry gear, the materials he's working with, the whole caboodle.'

She stifled her natural inclination to laugh but didn't miss the glint in his eyes, or the half-smile that told her he'd hit on an idea that he liked. And had she heard him correctly? Had his *I* subtly become *we*?

'It occurs to me that if we were able to...' He stopped mid-sentence, and raised his hand. 'Shhh.' He pointed towards the door.

'Someone there?' She mouthed the words. He nodded, pushed his sketch map and his radio into her hands. 'Drop them down into the garden, if you have to,' he whispered. He waved his hand towards the balcony. She slid back the door, stepped out and pulled the curtain across the opening.

He opened his door. 'Hello? Madame? Anna?' There was no response. He peered both ways along the corridor, dimly lit by the emergency lighting. 'Anyone there?' he called.

After a second or two, a voice came back. It was soft but crystal clear. 'Dr Chris. It's me... Bess.' He peered along the dark corridor and could just make her out in the flickering light. She was hunched up against the wall at the top of the concrete stairway.

SALTY SHOES

Nothing much in life had ever surprised Christopher Jamieson, leastways not that he'd ever admit it. But now, as Bess emerged from the gloom dressed almost entirely in black, and a large silver torch dangling by string from her wrist, his self-image folded in on itself. He was lost for words. How could this mild-mannered, middle-aged woman have possibly got safely past at least two lots of armed men intent on preventing all movement into, out of, or around the town?

'Bess… in here!' He pulled her gently into his room, closed the door behind her and slid the security chain into place.

'How on earth did you get here? Can people go out now?'

'No, Dr Chris. No-one can go anywhere. Except, this morning, a foreigner came and told Mina and me to go up to the clinic. He took us up there in a Land Rover. There is one dead man, a local policeman – he's squeezed into the fridge – and there're two other men who are injured. One, I'm sure, is a local from the north; the other is a foreigner. We had to treat them and were told we must go up morning and evening to make sure they are all right.'

'But how did you get *here*?'

There was a wariness in his voice, an edge of uncertainty and concern. She'd have to explain very carefully.

'I came along the shore from behind Valli's compound to the Mirabilé gardens, beyond that little bay. Our compound goes back a long way, you see, and there's just a small cliff face down to the water. When Mina was young, she used to climb down into a tiny cove there and then walk below the cliff face to the hotel gardens. That's possible when the tide is out and the water is quiet, and even when the tide is full, the water's only a couple of feet deep. I came that way.'

He glanced down at her boots. They were still wet, but there was a thin white salt crust line beginning to form on the leather.

'And the tide is about half-way in – or out – now?'

She nodded. 'That's right – out. But I need to tell you why I've come, and first, I must show you this. Excuse me, a moment.' She turned away from him, reached into her bra and carefully extracted a folded piece of paper. It was a page from an out-of-date diary. On it, in handwriting he recognised immediately, was a list of numbers alongside days and the names of fungi.

He stared at the piece of paper, not believing what he was looking at. 'I really don't know what to say, Bess.'

'I can see it is not what you expected. I'm sorry.'

'Goodness! No need to apologise. Look, before you go any further, there's something you should know. My colleague, Emmeline Freemont, is out on the balcony and will have heard everything we've just said, but don't worry, it's not at all a problem. Just a moment.' He crossed the room. 'Em,' he called softly. 'It's OK. Come back in.'

Em stepped into the room.

'You're Dr Em!' said Bess, relief in her voice. 'Lots of people have told me about you: Mina, Meera, my embassy link.'

'Hello, Bess, and my apologies for concealing myself like that. We weren't sure who was out in the corridor. Can I ask if you've been in touch with the embassy since this thing started?'

'Yes, three times today already. I talked to Meg at ten, I told her what was happening, and later in the day she called to say that the national news had announced that the ferry from Ivundé had broken down. Then, this evening, she asked if everyone in the Mirabilé was OK. I told her I'd come over and check.'

'And she approved of that? You surprise me.'

'No! No. She was very reluctant, but there's another reason. I – we – need help. We have a technical problem. I have to change the way my transmitter works. It's quite urgent.'

Em looked over at Chris Jamieson. 'Co-ordination?'

'Could be.'

'Yes,' Bess said. 'That's the word she used. She said you could help, Dr Chris.'

'Possibly, Bess, but I'd need to see what your present set-up is like and find out what capacity the embassy needs. Any chance we could get round to your place right now so that we can talk to the embassy?'

'Yes. We can do that, Dr Chris, but you'll need stout shoes… and they'll never be the same again!'

•

Bess led them along the rocky foreshore below a low cliff face, a wide swathe of light from her torch picking out a path through numerous ankle-twisting, lichen-covered rocks. Within yards, they were in ankle-deep water and moving more cautiously, their feet probing a rocky sea bed. Ninety-odd yards or so further on, they came to a tiny pebble inlet, scarcely ten feet across at the mouth. The rock face at either side of the apex was ridged, step-like. Using her torch, Bess guided them up in turn. She then switched it off and, in the dark, climbed up and joined them at the top.

'Follow me.'

'Any snakes here, Bess?' whispered Em, disturbed that they now had only starlight to see by.

'Oh, those silly things!' said Bess. She sounded quite dismissive. 'Don't worry. The ones that don't run away know me anyway, but keep close behind me… you know, just in case.' And she laughed.

They made their way up a slope through heavy bush, and as the ground began to level out, they came up against a high wooden takamaka fence. Bess switched on her torch, bent down, heaved at two planks and pulled them apart, making a triangle of space just large enough for them to crawl through.

'Sorry,' she whispered, 'children size! Anyway, we are in Valli territory now, and safe. The house and shop are up ahead. That light you see – that's Meera. She's still up. She worries when I'm not in. That block-shaped building to the right is the storeroom and garage. It's where Valli repairs his Toyota and keeps his private petrol pump. We have an electricity generator in there. That's what you can hear.' She hesitated. 'And, on the left here is my studio. It's where I paint and listen to music; well, that's what we say. Come on in.'

She closed the door behind them and switched on an overhead fluorescent strip. 'Welcome to my arts and crafts studio! And there on the bench and shelf above is my equipment.'

On the bench was a military field-transmitter. Arranged neatly either side of it were other bits of equipment: a laptop, headphones, a microphone, speakers. On a shelf above, were numerous bits and pieces: a roll of coaxial cable, lengths of aerial wire, radio and computer parts and an assortment of tools.

Chris pulled the transmitter forward and felt along the back. 'This connection out of the back, Bess – an aerial?'

'Yes. There's a hole in the side wall over there and the wire hangs down the back of the shed. If the weather's bad, I clamp more wire on the end and I hang it over the bushes.'

'Quite a set-up,' he said. 'It must stress the power supplies to the house when you're using it?'

'Only when the town main power supply is down, but I usually only switch it on late at night; there's better reception then. When we're on generator, they have to switch everything off in the house and sit in the dark. It's funny, really, but Meera stops talking when the lights go out. Anyway, you said you need to speak to the embassy. I think I can get them right now.'

The response was almost instant. *'Hold a second.'* It was a woman's voice. *'I'll get your respondent.'*

'Who's that, Bess?' Em whispered.

'I think maybe she's called Sybil.'

'Megan here.'

'Bess leant over the microphone. 'It's me, Meg. The doctors want to speak to you.' She passed the microphone over to Em.

'Em here, Megan. We secure?'

'We think so, but no choice. I'll get straight to it. We have to implement this co-ordination thing or we're out of the chain, and London's adamant that we cannot afford to be. Our US colleagues say the present set-up, your end, is well past its sell-by date, and any communication is at serious risk of interception by the Chinese and Russian Indian Ocean fleets. So, we need to install the new top-line gear your end. We heard the US Secretary-of-State was resistant at first. No way was he going to let state-of-the-art communications stuff loose on some island in the Indian Ocean belonging to a Marxist regime. But I hear he had his you-know-what's squeezed. And of course, even if we had a choice before, we don't now: it's got to be done.'

'Understood. I'm going to pass you over to Chris.'

'Hello, Megan. I got all that. However, before we look at what's required, I need to send you something. I've just plugged a micro-card adapter into your helper's laptop here and linked it to the transmitter. I want to send you a report that Em and I put together. It includes visuals, a stretch of video and a detailed sketch map of the island, and another of the town. Your end needs to be able to download and copy.'

'A moment, Chris. I'll check on that. OK. I'm being told it's not a problem. Any channel will do. When you're ready, just send it.'

'Before I do that, you need to know for the record. I am personally unclear about the precise identification of the rocks and minerals in the report. I have a view, of course, a rather disturbing one, but nothing, and I repeat *nothing*, definitive can be said without detailed prismatic and chemical analyses.'

'That's understood, Chris. And now, our technical problem. Cheltenham has said that the transmitter there doesn't have the capability of a multi-link particle end-to-end encryption-based approach that's required. I have absolutely no idea what that means by the way; I'm just reading this stuff! Does it make sense?'

'Just about. But there's nothing I can do without an appropriate cypher module to wire into the transmitter. Even with it, who knows?'

'OK. Looking at these notes, I think they're saying the same thing. It also says they have the module thingy and housing down in Diego Garcia. There's a footnote saying it can be delivered by drone to the island – parachute or touchdown. Don't ask me what that means. Oops! And there's more. They want you people to identify a delivery site, pick the gear up and get it to the co-ordinator.'

Em nudged him, and put out a hand for the microphone. 'Megan, I don't believe I heard that! Don't the people out there realise how tied down we are here? We're in a permanent steam bath; there's a total curfew and we've got maniacs running around with automatic weapons. It's fine for—'

She became conscious of a hand firmly squeezing her arm. Chris Jamieson was shaking his head slowly. She stopped and took a deep breath. 'Ooops! Sorry, Meg,' she continued. 'My apologies; forget I said that. It's just that it's so frustrating.'

'Em, I understand, and I'm sure our masters do as well. It seems, though, that the situation is critical. We've reached a five-star red state and they're desperate for a solid, reliable conduit on the ground.'

Chris reached across for the microphone. 'Meg, the drone delivery problem may be solvable. The safe delivery to the co-ordinator really is something else altogether, but give us half an hour while we get our heads together. We'll get back to you. Don't be too hopeful, though. Em's description of the position here is spot on. In fact, she's even being quite restrained.'

'Understood. Half an hour.'

They sat back in their chairs, silent for a moment. Em's eyes were closed. 'I'm sorry I lost it, you two,' she said. 'I don't know how you stay so calm, Chris.'

'You really don't want me to answer that.'

'Dr Em, what did she mean by a five-star red state?' Bess asked.

'Anyone's guess, Bess. The language those people use can be confusing. It's sort of technical jargon. But, whatever it means, it sounds pretty serious.'

'I see. Thank you. Can I ask what kind of place is needed to land one of those drone things on?'

'Chris, you know?'

'Depends on the size of the cypher thing, but probably not much more than a precise geographical position – and that's easy – and a bit of flattish ground. What were you thinking, Bess?'

'Our compound out there is really big – football-pitch-sized. Could that be used?'

'Good idea, in normal circumstances, but those long-distance drones make a lot of noise. The risk to your family would be huge; there are armed men on the road just out there. No. It has to be well out in the sticks, at least a mile from where anyone might be. I was thinking, Em, didn't Danny say they could get out of their place safely?'

'It was Rosalie, and, yes, down the garden. But even if they could get to a drop site, how could the equipment be got back here to Bess? It's the same problem?'

'Not really. It's only half the same problem.'

'You're serious, aren't you?'

'Yes. Let's wake them up; they're ideas people.'

He took out his radio from his backpack and pressed 3.

26

WATCHERS

Sleep wouldn't come. It wasn't the enervating humidity; she was well used to that. It was rather her fear for the future and the tension that swirled like a living force round her head and between her and Danny. Their island, the place they called home, their refuge from the modern world, had been plunged into a terrible uncertainty. A pestilence had descended. Nothing could ever be the same again.

They'd sat up into the early hours going over and over the preparations they would need to make to leave the island, and they had been about to call it a day when Danny heard the low buzz.

The request Chris made initially seemed simple. Could they identify a spot well away from the road where a drone might deliver a small package which they could collect? That would be easy and virtually risk-free, Chris said. It was the follow-up bit that was the problem, but when the question came, they'd looked at each other and nodded in unison… and yes, they had an idea. Only later did they realise how tricky it was going to be.

•

By midnight, the site had been identified and the information passed through to the embassy and on to Diego Garcia. Four hours later, a UAV took off from the airfield with two small packages, one under either wing, latched into a missile pod. The control pilot, sitting in the operations room on Diego Garcia in front of a computer screen, fed in co-ordinates and sat back with his book and coffee as the drone headed west-north-west on auto-pilot.

•

The light was rolling in from the east as they crept down their garden and out into the scrubby bush that lay beyond. Once clear of any possibility of detection by the men up at the junction on the road, they relaxed.

In a while they turned east over clearer ground and along a gentle slope. Their target was a narrow stream that curved around a large patch of gently undulating grassland, almost enclosing it.

'We're early, Rosie.'

'I hope we got this right, *and* them!'

'Relax. It'll be OK. It couldn't be anywhere else, and those guys are good. Come on. Let's get our feet into the water… cool 'em down!'

•

At 0700, the drone was ten miles due east of Ivundé. The joint UK/US Diego Garcia commanders were standing behind the UAV controller as he sat staring at the screen. Next to it was a second screen, live but blank. They watched as he took over manual control.

'OK, Billy,' said the US commander. 'Call Seb in for the Predator and talk us through what's happening.'

'Right, sir. The over-watch Predator from Djibouti is in place – 8,000 up. Coming up on the other screen… just now. It's armed with double Hellfire 8-ZIs. Seb will take over control from Djib. Hang on.' They watched as the second screen became fully active. Seb settled in next to Billy.

'We'll now do a double check,' continued Billy. 'If the ground's clear, and the customers are there, we'll deliver.'

He manoeuvred the UAV into a gentle spiral downwards over the site. He looked across at Seb, who nodded. 'Yep. Keep going. We got two – a man, a woman – up the slope a bit… just there. Confirmed. No-one else visible.'

'OK, Billy,' said the American commander. 'It's *Go*. Put the gear down and get out of there.'

And so, within fifteen seconds of the appointed moment, the aircraft – its wingspan scarcely twenty feet across – floated down out of the sky. All Danny and Rosalie could hear was a high-pitched whine and the slow, rhythmic surging wind as the three propellers sucked in, compressed, and released huge volumes of air.

The plane hovered and landed… one second… two seconds. It released its deliveries, one from either side. In a further second it bounced forward along the uneven ground, picked up speed and began to lift up into the sky. At fifty feet, it turned eastwards on its journey back to Diego Garcia.

'OK, Seb, step one over. Your game now. Go over the instructions again,' said the US commander. 'We don't want any mistakes with this one.'

'I move the Predator up to 10,000 and follow the packages to final delivery. The window for that is max. twenty-eight hours, effectively twenty. Any threat to delivery and we move to weapons launch protocol. That and subsequent activation will be your joint decision. You will also jointly authorise discontinuation of observation and the return of the plane to Djibouti control.'

The British commander nodded and looked across at his American counterpart. 'I really hope to God that man, Jamieson, has a solid plan for getting the gear delivered safely.'

•

But, and not for the first time, Chris Jamieson didn't have a solid plan. He had the merest possibility of a plan. He was doing what he disliked intensely. He was flying by the seat of his pants and praying Lady Luck would be on their side. Had he known that an armed Predator would be circling high above Danny and Rosalie, tracking their every footstep, he might well have behaved somewhat differently.

27
ROSIE DELIVERS

'What d'you think's in them, Danny?' she whispered. They were sitting up against the inflatable, recovering from the final rush up the garden. 'Couldn't we have just a little peep?'

'No idea, my love – and no, we mustn't. We just get rid of them ASAP. Think… they've sent a UAV all the way up from DG with these packages. Ask yourself whether you *really* want to know what's in 'em. It's a dead cert *I* don't. Come on, coffee; then let's get the real show on the road.'

•

An hour later, they crept around to the Land Rover parked at the side of the house. 'I hope we can do this!' said Danny.

'Got to! As the British say, beggars can't be choosers.'

'Us Transatlantics say that, too!'

'OK!' She laughed, happy he was not too stressed by the whole business. She knew she'd need his strength. 'Just teasing!'

In a more amenable climate, pushing the Land Rover down the garden and across the east coast road onto the forestry track would have been relatively easy, not that they'd ever tried it before, but on that day on their island, the temperature – and worse, the humidity – were about as bad as they'd been at any time so far that year. And so, it took them a full half-hour, with numerous pauses, changes in position and regular liquid intake, to get the vehicle onto the track. Then it became relatively easy, requiring almost no control of the steering wheel, the vehicle's front wheels conveniently locking themselves into the ruts made by their repeated journeys over the years.

After sixty yards or so of gentle pushing, Danny leaned into the cab and pulled the handbrake up. 'OK, more than enough. They won't hear us start her up, even if they're awake. Get your pregnancy organised. I'll let Chris know what's happening.'

He eased the radio out from beneath the spare wheel on the bonnet and pressed 1.

Chris Jamieson had been sitting on his balcony for some time waiting for their call. His reply was instant. 'Danny. Thank God! Everything OK?'

'So far, so easy. We'll be at the end of the forestry track above the clinic in about forty minutes. May get a bit trickier then.'

'And that's what really worries me, Danny. Look, I've an idea about how I might get up there and meet you. It's not certain. I need to talk to someone first.'

'No, Chris. If you can do it, so can we. Rosie has a plan and is certain she can get in and out of the compound safely.'

'Well, if you're sure? But, if it looks to be a problem, call me.'

•

Rosalie was now prepared, with the two packages tied next to each other on a wide leather belt she'd buckled loosely at one side. Over it all, she'd pulled a long brown kabaya which covered her from shoulders to ankles.

'How do I look?' she asked, turning in a circle.

'You really don't want to know!' He gave a nervous laugh. 'Just remember your story: you're about to deliver… live in the forest… gotta get to the clinic. And don't forget that headscarf.'

•

An hour later, they were sitting in the Land Rover at the end of the track looking down towards the town.

'See anything, Danny?'

'Nope, nuthin! Place is dead. In fact, it's so dead, why don't you let me do this? It'll be OK.'

'No! We agreed! If there *are* any of those men there, and they see you, a white man, *and* an American at that, you wouldn't have a chance. I'm about to give birth, remember. They wouldn't dare to try to look at what's up my dress – or down! No. I'm off, and right now!'

She scrambled into the ditch and ran across the road into the light bush on the other side. Once there, she felt safe. She threaded her way down the slope through stunted acacia and thorn bush to the back fence of the clinic compound, and along it to a huge mango tree. The fence itself was a solid, six-foot high takamaka construction, but she'd noticed many times when visiting the clinic that there was a gap either side of the tree. She was certain she could get into the compound through one side or the other.

But she was mistaken; it proved impossible. Frustrated and angry, she propped herself up against the fence to calm herself down and think. She knew Danny would simply have pulled himself up one-handed and swung over the fence. That was his style, and what he'd been trained to do. For her, that wasn't an option, and she couldn't just push the packages through the gap and hope for the best. No-one – and anyone – might see them.

Then, there was something she vaguely remembered from her childhood. It just might work. She heaved her kabaya up over her head lightning fast, rolled it into a ball and shoved it through the wider of the two gaps. The belt with packages attached followed. Then, she eased her head through and looked round the compound. It was deserted. The only thing alive – if indeed it was alive – was the clinic cat, a black and white, nothing-in-particular stray everyone called Green. It was lying splayed out like a mini rug in the shade of the waste bin to the left of the clinic door.

She'd go... she twisted and manoeuvred her shoulders into the gap. It still seemed impossible. Then, a voice started up in her head. It was crystal clear. It was without doubt her long-dead father: *You know what you've got to do! Do it. Off you go, Rosie girl!* And she felt her whole body being twisted sideways and propelled through the gap.

She fell forward into the dust of the compound. Elated but scared stiff, and without looking over at the clinic, she slid her long dress back over her head and pushed the belt and packages up onto her stomach underneath it. Then, half-bent, face contorted in feigned agony and one hand holding the bulge at her middle, she stumbled across the compound towards the building.

She was half-way across when she saw movement just inside the door into the waiting room. Then, as imprecisely as it materialised, the shape receded; the doorway became a uniform black oblong again. A few more faltering steps and she froze as she heard the sound of men's voices, one, high-pitched, husky, angry, another, subdued and whining. Despair and annoyance flowed through her in equal measure. They had come so far. She wasn't going back. She geared herself up to produce the greatest performance of her life. Breathing heavily, she moved forward towards the door.

Perhaps again it was her father's doing, but there, suddenly, was Mina, standing in the open doorway, her eyes wide with both astonishment and alarm. She began tapping her closed lips repeatedly with her right-hand index finger. She moved her left hand, palm-down, back and forth at waist height. As she did so, she looked to her right, nodding her head slightly.

'Woman. In here!' The angry high-pitched voice from inside the clinic was now a scream. Mina swivelled round and disappeared back inside.

Rosalie moved to her left towards the bin. Green, the cat, was now on her direct route. He opened one eye, looked at her and then sank back into a stupor. He was no threat. She stretched over him, grasped the edge of the bin with her left hand and, with her right, she deftly pulled the belt and packages from beneath her dress and placed them carefully in the bin.

•

Ten thousand feet up, the Predator had been circling slowly for close on three hours. At one point, the operator had noticed that the signals from the two radio tags, one in each package, had been brought so close together the objects must almost have been touching each other.

And then, at four in the afternoon, he sent a code orange signal to the desks of the Diego Garcia commanders. Within seconds, they were standing behind him, looking at the screen.

'What we looking at, Seb?' asked the US commander.

'That's the clinic compound. Both packages have been taken through the fence at the back of the building – just there.' He moved the crosshairs into position. 'The gear has come to a halt against the wall of the building in some sort of shadow. I think they've been put in something.'

'What's that. Left of your marker?'

'Not certain, sir. It's alive, though. Got a strong heat signal… a dog, maybe.'

'Doesn't seem likely in that place, but OK.'

The UK commander joined in. 'What's happened to the carrier, Seb?'

The operator switched to the forward camera. 'There you go… a *she*, I'd guess, moving up the hill at the back of the compound.'

'Thank God for that! OK. Next, it *must* be a woman who picks up. If not, you know what we have to do. You got a description?'

'Two.'

'Right. Could be either.'

'I'll need to drop a couple of thousand, to sharpen the image. No risk.'

'OK. Do it and call us in for the pick-up.'

'Let's pray we don't have to go to destroy protocol, Marv,' said the British base commander. 'Though how that stuff could possibly be worth the lives of all those people astonishes me. There must be eleven or twelve aid people in the building somewhere – Swedish, Portuguese, French, British, Venezuelan. It's the bloody United Nations!'

'I agree,' said his American counterpart. 'And it's ridiculous sacrificing those people when everyone in the world will have that technology within a couple of years.'

'It's always the same. I've been thinking, if things did go wrong, couldn't we argue our destroy order referred to the *postmen* being waylaid and the gear taken from them? After all, the postmen have now delivered, so technically the order ceases to be relevant.'

'A good hair-split… and I like it,' said the US commander. 'We could even strengthen it by tying it into the rule book. One of us would authorise, and the other over-ride on the basis of changed circumstances. That would really muddy things up.'

'Nice point!' said the British commander. 'Plenty of wriggle room there! And to be honest, I think our governments would probably thank us and give both of us medals for not grossly offending a dozen countries by wiping out some of their citizens!'

'Yep. Certainly, but they'd still throw us onto the scrap heap, push us into some desk job and then quietly retire us gracefully, and with enhanced pensions. Mind you, thinking about it, there are probably many worse things that could happen.'

WAR OF WORDS 28

They were sitting around a table in the restaurant, bent forward, listening to the English Service of Ziaŵala National Radio broadcasting from the mainland. Their knees were touching and sliding against each other, sweat mingling, in an act of mutual support.

A government spokesman was reporting the takeover of the island:

'The *cowardly dog of a leader of the so-called National Salvation Liberation Army*,' he declaimed, '*has issued an evil, lying message from his mud-filled, coward's, hyena hidey-hole somewhere in the mountains, claiming that the population of Ivundé has risen up, to a man, woman and child, and has thrown out the local administration in the face of bullying, deliberate starvation and the repression of religious rights. Utter, utter lying nonsense it all is. You will all have heard these claims, repeated time and again, and you all know these are but diabolical, evil lies.*'

'*And,*' he continued, '*not only that but that stupid dog*

also claims that our representatives on the island and their families were put on the Friday ferry back to the mainland, and so their lives had been spared by the merciful Liberation Army.'

The spokesman then announced that the government had issued an official communique, which he would now read:

'We, the legitimate government of the Socialist Republic of Ziaŵala and all her outlying islands, reject out of hand the long, rambling, incoherent and ill-educated list of demands we have received. These so-called Liberation people are evil criminals... thugs... renegades... terrorists of the worst sort. They are mere cockroaches, and we will crush them underfoot, spreading their grey cowardice in the dirt. In addition, there is no truth, none whatsoever, that there is support on our sovereign island for these evil dogs. Further, no local officials have been ejected, not a single one. Indeed, as everyone in our great country knows, the Friday ferry has not even left the island at all. It remains there, nestled up against the pier!'

'Ivundé,' he continued, 'and all the islands lying off our coast are unequivocally an integral part of our beloved country. This fact is fully recognised by all peace-loving governments across the world. Nor have the people of Ivundé been repressed or bullied or had their religious rights supressed in any way whatsoever. The Socialist Republic of Ziaŵala recognises all religions, including the right to observe no religion at all.'

The newsreader then read out a personal message from the President to the people of Ziaŵala, assuring them he would very shortly take all necessary steps to bring Ivundé back into the national fold. This endeavour, which he would lead himself, had priority over all others.

And there, the broadcast ended.

The listeners sat back.

'Stupéfiant! What nonsense! Where are all these people rising up against oppression?' Madame said, grimacing and flicking her head in contempt. 'Right now, most of them are in their 'ouses – 'ow you say it – cowering under beds only wanting to get food, get water, get cool! What you think Dr Em? Will your country 'elp restore sanity?'

'I agree, Madame. It's astonishing, and I'm sure the United Kingdom will be at the forefront of the efforts to resolve the problem.'

Chris Jamieson was sitting back in his chair staring out across the gardens at the sea. 'That's right,' he said slowly. 'I was wondering, though, just who wrote that stuff. The rhetoric is quite remarkable, almost poetic. It's junk, of course. And Madame, you're right. I've not been here long, but from the little I've seen, the idea that anyone is oppressing anyone else is ridiculous. These people aren't like that; it's not in their nature. I was also wondering who the local representatives of the oppressors are who've supposedly been sent back on the ferry. Most government officials here seem pretty well integrated into the local community.'

'Ah! That's intéressant, n'est-ce pas?' said Madame, 'and true. Those officials come and they like it 'ere; it's cheaper. They save money. Best of all, their extended family on the mainland can't get at them easily and strip it off them. They like to stay and stay. Very soon they are locals; there is no difference. It's like the *Animal Farm*, n'est-ce pas?'

'But mainlanders mostly aren't going to be Islamic, are they?' Anna said.

'Some, of course, but many are Christians, and some, or, 'ow do you call it, *animisms*.'

'Animists?'

'Oui. They like the nature and things and sometimes they chase the local girls. Ooh la la! So funny. That's always a big problem. And, if they catch them, the men have to become Moslems, and they 'ave to go across to the 'ospital to get dealt with. Don't ask!'

'I notice that the broadcast didn't mention foreigners,' Anna continued. 'I suppose we're not seen as a threat to anyone.'

Jamieson looked across at Em. Her eyes widened fractionally. He'd be circumspect, but it was an opportunity to prepare the ground.

'You're right, Anna. They don't have to worry about people like us. Of course, there *is* the hostage question, but hostages have to have trading value. You know, hostages for money, safe passage, someone's freedom, or the like. I can't see how *we* could be used for leverage, but you never know.'

•

Em joined him in his room. 'Nine, Chris. Time for R and D?'

He went out onto the balcony, retrieved his radio and pressed 3.

There was a breathless excitement in Rosalie's voice. 'Dr Chris, we're back; it's done! I saw Mina. There were men in the clinic… so I had to leave the packages in the bin… she knows. Hold on a sec; I'll get Danny. He's out checking on our friends at the junction.'

•

The contents of the packages had already been laid out on a side bench in Bess's studio. The two main items were a small box-like housing unit and a cypher-conversion module, which appeared to be nothing more than a tiny bar of dense, hard black tar-like material covered with fine plastic and criss-crossed with silver flecks. It had a miniscule connector rod projecting from either end. Alongside the two items were a roll of the flecked plastic material, a small bag of connectors and screws and a set of operator's notes.

'I unpacked it very carefully, Dr Chris,' Bess said as she let them in. 'It doesn't look much.'

'These things never do. Of course, whether I can make it all work is a different matter. Mind you, it'll be a lot easier than putting together the transmitter you're using was.'

'That was easy! They sent a young man from UK. I just had to feed him compliments and Meera's Darjeeling and samosas. It took him two days. Since then, all I've had to do is press buttons and twiddle things.'

Chris touched the transmitter on the main bench to disperse any errant static electricity and felt around inside the cypher housing. In the corner, where the module would go, he felt a disc-like, thumbnail-sized raised area. It slid around under his touch. He manoeuvred it out to the opening, picked it up, glanced at it briefly and put it to one side on the bench.

'What's that, Chris?' Em asked.

'Nothing much… just a security tag.' He picked up the cypher module and located a second disc beneath a strip of black electrical tape along the base. 'We'll deal with those later,' he said quietly as he put it next to the first disc.

He sealed the box, soldered a lead from it to the transmitter and swathed both pieces of equipment in the ultra-thin silver-flecked shielding material, leaving only the operating panels exposed.

'Not tidy, Bess, but this covering material is important. It reduces the electro-magnetic leakage and prevents it being electronically detectable unless you're almost sitting on top of it. What we need to do now is to programme these channel buttons on the transmitter.'

'That's the bit I couldn't understand.'

'It's the way they write this stuff, Bess. They think if they write something in a way that's unintelligible, they're earning their salary. Right, you have twelve buttons but only need ten separate channels.' He looked at the operator's notes. 'They suggest you make number 1 the default master. It opens up all the channels together. That leaves 2 onwards to allocate to individual customers in any way you want. They're the places listed on the second page – the American Embassy, the British Embassy, the NSA, GCHQ, and so on.'

Em had noticed a growing concern on Bess's face. The poor woman had no idea what she'd let herself in for. From a lowly covert with basic transmitting equipment, she had been catapulted to the role of keeper of the keys, and in charge of some of the most advanced communication gear in the world.

'Bess, I think you may not have been told about these others,' she said. 'Our apologies for that.'

'Thank you, Dr Em. I realised when Meg first talked about other channels that it meant more links; I'm just surprised by how many. Dr Chris, could we do the allocation now? I'm guessing I start by pressing 1, and then I tell everyone which number they are.'

He nodded. 'That's exactly right, Bess. Go ahead.'

'I warned Meera earlier that the lights might just go out. She loves the drama of not knowing when. She calls it the nuclear fallout option.'

The speed of response from all the parties astonished even Chris Jamieson. Bess read out the key allocation list, articulating each number in turn, slowly and clearly.

'You can switch to stand-by now,' he said. 'That requires very little power. They'll need a bit of time to integrate their systems.'

'Wow! So easy. You're a genius, Dr Chris!'

'I think not, Bess. A fanatic, I'll admit to being. My wife calls me many things, and you can be sure *genius* isn't one of them.'

He picked up the notes again. 'I thought so. You need a crisis button. I suggest 12. Let me do that now. It's a one-time use. If you press and hold that for five seconds. the module software burns out and the equipment becomes a worthless chunk of metal, melted plastic and the odd splodge of gold. It's only to be used in an emergency. There's one other thing: if a button lights up, it's someone wanting to talk. They'll let you know who else to bring in. You might also find links are being made independently. Not too sure about that. I'm guessing.'

'Can I use this with those radio thingies you've got?'

'Yes, but I doubt we're going to be allowed to link in, Bess. There is something we *can* do, though, and that is allocate standard channel frequencies on your embassy transmitter, one for Dr Em and me and one for Danny and Rosalie. We can do that tomorrow.'

'And those disc things on the bench?'

'Nothing. Just security tags. They're not needed anymore. I'll take them and get rid of them.'

·

'You know, Chris,' she said as they were making their way back to the Mirabilé through warm, ankle-deep water, 'I've been thinking about this encryption thing and how complex security approaches have now become. I was trained, twenty odd years ago, in old-speak type things: code letters, text references, dead drops, microdots, numbers stations… basic tradecraft stuff. Now it's coding-decoding systems, quantum inscription, end-to-end encryption, and God knows what else. It's all double Dutch to people like me. I sometimes think I should get out of this business while I'm still sane and young enough to start a new career.'

He laughed. 'No. You don't want to think like that. All you need to do is beaver away at the paperwork, get yourself liked, make yourself indispensable, understand the figures – the money, the key data – that sort of thing. You'll soon get yourself promoted and *then*, you can be as technically incompetent as you like. Just think, since when could those on top actually do what the underlings and technicians do? Never. Haven't you noticed that the technician types just don't rise through the ranks? The thing is they know what they're doing; they understand all that technical junk, so it'd be a real mistake for those at the top to promote them.'

'You're a dreadful cynic.'

'Maybe. My wife certainly thinks so. She says I've seen too much.'

'Can I ask you about something else… those security tag things. You sounded just a bit devious when Bess asked about them. What are they?'

'They're exactly what I said… security tags. They're just positional radio chips that give off regular electronic pulses every few seconds, which can be tracked.'

'OK; so, why would anyone want to do that?'

'Well, you know… security.'

'But that's it! I *don't* know! What do you mean by *security*, for God's sake? What could anyone have done about it, if there had been a problem?'

He'd have to come clean. 'Well, the people out there would want to know that the equipment got to the right place, and it's obvious that whoever put the chips there expected them to be discovered and removed. I wouldn't have been able to put the cypher module into the housing in the box with the tag in there; the same goes for the other one. The degree of fit-tolerance is miniscule – sub-millimetre level.'

'You're still obfuscating!' she replied, deciding she'd give him a bit of his own fancy language back. 'What could anyone have done, if the gear had just been left out in the bush, or fallen into the hands of the baddies?'

He stopped, leant back against the cliff, looking up at the stars. She came up alongside him. 'You OK?'

'I'm fine, Em. I'm thinking about what you've just said. Don't take this the wrong way – but I think there may well be an armed UAV tracking us along the shore following the signals from those tags.'

'You mean right now we're a *target*?'

'Yes, if you look at it that way, I suppose we are. Well, technically, *I'm* the target.'

'Lord! That's *not* a lot of reassurance! I'm standing right next to you.'

He laughed. 'True. But if someone did press the button, you wouldn't have time to worry about it. Anyway, remember, we've just used the communication system, so they *know* the gear is where it's supposed to be. They'll realise what we've done... I guess.'

'I don't like that. Get rid of the damn things! Throw them into the ocean!'

'Could do that, but the chips probably have a good six months' life in them. I wouldn't want to waste them, and who knows, we might find a use for them.'

'Well, you're welcome to keep them. I certainly don't want them anywhere near *me*! And anyway, why anyone should be so concerned about a bit of radio gear that they'd blast whoever to smithereens to prevent it going astray baffles me.'

'I don't disagree, Em, but that gear is state of the art; it's secure plus –for the next few years, at least. At present, anyone who managed to tap into the signals from it would get indecipherable gobbledygook, and remember, this country is a pseudo-Marxist fruit-and-nut case.'

'Yes, I get all that, but that takes us back precisely to the issue of what's so critical about this place. So far, everyone – well except, you – seems to think there's gold here.'

'Not only me, I think. You'll remember that pixelated patch on the satellite image. I'd guess your people did that deliberately because they noticed something odd about that area, something that disturbed them. They're not sold on the gold thing, either. They're not certain, of course, and they weren't going to let us know what they think; what we don't know won't hurt us.'

'But my Director would not be so devious as to not let me into what they knew.'

'Now, there's a thought, Em, and one I wouldn't want to comment on. Haven't you ever wondered why Burnett insisted that you get hold of *me* for this job? It just may be because I know certain things and have particular skills. They need corroboration. Anyway, for that matter, why do you think you're here with me? Forget the civilian ethic thing; Burnett doesn't give a hoot about that in my case. No… I think you've been sent here to be the co-ordinator of this business.'

'Co-ordinator! Stuff and nonsense, Chris!'

'Not really. Look what's happening. Between us we are now determining all the significant processes and activities. Bess is our apprentice. She knows that. She's as smart as they come. She's learning. It's about the future, and her role in it, and there you have it… and the gold thing. I'd forget that one, if I were you. I've a feeling we're dealing with something much more disturbing. Anyway, let's get back to the Mirabilé.'

•

Madame and Anna were huddled over a table in the restaurant when they arrived back in reception.

'Look at them!' Em whispered. 'Surely, they're not still listening to that radio nonsense.'

'Who knows? Let's go and see.'

'And where 'ave you two doctors been?' Madame asked, an air of ownership in her voice. 'I knocked on your doors an hour ago!'

'Out in the gardens studying the night sky,' Chris replied. 'The bit just above us here is beautiful, a magnificent star-spangled wonder.'

'Zut Alors! You 'ear that, Anna, and no theories! Come, sit down, you two. So much is 'appening. We were listening to the National Radio and suddenly it disappears – dead as the Dodo… Poor Mauritius! Immédiatement, a new station starts, and so loud! It calls itself Radio Free Ivundé. So, we are free! It says we are now a revolutionary republic. Hah! And what does that mean then? Everything is in the local language, then English, then French. Tomorrow, men can go get food. Women can get water but must wear the scarf on the 'ead and a long dress. But fishermen must *not* go to sea! Poor things. 'Ow will they feed their families? And all foreigners and people from the mainland must not leave their 'ouses. They *even* talk about my 'otel. They say the people 'ere must stay 'ere. They must not go out. That's us!'

29
FCO FLUNKY

The Watchkeeper communications drone was inaudible and unseeable. Indeed, if radar had been sweeping those skies, the drone would have created the merest microsecond pixel-twitch only. For over twenty hours, it had been transmitting photographs and video south-east to Diego Garcia. And, when Radio Free Ivundé started up, the UAV picked up the broadcast and relayed it on.

•

In the communications complex in Cheltenham, late on that Saturday evening, James Burnett and his head of technology were meeting with Leon, the Deputy Director of MI6, and a senior FCO adviser.

'How does this Jamieson stuff fit in with what *you* claim we already know?' asked the Foreign Office man, his tone suggestive of an interrogation.

'Pretty well, Clive… as far as we can tell,' said the Director.

'As far as we can tell! What's that supposed to mean?'

'Well, Dr Jamieson is being very circumspect and careful. He's only his eyes to go by, after all. Even so, we are in agreement with him: the gold thing looks like a bit of invention, a cover.'

'You mean a story? A fairy tale? If that is so, Director, it would presumably be in our interest to inform our Chinese friends. It would put them out of their misery. Their visiting fleet is only a few hours out from the island. We don't want them blundering in chasing a myth. We'd also get brownie points from them for telling them what we know.'

The man's manner was irritating, but he was right. No-one wanted China to get a military foothold in the Indian Ocean. They already had far too much economic leverage on the African continent.

'I don't disagree with that, Clive,' Burnett said, with as even a tone as he could muster. 'But there's the problem of how we feed the information to them, so they'd believe it and not treat it as a bluff or double-bluff. A simple assertion wouldn't be good enough. The best way is for your people to arrange something which would let the Chinese discover that position for themselves.'

'All right. Possibly. I'll talk to the Minister about it in the morning. Now, the second bit of the agenda – these notes and things Jamieson sent through – and can we do this quickly. I'd like to get home while there's some night left!'

The Director's response was cut short by the orange light flashing on his desk.

'One moment, please.' He went over to his desk.

'Right now? Through DG? Language? Doesn't matter. Take it back to the beginning and put it through to my office. We might get something out of it.'

•

'That's not much use to us,' Clive said after they'd listened for a minute or so to the relayed Radio Free Iuundé broadcast. Anyway, what's the lingo?'

'Ziaŵalan, or whatever they call it,' said the Director. 'We can get it translated.' He turned to his technical adviser. 'Peter, could you chase that one up? Give it priority. It might be difficult. We may have to go outside. Pay whatever's necessary.'

At that moment, and without warning, the broadcast switched to English. They all leaned forward, focussing on the heavily accented voice. After five minutes of forceful rhetoric, the language changed yet again; this time to French, and a different speaker. The Director cautioned the others to wait while he checked that the versions matched.

The broadcast ended abruptly.

'Peter, cancel what I just said. I think we can be sure we've just had three identical versions: one local, one English, one French. Can you check with DG about source and strength? Make sure the embassy in Ziaŵala is brought into that loop? Oh, and get someone – right now – to transcribe and make copies of the English version for our visitors here.'

He turned to the Foreign Office man. 'Well, Clive, there you go. We have a very convenient solution to our China problem. Fate has thrown the dice in our favour for once. The Chinese will have picked that stuff up loud and clear. We don't need to say anything to them. We let them come to their own conclusions. I would suggest, though, that we give the Russians a copy. One of their Indian Ocean listening stations will have heard it, of course, but we wouldn't want to admit to knowing that.' He smiled. 'It'll show our desire to be open and to co-operate. They might even reciprocate; their guy has been visiting the place regularly.'

'Thank you for that advice, Director Burnett, and I will inform the Minister of your views, though as you are aware, such matters are subject to guidance from my office. In any event, what is your broader reasoning? I don't see how this solves our China problem.'

Burnett sighed. He'd have to spell it out for the fool. 'It's simple, really, Clive. Both the Chinese and the Russians now have an explanation for all the covert activity on the island. That broadcast is clear. Ivundé has been taken over by a group of local religious extremists. And that – if you think about it – leaves the gold story a cover-up, a subterfuge, put out by those people to divert attention from their real purpose. The Russians don't have a gold hang-up anyway, and China will now ask itself whether it really wants to get involved in a local religious squabble, with all the regional and international opprobrium that would bring.'

'But they mightn't see it that way.'

'No, Clive. Indeed, they might not, but the Chinese government is as smart as it comes in these sorts of matters. Put yourself in their position. Wouldn't you *at least* reflect on the situation and pull back from any immediate action to give yourself a breathing space, make a few enquiries, see how things develop?'

'I see. All right. I'll go over all this with the Minister in the morning. Now, you say your people, using some sort of expensive spectrum analysis, and then this Jamieson fellow, by just looking at the stuff, have come up with broadly similar conclusions?'

'That's correct, Clive, but remember, Dr Jamieson is *not* able to be definitive in any way. He is speculating. Nonetheless, we can state that our conclusions are *very* similar, not merely broadly.'

'That's just semantics! You have a written summary for me, of course.'

Officious sod, thought the Director, as he moved over to his desk to retrieve the papers. 'Here you go. The second page contains explanatory technical notes. The whole thing needs to be looked at by the Chief Scientific Officer or relevant specialists on the Science Advisory Committee.'

'I believe I said earlier; action on this matter is the Minister's prerogative.' Clive stared at the first page. 'Anyway, what is this stuff? Looks like a load of Greek mythology twaddle. The Minister will have no idea what it means. Don't you have a layman's version for him?'

'With the greatest respect,' said Burnett, trying – but failing – to hide his annoyance, 'that is precisely *why* I suggested it should be referred to the science people. GCHQ is a communications surveillance and analysis service. My staff aren't physical science specialists.'

'I see,' said Clive, 'and these notes on the second page – are they relevant?'

The Director smiled to himself. 'They're not long and quite intelligible. I'm sure you'll find time to read them before your meeting with the Minister in the morning. They list the things needed to get an accurate baseline picture of what we're looking at, including chemical analyses and an on-site quantity and qualitative survey. Oh, and by the way, I believe the Minister knows about this whole matter.'

'I don't know how *you* would know that but, fine, this is all *I* need. Now, the final bit of our agenda: these people who've managed to get themselves stuck on this damned island, and who you claim we are responsible for.'

'I don't *claim* anything, Clive! It's obvious.'

'Who are these people? Why isn't our embassy dealing with it? That's what we have those overpaid and underworked organisations for.'

'Our embassy *is* dealing with it, Clive, and we are in touch daily with our ambassador about the matter, but the Minister will need to make decisions.'

'I see. Numbers? Nationalities?'

'British, French, New Zealand, Swiss, Portuguese, Norwegian and Swedish and a dual UK-Zimbabwean, with seventeen individuals in all. The Americans have six nationals and a couple from Latin America on the island.'

'Right. So?'

Burnett was disturbed by the man's lack of awareness. 'Well, in effect, they're all hostages, or are likely to be very shortly.'

Clive shrugged dismissively. 'What do you mean, *hostages*? You've seen the reports. They aren't in any danger.'

The MI6 Deputy Director, Leon, who had been silent thus far, looked up from his notes, thoroughly fed up with the man's ignorance and his officious hectoring tone. 'Clive, did you not *hear* what was said in the broadcast? Anyway, it's so damned obvious! Every foreigner on that island is now a hostage and that's *exactly* what I'll be reporting back to my Director. I guarantee, *now*, that he'll be on the phone to the Cabinet Office first thing tomorrow. That is, unless *you* know something we don't which assures the safety of those people!'

That's style, thought Burnett, *doesn't give a toss.*

The Foreign Office man fumbled round for words. 'Well, you know what I mean. No-one's made any threats or demands, and so I can't see why they should be regarded as hostages.'

'I suppose it comes down to those damned semantics again,' said Burnett. 'Look, I speak for both our agencies, when I say the Minister must be made aware that it's overwhelmingly likely those people will shortly become a bargaining pawn. I'd give it forty-eight to sixty hours.'

The MI6 man nodded. 'And I agree with that.'

'Clive, a friendly word of advice, if I may,' Burnett continued. 'The press will get hold of this thing by late tomorrow, and then it's up in lights: BBC, SKY, CNN, NBC, RT, RTF, CBC, Al Jazeera. God knows! You name it! And your office will have to answer calls from the embassies and aid agencies of the countries of those stuck on the island, to say nothing of their relatives, mothers, fathers, children.'

'I understand,' Clive said quietly. 'I need to go now.' And, as the man shuffled out of his office, Burnett could see that an intense weariness had descended on him.

Leon broke into the Director's moment of reflection. 'God! James, where on earth do they find people like that? Surely, the Minister has someone more competent than that twit!'

'Don't count on it, Leon. I meet such people regularly; I have some of my own jobsworth crew. I'm guessing the Minister's just using him as a gofer. It may even be a back-covering thing.'

'Anyway, where do you think this whole business is going?'

'I wish I knew, but I guarantee the Minister will phone me tomorrow after Clive's given him a headache. Maybe I'll pre-empt that. Anyway, what does MI6 make of the weapons that Jamieson photographed?'

'We've had a quick look and we calculate there're many more guns than baddies. That suggests there's another crew hidden away somewhere.'

The Director sat quietly for a moment or two. 'What's our Security personnel position like in Ziaŵala?'

'Not good – a couple only.'

'The Americans?'

'Who knows? They claim about the same. There's also that Stryker character on the island, though last thing we hear is that he's gone missing.'

'We heard that. He's probably squirrelled away somewhere, watching, and waiting.'

'What for?'

'Lord knows, Leon! What sorts of things do American agency people who claim to be majors and call themselves Stryker watch and wait for, anyway?'

'So it may finally be the cavalry, then. That would generate some heat.'

'Don't I know it!' said Burnett. 'One lot would call us colonialists, another lot neocolonialists. To others, we'd be evil Crusaders. Anyway, Leon, enough! It's late. Let's get back to our long-suffering families. I'll see you at the meeting on Monday. Things should be clearer then.'

Burnett sat back, mentally running through the options for moving forward, none of which he concluded was worth pursuing. He leant forward and pressed Red 3.

'*Yes, Director.*'

'Peter, can we get in touch with our Ivundé co-ordinator?'

'*You mean right now?*' You'll appreciate it's well past midnight there?*'

'I know. Try, anyway, and bring in the embassy night-bird.' He sat staring at a copy of Chris Jamieson's sketch of the island in a folder on his desk. There was no way back, and he knew it.

Red 3 came on. '*Got it, Director! Embassy's listening in.*'

'Excellent, Peter. I'll close down when I've finished. Thank you for staying on.'

30
TEDDY BEAR

Bess had created a sleeping pod in the narrow storage area beneath the transmitter bench. Earlier, Meera and Mina had noticed the weariness in her face, the slumped shoulders, the smile that had lost its sparkle. They sensed she was under great pressure in a way they had never seen before. 'Sleep in the house, Bess,' they'd pressed, but she'd have none of it; she needed to be next to her transmitter, ready for the next contact, from anyone, anywhere, at any time.

And now – well past midnight – she retired to a single mattress she'd found in the storeroom. She'd earlier raided Valli's Toyota and taken a small dashboard fan. She'd put this on the ground next to her face to break up the worst of the humidity in her airless enclosure.

•

It was around one-thirty that a low-pitched buzz began threading its way through the whirr and squeak of the fan.

She opened one sleep-laden eye. There was a blue glow rolling around her shed. She crawled out from under the bench, sending the fan flying, and pulled herself up onto a chair. '2 – GB,' she muttered.

'Yes. Co-ordinator here.' And as she said it, she realised how pretentious it sounded. She had thought at one point that she might use her own name but had quickly backed off from that idea. Her anonymity was sacrosanct. She knew that, and anyway it would be presumptuous.

'Co-ordinator,' she said again, this time more hesitantly.

'Hello, Co-ordinator.' The voice was metallic, but clearly male. 'Exciting name you've got there.'

So, it *was* pretentious. 'I agree,' she replied. 'I'm thinking that, too. I may change it. How can I help?'

'We've a problem that needs a solution your end, but first we'd like to run a few things past you and the two doctors.'

'I'm afraid they left more than an hour ago… maybe two hours. They'll be fast asleep in the hotel. If it can wait till tomorrow a.m. – sorry, I mean today – I can get a message to them. I'm sure they'll get back to you. Of course, if it's urgent, I can go and get them right now.'

'No. Tomorrow mid-morning your end would be fine. When you see them, could you let them know that we need a definitive picture of the type, quality and quantity of minerals on the northern site. Our discussions here have led us to believe it can only be done through a hands-on survey, and for that we'd need to get someone covertly onto the island with the right equipment.'

'I understand. I'll get the doctors here about seven, eleven your end, but can I say even now that getting someone here safely would be very difficult. *I* think impossible.'

'Yes, and we've more or less come to that same conclusion, but we'll talk it through in the morning. Now, go back to sleep.'

'Will do. Over. Out.'

She smiled. She'd made the equipment work, *and* she'd been empowered. Now, maybe, she could get some sleep. Something would have to be done about that name, though.

She rolled back under the bench, righted the fan and lay still. Her focus began to drift.

•

She's lying in deep, dry, yellow grass, rigid, fearful for herself, fearful for her mother down there in the village, hiding somewhere, fearful for her neighbours. Her heart sounds like the loudest drum she has ever heard. Surely, those terrible men must hear it! She presses her hand tight against her chest – left side her mother once said – and pushes it into silence. She watches, screaming silently, as the bandits fling flaming pitch-tar torches into the houses of her small Christian community. Thick, black smoke comes rolling up the hillside. It envelops her. It is acrid and choking. She buries her face in the grass.

She's standing in the smouldering ruins of her house; her mother lies dead at her feet. It is as though she is asleep. She is so beautiful. She is untouched by the fire, but around her everything lies blackened, destroyed.

Suddenly, the fierce, cruel matron is waving her fists and baring her teeth at her. Then she charges towards her, and the face melts away. In its place is the smiling British lady from New Delhi, who takes her by the hand.

They are in the sunlight and walking into a fine school full of young girls, all laughing and shouting, all in pristine blue and gold uniforms.

It's the school oath; she learns it off by heart. 'I promise to do my best to tell the truth and be honest at all times. I will always be reliable, disciplined and responsible, upholding the honour of my God, my family and my country.'

Then, there, in her bed in the dormitory, lies a present from her fine British Lady, her saviour, a woman blessed by God with the gift of absolute love. It's the biggest and best present in the world. The best present ever.

'That's it! That's it!' she hears herself shouting. Her voice wakes her up. '*It's Teddy Bear!*'

And, in a second, she is fast asleep.

31

DISTRAUGHT

The Chinese ambassador's breakfast dumplings were particularly fine that Sunday morning and he wondered idly how on earth his cook had managed to find the ingredients in the empty-shelved shops of downtown Mulamuezini; he'd think to ask him sometime.

Next, it was Oolong Gold, his favourite morning tea. It came meticulously laid out with serviette on an oblong silver tray, which sparkled in the morning sunlight, not a fingerprint evident anywhere. His Oolong Gold deserved no less. It had come many thousands of miles, specifically for his table, from an estate drawing its water from the magnificent Lancang river. His tea required his undivided attention, with its fine swirl of blacks and browns and its aroma redolent of hibiscus. It was a miracle of natural processes, God-made and God-given. Above all, it was a liquid that could not and must not be rushed.

And so, his cypher clerk, when he rushed in unannounced, was endlessly apologetic and full of "Your

Excellencies. There was an urgent summons to the presidential palace; attendance was required immediately. The ambassador was frustrated and more than a little annoyed. Though on reflection, later, he realised he shouldn't have been surprised; he should have expected it – and at short notice. Certainly, Beijing had anticipated it, and warned him.

His Foreign Ministry had sent him a top priority message earlier that morning. It was brief and unequivocal. Under no circumstances whatsoever was he to offer any more than material aid to the government of Ziaŵala. Guns, ammunition, the odd armoured car – even money – were all possible, but that really was *it*. The island business was a small, local fundamentalist conspiracy fermented by a few out-of-control criminal and extremist religionaries. Ziaŵala was on its own on this one. China could in no way become directly involved in the squabble.

The directive had ended with a footnote stating that the Chinese naval group, at that point in mid-ocean, was being ordered to head back towards the Indian sub-continent and that the British, American and the Russian Governments were being informed of this decision. No other action was planned or under consideration.

The ambassador knew that the flagship would have heard the Radio Free Iuundé broadcast and relayed it back to Beijing and, while Ziaŵala might well be a member of the Communist camp, albeit superficially, he quite understood this was insufficient to justify physical intervention. His country's extensive political and economic stake elsewhere on the continent and in the Gulf region to the north would be put at great risk were they to contemplate using force in such a trivial affair. It would be seen as gunboat diplomacy of the worst sort. The loss of face would be overwhelming.

And now, as he made his way out to the limousine waiting to take him to the presidential palace, Ambassador Lee Kwong Wei knew full well he wasn't going to be asked simply for AKs, land mines or rocket launchers; Ziawala – indeed the whole continent – was awash with such weaponry. No, he was certain he was going to be asked for the very thing he couldn't give.

•

The President, in regal pose, besuited, hands clasped across an ample stomach, was waiting for the ambassador at the foot of the marble steps, which swept in a great arc around the front of the fine colonial building.

As the car came to a gentle stop on the white-painted cobbled parking area next to the flagpole, the ambassador leant forward and said quietly to his chauffeur in Hokkien, 'These are fine gardens, Kong, very uplifting of the spirit. Walk a little, study them, enjoy them, but do not wander far; stay in sight of the car, at all times. I believe I may not be with the President very long. Shall we have a small wager – one yuan? Set your watch; I predict ten minutes.'

The President came over, arms outstretched. 'My great friend, Ambassador Lee, I am so very happy you could find the time to drop in, and on Sunday as well. You demonstrate the devotion of a true diplomat. Come into State House. Let us have some mid-morning tea and some of the finest fruits of this great continent, grown here in my very own orchards.'

The President led the way up the marble steps and through the main entrance. 'We will, of course, use my Number One reception. From there, while we discuss, we can look out over my gardens.'

'And very fine gardens they *are*, Excellency,' said the ambassador, wondering, as they settled into fine leather armchairs either side of a low table laid to tea and fruit, whether he or Mzinga would be first to kick the ball into play. He didn't have to wait long for an answer.

'This Ivundé thing,' said the President, staring out of the window and waving his hands dismissively, 'it is but a small matter, a family squabble, you might say. Mmmm. Yes. That is right, just a little family dispute… part of the human condition, wouldn't you say?'

'I would, indeed, Mr President, yet it is still an annoyance, when there are so many other more important matters of state to deal with.'

'Yes! As always, you are so right, my wise friend. Such trivial things divert us from our constant, heroic efforts to improve the lot of our fellow countrymen – those who toil in our fields, hunt in the bush and net the seas, and all for the common good. But here! Have tea and papaya, or perhaps you prefer mango, or indeed both?'

'Tea would be very welcome, sir, and thank you.'

'As I am sure you know, Ambassador, you, yourself, and your great country are our closest friends, and we your most loyal partners and supporters. Thus, when I woke this morning, it was with the thought that solving this Ivundé triviality together offers us a magnificent opportunity to consolidate our close ties. It will bring great benefits to both sides – indeed all sides. The Ivundé family dispute is, you might say, a great blessing in disguise, a tiny cloud that brings with it a fine silver lining.'

'I agree, Excellency, and, as you know, we have already co-operated so well on many things – agriculture, health, industry, education – and all very successfully. I can assure you we will continue our support and co-operation.'

'I thank you for that assurance. It is a wonderful vote of confidence in my government, and my leadership. But this Ivundé matter, Ambassador, do you have views on it?'

'Sir, I am, of course, not in a position to know the details, but I have great confidence that the military training we have provided to Ziawala over these last two years will pay dividends if your government needs to use a little compulsion – force even – to resolve the problem.'

But, as he said it, Lee Kwong Wei knew that it was utter nonsense – a vain hope, indeed – to believe that the local military could push determined rebels off the island. All the reports of their own military trainers and advisers were abundantly clear: the Ziawalan forces were not up to anything more than looking well-groomed on Armed Forces Day as they marched up and down Independence Boulevard, bayonets and buttons glinting in the sun, with their only functioning armoured car following on behind. An effective fighting force was at least ten years away, if ever.

'And of course, it is very true,' said the President, smiling, 'very true, indeed! I have the finest generals on the continent. With their men, they could squash those Ivundé dogs as easily as I can squash… this fly.' And, as he spoke, he flung his right hand out violently above the fine Georgian silver sugar bowl and scrunched his hand into a tight, trembling fist. He then proceeded to roll his fingers across the palm of his hand, reducing the hapless creature to a fine black paste.

The ambassador sighed inwardly and thought wryly how such fine fly-catching skills would once have been highly regarded in his own country. However, he now sensed the President was gearing up for the real kill and even with his finely-honed diplomatic skills Lee knew the challenge would certainly be beyond him. It wouldn't be the manner in which he would have to say no; rather it would be the saying of it in the first place. There was absolutely nothing he could do to avoid causing great, irreparable offence. His fabled ambassadorial ability to smooth ruffled feathers would be put to the sword. While Beijing wouldn't be worried about such an outcome, *he* definitely would. He quite liked the country and its wonderful, endless chaos. He even quite liked the President and normally got on with him well, despite the man's corrupt practices, with his regular visits to the Central Bank "to check on the figures", as he would say.

'The thing is,' continued the President, calming down as he returned his gaze to the gardens. 'Yes, the thing is… the island is so remote. There are many, many miles of ocean to traverse between here and there, and I think you know we have only just begun training our naval forces. Thus, getting my army boys there to chase those evil people out will not be easy.'

This, at least, thought Lee, was perfectly correct, though even with a functioning navy the result would be the same. More to the point, though, he now knew the precise angle of attack and his instincts told him it was time to move fast. He'd strike first. He might in that way prevent a much bigger loss of presidential face, one from which neither of them would ever recover. Things once said cannot be unsaid, though whoever says them first can exercise some control over the consequences through the manner of their saying.

'You're very right to have those concerns, Excellency. Indeed, I was just thinking on the way here what a pity it was that our naval group has had to turn back. Otherwise, of course, it would more than willingly have assisted directly in this matter.'

Mzinga froze. Had he heard this right? Surely, it could not be so. Slowly, a mixture of disbelief and horror spread across his face. Lee steeled himself.

'Turned back! How's that possible? When did it happen? I don't know this. No-one told *me*! It cannot be true!'

'My apologies, Mr President, sir, but the news only came in last evening, and very late indeed, and even at that late hour, I immediately instructed my First Secretary to let your protocol office know, and to inform them that our fleet has had to turn around and head back to India for technical reasons. I fear the lady may have been delayed a little, or maybe she was just not able to get through. Late Saturday is not the best time to contact anyone.'

But the President wasn't listening; his hands were twitching, his round face twisted in fury, and Lee knew his only hope now was to get it all out quickly. 'It seems, sir,' he continued, 'it was unavoidable. Our command and communications ship – our flagship – broke down late yesterday afternoon in mid-ocean with very serious engine trouble. It is now limping back on one propeller towards the sub-continent with the other vessels in support. We are going to have to postpone our programme of courtesy calls, both here and elsewhere on the continent.'

'You people!' the President spluttered. 'Is this how loyalty is repaid? How can it be so? You have the biggest and best navy in the world. Your engines do not break down; they are the best in the world!'

'I can only apologise profoundly on behalf of my government, Mr President, but we do not have the capacity to help at this time in the way you want. Of course, in the meantime, if you could let me have the full cost of the many preparations that have undoubtedly been made for our naval visit, I will personally see that appropriate recompense is made – with added compensation as well. In addition, my government would be very happy to provide any weapons you require for your armed forces, so that they can deal with this business.'

The ambassador knew he was offering crumbs, and while the additional financial reward might calm the President a little, it would not help the man deliver on the promises he'd rashly made to his people on national radio.

Mzinga was now looking down at his hands. They were clutching his knees. He was shaking his head slowly from side to side and muttering to himself.

Lee stood up quietly, excused himself, and slipped out silently from the room.

•

As he was being driven back to the embassy, an English saying he'd learnt at university, and had found so descriptive of many situations in life, came to mind. He leant forward and tapped his chauffeur on the shoulder. 'You know, Kong,' he said in English, 'one must never count one's chickens before they are hatched.'

His chauffeur smiled and nodded wisely, though he had not the slightest idea what his ambassador had just said to him.

Then, the ambassador added in Hokkien, 'And you owe me one yuan.'

PSYCHIC DISTANCE

The traffic on the outskirts of Cheltenham had been reduced to a snail's pace as the cars negotiated the flooded areas along the main roads.

James Burnett leant forward and slid back the heavy glass divider. 'Ralph, we're running late. I need a word with night-bird before he goes off duty. It was Mervyn last night. Can you patch me through?'

Mervyn was a favourite. He was over-verbal, but infinitely patient and reliable, and one of the safest administrative hands in GCHQ. His voice came through, slightly distorted. *'Night-bird.'*

'Anything overnight? Indian Ocean?' Burnett asked.

'Nothing earth-shaking, Director. Mostly routine. There was one marginally interesting Indian Ocean thing from DG. It seems that Chinese flotilla, which I believe was heading west towards the African continent. At least, last time—'

'Yes, Merv, get on with it. What about it?'

'Sorry. Yes. Well, it just sort of turned around after midnight, GMT, and it's now heading, full-steam, towards the sub-continent. The Indian FM asked our Delhi High Comm. if they knew what it was about. Our lot said they don't know and would ask around. The High Comm. told us the Indians didn't seem too fussed. I suppose they're used to everyone paddling round in their part of the pond. Anyway, I've recorded it in the—'

'Excellent, Merv, and that's all I need to know. Can you do me a favour on your way out? Check the logbook to see what time Harry's going to be in? He was up late last night. I need him this morning. He knows, but could you just remind him? Catch up later.'

•

Radio Free Ivundé repeated the *"Communique of the Free"* – as they called it – of the previous evening, every hour, on the hour, and in the three languages. In response, a few of the bolder men in the town ventured out looking for food supplies, only to see heavily armed men in groups of two or three at every junction, the shops still closed, the market deserted.

Up the road from the Mirabilé, the three gunmen were now sitting under the mango tree, talking. In the middle of the group was a heavy machine gun mounted on a tripod. It was pointing directly down towards the Mirabilé.

'Mon Dieu!' said Madame Lemessurier as she came into reception. She had a bread roll in her right hand, which she was waving vigorously in the general direction of the main entrance. 'Anna, look. Out there! Why are they pointing their nasty gun at my 'otel? Pourquois? What for? What 'ave we done to 'urt them? We are 'armless.'

'I'm sure it doesn't mean much, Madame. After all, they've got to point the gun somewhere. It's just by accident it's pointing our way. Which reminds me – well your bread roll does – I was just thinking we should check what food supplies we have. We need to make an inventory, and there's the generator fuel, as well.'

'Did I hear something about organising the food and fuel supplies?' Em said, as she came in from B Wing. 'That sounds a jolly good idea, and here comes Chris. He'd *love* to help, I'm sure.'

'Help? With what?'

'We're all going to make an inventory of the Mirabilé's food and fuel stocks.'

'An excellent idea!' he smiled, 'but, not me, too many counters will get the sums wrong. Anyway, I can't add up. I'm a trig man. I like spaces shapes and sizes. Em, you got a moment?'

He drew her to one side. 'Bess has managed to get our radios linked into her old transmitter. She's just called. We've got to go round there. Your boss wants to talk to us.'

'You mean right now, in broad daylight?'

'Sure. If we go out through the emergency exit at the end of A Wing and along through the gardens down to the shore, we'll be well out of the line-of-sight of the guys up the road.'

•

Bess closed the door behind them. 'Your Director called me in the early hours. He asked about a minerals survey on the northern site. He said they want to send a specialist, plus equipment. I said that would be impossible. He'd like to speak to you two about it.'

'And that was exactly the right answer, Bess,' Em said. 'Chris?'

'Yes, absolutely. They'd have to put a ring of steel around the place and send a helicopter with specialist surveyors with a pile of gear. There's got to be another way—'

He was interrupted by knocking on the back wall, where the shed joined Valli's garage.

'It's OK. Not a problem,' Bess said. 'Three taps; that's Mina with refreshments for everyone from you know who. She doesn't come in much, and Meera and Valli never. It's sensible. What you don't know, you can't let slip out by mistake one day. Valli even says my shed is not really here; it is but an illusion, an oasis, that the thirsty man lost in the desert sees, yet can never reach. One moment, while I collect the tray.'

'Em, you'll remember that WMD Iraq debacle,' Chris said quietly while Bess went out to Mina. 'I guess that's why they want a professional quality-quantity analysis. They need unequivocal evidence to back up my view of things.'

'Hold on. She's coming back.'

'You know, you two,' Chris said, as Bess rejoined them, 'we're all being a bit slow here. Psychic distance and the thought of those samosas has given me an idea.'

'You off again, Chris! I apologise for him, Bess. He likes talking in tangents. Right. What nutty scheme have you come up with now?'

'Well, here's the funny thing: what's required is already here.'

'Nonsense, as I said, Bess; but go on, Chris, what do you mean?' asked Em.

'I think we can safely assume that the Colonel and his men have been running around gathering geological samples, along with a bit of arms smuggling. Now, if we add Zhou, a highly qualified, professional scientist, and what I saw in that laboratory of his, I'd bet anything we have exactly what our lot are looking for. There's no need to replicate the whole process. Zhou has the data, and all we have to do is steal it from him.'

Em was shaking her head. 'Oh, no, Chris. I really don't think I like what you're saying. How do you propose we go about doing that? You've already rampaged across that site with Danny. Is Zhou – let alone the others – going to let you waltz in again and this time steal his research? And just supposing we – and I suppose you mean *we* – could even get to him, what then, threaten to shoot him if he refuses to give us the answers?'

'That sounds like a good tactic to me,' he said, laughing. 'Of course, the shooting'd be your job! Let's talk to Burnett.'

'OK. But I just know he won't support the idea. It's reckless, full of dangerous unknowns!'

'Unknowns are the least of our concerns, Em, and they're only dangerous when you know them. The consequences of the wrong people getting control of what's here are far worse. We have to get on with it. It's now really a question of the better or worse of two evils.'

'*Two* evils?'

'Yes. What exists here, and the knowledge of it. Bess, can you get the Director, GCHQ, for us?'

Seconds later, James Burnett came on the line.

Jamieson touched Em on the shoulder. 'You start,' he whispered. 'I'll come in as and when.'

'Director. Em here. We've been talking through the problem. We agree that getting someone onto the island to do an analysis is quite impossible. Chris has a different idea. He is actually suggesting we break into the site yet again and this time *force* the Chinese scientist to give us all his data. He says it's our only option; to me, it's far too risky. What do you think?'

'Em, thank you. Look, I don't disagree with what you're saying. But this matter is more than pressing, so at least let's talk it through. Can you please put Chris on, and Coordinator, please bring all your other links into the debate.'

'Chris,' Burnett continued, *'we've always realised that sending someone in plus equipment is a no-goer. If we went with your idea, though, how would you get up there, onto the site, and into the building?'*

'The last two aren't a problem… done them already. The difficult bit is getting up there. There may be a way, though.'

'And I think maybe I don't want to ask what that is,' Burnett continued. *'Anyone listening out there, you have any ideas?'* He waited for a moment or two. *'The silence is deafening,'* he continued. *'OK, Chris, if you think it can be done, it has to be only on the basis of no undue risks.'*

'I understand.'

'Everyone, out there. Any objections? Questions? If not, let's assume it's a Go. Right, Chris, is there any way we can assist?'

'A couple of things. First, do you have a UAV monitoring update?'

A new voice cut in. *'DG control room here. Something happened a couple of hours ago. A Q16 observed forty, four zero, approx. new military, plus cargo, land from a Romeo-*

class North Korean sub on the north-east coast. It followed them down to the northern site.'

Burnett came in. *'Good Lord DG! You might have let us know this earlier. That really puts a stop on things, Chris.'*

'No. Hang on, Director. Correct me, but doesn't what we've just heard mean it's now more critical than ever that we get this done?'

Em shook her head in desperation. Perhaps if she didn't look at him, he'd realise the futility of continuing and the whole idea would just melt away.

'I can't see how, Chris,' Burnett replied. *'But you're on the ground. What exactly do you have in mind?'*

'We have a number of things going for us: first, the security system on the site is crap. Second, those guys off the sub are going to feel super-secure; there are no threats. And, after three… four… five days in the thing, they're going to be absolutely exhausted. If we choose our time right, they'll all be asleep. Third, I know exactly *where* they'll be sleeping and it's well away from where our scientist is. Anyway, neither Em nor I is suicidal. If we turn up and there're PRDK regulars wandering all over the site, then, of course, it's off. We'd just turn around and come back.'

Burnett came in. *'It still sounds very high-risk… Em, how do you see it?'*

She had her eyes closed.

There was a prolonged silence.

'Em?' Chris nudged her. She shook her head. 'Sorry, Director, if I might speak for her. She's thinking, and I'd say she's feeling overwhelmed with joy at the prospect. Em, for God's sake say something,' he whispered.

She sighed audibly. 'Yes. Yes. OK!' She spat it out. 'I'll go with this, Director, but *I* decide if we back off.'

Although he recognised the overwhelming concern in her voice, Burnett knew there were no other options, short of a direct assault and a bloodbath.

'*OK. On that basis, and only on that basis,*' he said, '*we'll go with it. Objections, anyone? None. Right, Chris, any other way we can help?*'

'Yes. We could do with a communications UAV over the place tomorrow night for three hours from 2330 on and programmed with P2P to/from the radios we got in Djibouti.'

'*Djib in. Can do that. You'll need to open another channel on your radios. We'll download the code for that to you just now.*'

'Thank you. Oh, and one other thing.'

Lord! Hate it! Hate it, thought Em. *Why couldn't he have told me beforehand about all his hair-brained ideas? What could he possibly want now?*

'We may need a deal-breaker,' Chris Jamieson continued, 'something we can put on the table, an offer the scientist can't refuse, and forget money or any threat to shoot him. None of that will work with that guy.' There was silence... then a voice came in, one Chris had not heard before. '*Understood. We'll consult on that and will have answers, if and when they're needed.*'

Burnett came back in. '*Well, if there's nothing else then, Chris... Em, all we can say is thank you and we wish you well.*'

Chris Jamieson signalled to Bess.

'Teddy Bear in,' she said into the microphone. 'Before you all go, you need to know that's my new name: *Teddy Bear*.

I know it sounds a bit silly, but I don't like that *Co-ordinator* thing. So, hello, everyone… and goodbye, everyone. Oops! No, not you, Director, Dr Em wants to speak to you on a personal matter.' She waited a second and then deactivated each of the outliers in turn, leaving only Cheltenham live.

'*Em?*'

'It's my mother, Director.'

'*Yes, of course. Well, so far, so good. She heard something on the BBC about the island. I had a word with her – quite a long one as it turned out. She seems a very knowledgeable lady. I see where you get your alertness and strength from.*'

Em winced. 'I'll pretend I didn't hear that, Director.'

'*OK. Anyway, it doesn't seem to bother her. She said you were always getting into scrapes when you were small. And Cedric is getting on well in the kennels. Your mother goes to see him every day to check he's all right and being fed and watered properly… Ahhh, yes. There's something that she particularly wanted me to tell you. She said she had some important information about your father she'd let you have when you got back. That's about it.*

'*And Chris, I spoke to Martha about what's going on out there. She simply said she'll see you when she sees you, and to make sure not to forget her favourite from the duty free in Heathrow on the way back. Over to you, Teddy Bear. You know, I quite like that name. It's got character. Speak later. Out.*'

•

'OK, Chris,' Em said, as they made their way back along the cliff face. 'Tell me how we're going to get up there?'

'We need to think about that one.'

'But you told them you had an idea!'

'I did? I suppose there must have been something in my head at the time. Right now, it's sort of out of reach. It'll come back.'

•

Anna waved them across into the restaurant as they wandered into reception. 'We've just had the latest pronouncement on the radio. They've changed their name yet again. Now, they're the "Defenders of the Revolution". They say everywhere is peaceful and all shops *must* open this evening. Any shop owner refusing to do so will have his business confiscated and he will be treated as an enemy.'

'Anything about foreigners?' Em asked, as casually as she could.

'Not a word,' said Anna. 'But they did say no-one is to move out of their area – whatever that means. Oh, and no-one is to use a vehicle of any sort. I guess that includes bikes. Anyway, how about afternoon tea? Meera gave me half a ton of Darjeeling just before this business began.'

'And I will go and get some bananas from my garden,' said Madame, 'those small sweet mille type. Magnifique they are, and some strawberry jam, and we've lots of fine, tough, rolls!

She turned and strode off into the kitchen.

PART FOUR
ALL HANDS

CURFEW BREAKING

Danny lay as flat as he could get on the burning earth, peering through the minyara hedge. It felt as though the afternoon sun was melting the black lion on his T-shirt into his back. He slid his binoculars up along the river of sweat running down the bridge of his nose and gently eased aside bits of hedge that were obscuring his view. He'd seen something but needed to be sure. He watched a few more seconds. 'Yep. Definitely,' he muttered. The men were slowly dismantling the machine gun bit by bit and putting it back into its wooden crate.

He felt Rosalie wriggle up alongside him. 'Something's going on,' he whispered. 'You look. I think they're off.'

'I know! Packing up! Radio. Just now,' she hissed. 'Came to tell you. They say they've instructed their loyal volunteers to adopt a low profile. To these guys that means they can go home and sleep! They're allowing people out, as well, but no-one can go anywhere! What *I* think is that we sit out on the veranda tonight with a couple of home-brew specials and watch the sun sink into the trees. Right now, though, we need to tell our hotel team what's happening up here.'

They crawled backwards to the driveway, got to their feet and crept round to the back of the house, where they propped themselves up in the shade of the inflatable.

Rosie twisted sideways, stretched back and felt round for the radio, which had been taped lightly to the underside of the inflatable. She pulled it away gently, settled back, and pressed 1.

Within a few seconds there was a response.

'Chris? That you? Our friends up on the road are packing up. We think they're leaving!'

'That's good,' he replied. 'Makes sense. I was just about to call you. I'm afraid we've another problem looking for a solution.'

'Go on,' said Rosalie. 'This household is good at solutions. Good at creating problems, as well!'

'I hate to say this,' Chris continued, 'but we've got to go back to that place up north again, and it's got to be tomorrow night. We were wondering whether you two could think of a way we might do that. The roads are out, of course.'

'Danny, you hear that?' said Rosalie. 'Can we get them back up there? Can't use the road.'

There was silence for a moment. Danny came in. 'Hi, Chris. We could probably take the boat down the short stretch of track to that bay on the east coast.'

'No, Danny. Not safe. That submarine is still there somewhere and there may be armed men camped out on the beach.'

Rosalie had been listening intently. 'Danny! Danny!'

'Shhh! Rosalie. I'm thinking.'

'But I've got it!'

'Hold on, Chris... got what, for God's sake?'

'The solution! The answer!'

'You mean you have an idea?'

'Yes!'

'OK, Rosie, let's have it.'

They all listened carefully as Rosalie went step by step through her idea. 'A dead cert!' she concluded. 'Oh, and Danny's smiling,' she added.

Chris looked over at Em. 'What d'you think?'

She shrugged. 'I suppose it *might* work. What choice do we have?'

'I guess you two heard that. It means we really like it; so, tomorrow, half-six – plus or minus fifteen – forestry track behind the clinic. If we don't turn up, don't even think about coming to look for us; just get back home.'

•

Early next evening, Bess met them at the opening in the fence. She led them up through the garden, into the house and through to the garage. There was no sign of Meera or Valli. 'On the roof – late afternoon tea,' Bess said. 'Mina will be down just now. She'll drive. If you can get yourselves wedged into the back of the truck, I'll throw a mattress over you and a couple of hessian sacks. It'll take us about five minutes to get there. Mina drives very slowly. It'll be OK, though. They need us and haven't bothered us the last couple of evenings.'

•

'It'll be an hour's walk and another on the water, plus or minus,' Danny said. 'Depends on what gear we can find on the beach. We need to go carefully. It's ankle-breaking stuff out there, and there'll be snakes around. We can use our torches.'

'Snakes!' said Em. 'Huh! I've decided they're much over-rated. They'll hear us coming and run like mad.'

Chris Jamieson smiled. She was learning… maybe. He did notice, though, how she quickly manoeuvred herself to the end of the line as they headed out over open ground.

•

Danny walked along the shore with his torch, inspecting each of the fishing boats pulled up onto a flat sandy area, well above the high-water mark. 'Got one,' he called to the others. 'It's got a decent-looking Yamaha 40 and I've seen another engine that'll do as a spare. We just need to find some extra fuel, oars and rollers, and then we're good to go.'

'This is a Danny belt-and-braces job,' Rosalie whispered to Em. 'He loves overkill!'

As they headed north, the swell, which was initially heavy, gradually became more subdued as the tide fell. And it was just before eleven when Danny turned the boat in towards the shore, throttled back and switched off the engine. He tilted the engine up, clambered forward to the centre seat and lifted the oars into the rowlocks.

'Use the torch, Rosie. We need to be over to the right a bit. When you see the darker patch in the rock face, that'll be it. Left-and-right me to guide us in.'

They gradually manoeuvred the boat up into the cove, where Danny held it steady with the oars, pushing the blades alternately into the water, as the others clambered over the front onto the beach. He followed and then, using the rollers, they heaved the boat onto the dry sand area up against the cliff face.

'Right. Final quick check,' Chris said. 'Three radios: Rosalie – you've got yours; Danny, you take this one; Em and I have the third; that's the master. It's also in contact with a UAV circling above… I hope. I'd better just test that… Hold on. Something doesn't make sense.' He pressed the UAV coded button. 'Jamieson,' he said in a low voice into the microphone attached to the collar of his safari jacket.

There was a half-second delay. A metallic voice came in. *'DG.'*

'Do we have a problem? I've got a second active external channel,' Chris said calmly. 'What's going on?'

'It's OK. That's Stryker. He's been brought into the link.'

'Lord help us! Where is he?'

'Four-eight-five yards north-west of your position.'

Em's head was pressed up against Jamieson's during the exchange. 'I hear that right?'

Jamieson switched the volume up. Stryker's voice came in loud and clear. *'Yep, and I can hear everything you're saying!'*

'Where exactly are you?' she asked.

'Hill – your left, overlooking the site. I can't get into the place from here. You need to know there are fifteen to twenty in the hangar right now, and another lot off somewhere in a truck. I've put some plastic on the fence left of gate. I'll trigger

that if everything falls apart. It'll make one hell of a bang. It should draw them off while you get clear.'

'Thanks, Major,' Chris said. 'There're four of us. Em and I will be going into the building. Danny will be up on the flat above the excavation area, your left; he's been there before. Rosalie is down with the boat. They each have a radio. Em and I will use mine.'

'Got that. Listen. It's critical I go back south with you. I'm getting hungry! Living off the land in this place is no joke. How do I get to the boat?'

'Follow the fence down to the cliff face. It'll take you about fifteen minutes. At that point, you just need to slide down. It's not too steep and maybe fifteen, twenty feet.'

'OK. I'll move as soon as you're inside. Can't help you a lot after that.'

Chris turned to Danny. 'We should be out of the building by 0200 at the latest. If we're not, something's gone wrong. Get back to the boat and then head south with Major Stryker. Throw your radios in the ocean. Go home and keep your heads down.'

34 DENIAL

Zhou's Confucian calm was sorely stressed. From first light, Goliath had been thumping to and from the radio room in his bright orange, metal-studded boots, and the building had been reverberating with endless, repetitive haranguing radio transmissions. Even in his laboratory, unpacking the equipment, he was constantly being peered at by small groups of North Korean Special Force men, who insisted on wandering in and poking delicate bits of equipment, perversely, as young children might. They'd chattered incessantly, making crude comments about his rotund figure, the food he ate, his clothes, his general demeanour. To Zhou, the idea that these uncouth idiots could in any way be supporters of a religious revolution was the ultimate in irony. Not that he believed it was that for one moment. The religious thing was all a pretence. These thugs were there for an entirely different and much more sinister purpose.

Early evening had brought some limited respite; the first lorry, and then a second an hour later, had rolled in from the north coast bringing back the day shift, each vehicle then leaving in turn with the night shift.

Once the second lorry had left, Zhou listened as the DPRK officers – with Goliath in attendance – interrogated their men on the events of the day. They screamed questions at the assembled men and lambasted anyone who dared hesitate or give them answers they didn't want to hear. It occurred to Zhou that Goliath couldn't possibly have the slightest idea what was going on. The commentary he was getting from one of the officers – the interpreter – in broken English was inaccurate in the extreme. There was hardly an iota of reality in anything anyone was saying. It was fairy tale stuff, but all the more disturbing for that.

By 2200 hours, there was relief as silence descended on the building. The day shift had settled down to sleep after their heavy evening meal, and the radio transmitter had been turned off. He was now able to work at the delicate task of putting together the instruments he'd need for the next phase of his work.

By midnight, his concentration had begun to waver. He had to rest; tiredness would lead to mistakes. In any event, those numbskulls would wake him up at dawn, banging around, shouting comments at each other, and dropping things all over the place. No doubt, that infernal transmitter would again be blaring out its inane, haranguing messages.

Each night of exile brought for Zhou its own quality of nightmare; and that particular night his nightmare, though seemingly harmless – frivolous even – was so frustrating, it was horrifying. It sprang into life moments after he closed his eyes.

He finds himself surrounded by wooden blocks, very simple objects of the sort children of two and three build imaginary houses with and then knock down with shrieks of delight. They are the colours of the rainbow, red, orange, yellow, green, blue, indigo, violet, and easily distinguished. He is compelled to do the most straightforward thing in the world. He must construct three-block towers, each block of the same colour, in a straight line from one wall to the other of the tiny room he is entombed in. When the line is complete, he knows he will be able to escape from his claustrophobic, miniscule prison. Outside, his wife and daughter are waiting for him.

There's a problem. No matter how hard he tries, how often or how quickly – and he is lightning fast – blocks of the same colour refuse to stay together. He puts a red on top of another red but the one beneath turns green. He tries to take it back; it wriggles out of his hand and drops onto a blue. Again and again he tries. Nothing stays in the right place; nothing allows him to do what he is compelled to do.

Ridiculous… unscientific… impossible… the words loop through his brain. These coloured cubes surely can't be real, their smooth, weightless glow simply a chimera, a mirage never to be reached.

Without warning the blocks, the colours, the room all disappear into a mist of shape-changing figures which gradually rearrange themselves into another, much more frightening nightmare.

From the mist two wavering, shimmering shapes materialise. They stand above him. They are body-stealing aliens. One of the figures is female… he knows. She pushes a long, fat, black barrel-shaped finger onto his forehead. She is preparing to drive it into his brain and steal his mind. Another finger on another hand hovers within inches of the lower half of his face. She steadies it to jab it up his nose. And then the other figure, a male... he knows. It stands motionless. He's puzzled. It should be moving round him, over him, through him.

The silence is broken. The female speaks, her voice hissing and insistent.

'Wake up! Shhh! Do not move; lie still.' He shakes his head, and squeezes his eyes shut. He'll drive these apparitions away. It doesn't work. They are both still there. The pain begins retreating from behind his eyes and to shrink into the centre of his brain.

He opens one eye, then the other; he flexes his hands and tenses his ankles, and his consciousness and rationality began to assert themselves.

The man has now moved close to him.

'Dr Zhou... Dr Zhou,' the man's voice is soft, and even-toned. 'We are *not* here to harm you. We need your help.'

But they must mean him harm. He needed to understand. 'Who are you?' he replied in a hoarse whisper. 'What are you doing here? You must go. I cannot help you.'

'You can,' the man said. 'We *know* you can. We do not have much time. All we require is a copy of your research data, and then we will leave.'

Zhou, now fully awake, decided he'd give them the only answer he dared. 'I do not understand. I have no research data. There is nothing of value here. My job is simply to look for gold deposits under this site before they build a school here.' But, as he said the words, it struck him he'd seen this man before, not his face, but rather his overall shape and size, and he knew instantly his story was not going to be good enough. He fell silent.

Chris Jamieson saw the resignation in the scientist's eyes and the tensing of his jaws. He looked at the pistol still pointing at Zhou's forehead, nudged Em and inclined his head sideways. She hesitated, and then slowly lowered the weapon to her side.

'Yes. I see you remember,' Chris said. 'I was here. I set off the alarm in the radio room. I am a scientist like you and have read all your publications. I also know you and your family are in a most difficult situation in Pyongyang.' He glanced across at Em. She was frowning. 'Dr Zhou,' he continued, 'a scientist of your standing would *not* have been brought to this island merely to look for gold. That idea does not make any sense. In any event, during my earlier visit, I saw the boxes of weapons *and* your laboratory and the material in the containers along the far wall. None of it has anything to do with gold.'

Chris paused. He'd give the man time to digest his assertions.

'Our requirements are straightforward. We need to know the types, qualities and quantities of the minerals you have found here on the island. If you can help us with this matter, we will go and leave you in peace. No-one will ever know we have been here.'

Em brought the pistol back up again. Chris was beginning to sound all too reasonable. It was her turn. 'Dr Zhou, it's simple. We want your data, and we don't have time to bugger around. Sit up! The information. Documentation. All of it. *Now!*'

Zhou was well-acquainted with the good-cop-bad-cop routine. He'd been through it more than once. His own people were past masters at the game. And yet, the man didn't quite fit that picture. He seemed genuine – even honest – and maybe he actually *was* a scientist. Perhaps if he gave them something, some truth that made sense to the man, that would be enough for them.

'I was brought here to research the precious mineral deposits on the island. I have found a few, but they are not worth exploiting. My documentation is in the laboratory and there are many men with guns sleeping next door. It is impossible to walk through them to get it.'

'Not good enough!' hissed Em. 'We *know* you are lying, and we know about those DPRK Special Force men next door, and your relationship with the Colonel and his men.'

Chris could see Em's heavy approach was going to get them nowhere. This man was far too smart for that. And then, almost as though someone out there in the ether had read his mind, a voice started up in his ear-phone. It made him jump. He signalled Em to put hers in.

'Go easy! We have an offer. We can pull him out of there right now and get him into hiding. DG says they can get a boat with a helicopter up there within thirty hours to air-lift him off the island.'

Chris looked across at Em. She shrugged. She'd got the message. 'Dr Zhou,' Chris said calmly, 'it must be very difficult working here and with those men next door looking over your shoulder at your every move. I would find it immensely difficult in your position.'

This caught Zhou off-balance. Threats, he understood – even if he didn't believe they were real. Explanation and logic were also understandable. Empathy, albeit contrived empathy, was something else altogether.

'Our contacts are suggesting a way forward,' Chris continued. 'We know you have the information we require, and if you could let us have it, we can arrange to get you away from here right now. The authorities we represent would then get you off the island and take you to a place of safety.'

Zhou stared at him. It was a nonsense, of course. Even if they could get him out of his prison, the Colonel and his men, let alone those Special Force people, would tear the island apart looking for him. They couldn't afford to lose him or his data.

'No. That's impossible. They will find me and kill me. I have to stay here and do my job. I have no choice.'

Chris took a deep breath. 'No, Dr Zhou, it's perfectly possible. Consider this: we are here in this building, yet all the roads on the island are patrolled by heavily armed men; we have managed to get onto this site, yet it is encased in security systems. And now, here we are in your space in this building almost in touching distance of those armed DPRK men. One could argue our presence here is impossible. Getting you safely away and off this island is perfectly feasible.'

Zhou sat quietly shaking his head. 'You do not understand. I *must* go back to Pyongyang.'

Something had to be worked out. And then, Chris knew the answer, and even before he'd formulated the question. He'd noticed the photograph in a small wooden frame when he'd first come into the room. It was propped up on a book on the top of a single-drawer cupboard on the far side of the sleeping mat. It stood out against the stark metallic emptiness of the place. He leant across Zhou and picked it up. 'Your wife and little girl?' he asked softly.

Zhou nodded, apprehension and alarm evident in his face.

'It can't be easy,' Chris continued, 'living in a faceless, cold tower block in Pyongyang, and having to work in a munitions factory. So, what if we could get your wife and daughter safely out of North Korea so they can join you?'

'No. That cannot happen,' said Zhou. 'If I do not complete my work here and go back, it will be terrible for my family.'

Chris checked the drone link... Green. They were listening. He'd found the lever, but the pressure needed refining and reshaping. He took a deep breath. 'Let me rework that. What if you complete your work here and return to your family, and then we arrange for all three of you to leave North Korea together?'

A rapid exchange over the radio brought him to a halt. That'd got them twitching. He touched Zhou lightly on his shoulder. 'Shhh, one moment.'

'*Hold on. This is getting slippery,*' a voice said. '*We could lose him. He could walk away.*'

There was second voice. '*Yes, but what else can they do – try to drag him out of that place screaming? Then we'd lose him and them, and the data. We won't have another opportunity. If he goes for it and we get the data, we'd have a hold over him. I say we let the doctors get on with it. They're sitting looking at the guy for God's sake!*'

There was a momentary silence.

'*Dr J. We need a little side-conference here to clarify something. We're going to close you down for a few seconds. Don't go away!*'

Chris turned to Zhou. 'My apologies. We're waiting for

clarification, but what do you think about what I've just said?'

'It's still not possible. None of us could go back to China. I would be imprisoned, and my wife and little girl sent back to their village with nothing.'

Jamieson nodded.

The radio came to life again. *'Anything else come up?'*

'Yes. Going back to China's a problem.'

'We figured that. We don't want him back there, anyway. You can assure him of that. OK. You can go ahead. Everything is on the table! We get the data, and the scientist must – we repeat, must – be part of any deal. If it's his family as well, so be it.'

He turned back to Zhou. 'Right, I can now confirm the offer. You will finish here and go back to the DPRK. We will then arrange for you and your family to travel safely to the West. Once there, your skills and knowledge can be put to good use.'

This had to be a nonsense, thought Zhou, *but what if it were possible – safety and security, his wife and precious daughter by his side, and a professional future?*

'Who *are* you people?' he asked, desperately trying to get a handle on the situation. 'How do I know you will keep your word?'

Chris sensed they were turning the corner, but this wasn't territory he could get into. He looked over at Em. 'Who are we?'

She'd got the message. She'd play it straight down the middle. She looked across at Zhou. 'I'm a representative of the British Security Services. This man is an academic and a scientist who works for us as a consultant. Right now, we are talking on this radio to very senior representatives of the British and US Governments. They can hear everything we are saying. Above this site, there is an unmanned aerial vehicle providing the communication link.'

'*Excellent summary, Em!*' said a voice in her headset. '*We have a representative from the US State Department on the line who would like to speak directly to Dr Zhou to help move this along.*'

Chris turned the volume up three clicks on his radio and passed it to Zhou.

Zhou pushed the radio up against his ear and sat listening in silence, his face betraying no emotion, as a State Department official detailed a meeting held in Seoul with Zhou's brother less than twenty-four hours earlier. It contained information only he and his brother would have known. It ended with a brief recorded message from his brother in their Chinese dialect.

'Thank you,' said Zhou, as the recording ended. He passed the radio back to Chris. 'And are *you, personally,* able to guarantee this promise?'

'Dr Zhou, I have no power to guarantee *anything* at all. However, I have *some* influence and I will do everything I can to see that this promise is kept.'

Zhou sat staring at the back of his hands for a few moments, shaking his head slowly from side to side. He sensed the equivocation in the response, but how could it be otherwise? It was, at least, truthful.

He looked up. 'Can I have my photograph back? What do you want to know?'

RESOLUTION

'First. What minerals have you found?' Chris Jamieson articulated each word slowly, precisely.

'It is very complicated,' Zhou replied, 'but I have it all documented. It's in my laboratory.' He smiled weakly. 'I can get it for you. Those men are sleeping now – full of rice! They won't even hear me passing amongst them.'

Chris hesitated a second. He decided it was a risk worth taking. 'Right. So will you please do that.'

Zhou threw a green T-shirt over his head, pulled on khaki shorts and, without any attempt at stealth, walked out into the narrow corridor outside his room.

'God, Chris, you do take risks!' Em whispered, as they both moved up next to the open door. 'What do we do if they come rampaging in here?'

'They won't.' He shrugged. 'And if they do, so be it.'

Within seconds, Zhou was back. He was clutching a beige spring-back file, which he passed to Chris. He then sat down cross-legged on the edge of his sleeping mat.

Chris skimmed through the sixty or so pages of text and diagrams the file contained. 'Thank you, Dr Zhou. I believe this is what they want. I'm puzzled, though. You said earlier you had to stay to complete your work. This seems complete, though. What else is there to do?'

A metallic voice started up in his ear. *'Yes. There's other stuff. It's why those boxes came off the sub with the Special Force people two days ago. We want that data as well. Deal's off without it.'*

Chris looked across at Em, eyebrows raised. He watched her lips form the words, 'No idea,' and the shake of her head. He turned to Zhou. 'I'm afraid I don't understand, but we are being told you have something else that they want related to the reason you have to stay on here.'

Zhou sat silently, impassive. He knew he was trapped; there was no going back. He'd already signed his own death warrant. If his masters had even the slightest inkling of what he had revealed, it would be the end of him, and worse, also his wife and daughter.

He sighed, put his hand under his sleeping mat and slid out a slim beige folder, and passed it to Chris. 'This is what they're asking for. I was sleeping on it.' He forced a half-smile.

Then, he froze. 'Someone in the corridor,' he hissed. Against the background hum, and the creak of the building, he'd heard someone moving outside his room.

They waited, listening, ten… fifteen… twenty seconds. There was a loud clang, which reverberated throughout the building.

'It's someone relieving,' Zhou whispered. 'He pulled the personnel door hard on the way back in. They do that; they like to make a noise.'

A voice came over the radio. *'What's happening?'*

'Nothing. False alarm,' Chris said quietly, 'and I believe we have what you want. I have a file of seven pages. Give me a moment.'

He scanned the document and then reread the first two pages, containing the terms of reference and the design parameters. He pursed his lips and pushed out his cheeks. He'd make the listeners wait a bit longer. There was something he needed to understand.

'Dr Zhou, before we go any further with this, it would help if you could explain *your* position in all this and who you are doing this for. The connections and reasons aren't clear.'

A voice came over the radio. *'For God's sake don't worry about that, Dr J. Just tell us what you've got there.'*

'I don't know who said that but I'm looking at this stuff, and I can assure you that you *do* need to know what Dr Zhou's position is – even if you don't realise it yet.'

There was no response. Chris smiled; he quite enjoyed generating offended silences. He moved his radio towards Zhou. 'Please. Explain what is happening. Your position… the context.'

Zhou surprised even himself. He felt an overwhelming sense of relief. He could let it all come out. The bridge had been well and truly crossed.

'I work in the Pyongyang weapons development and procurement centre.' The resignation was there in his voice. 'My research project is explained in that folder. One day, they brought me here to evaluate the rare-earth deposits. That is done. Now I must stay to complete the next stage of my research; it requires rare-earth minerals of the finest quality. The equipment I need came with those men in a submarine. I can only return to my family when my controller is satisfied with my progress...' He stopped. 'You look puzzled. I have not explained it well?'

'You've been very clear, Dr Zhou,' Chris said. 'It's just the rare-earth thing. Why don't they import it from China?'

Zhou nodded. 'I explain. Two North Korean generals were guaranteed money by an Arab middleman if they could arrange for me to do the rare-earth evaluation. So, I was just part of a secret trade deal. Then, Goliath, one of the Colonel's men, made a big mistake. He sent my first report to the Security Bureau in Pyongyang – and the secret was out. Those generals escaped the machine gun. Of course, the Supreme Leader fears the military. Then those generals and the Kim family got together. They see great personal wealth and power coming from this island. My value is now magnified many times: I am no longer a simple trade deal. My research is to be given to those Arabs *and* the DPRK military. For that, they will let the Family and the generals share in this mineral business. So now, I stay here with those Special Force thugs who have been sent to protect the investment – me!'

'Lord! Talk about truth being stranger than fiction!' Em said under her breath. She then asked quietly, 'And China?'

'Ah! Yes. The Family, the generals, the government do not trust each other, but they hate and fear China more. They must conceal me. In my workplace in Pyongyang, I am number Seventy-Seven. I work in Hall D, Position 3. My name does not exist; my family does not exist; my research does not exist. And now, I am more dangerous and in greater danger than ever. For the moment I am safe. Parts of my work – in that second folder – require equipment that cannot be brought to this place. I must go back to my workplace to complete it. The Iranian Colonel does not know this. He believes my research will be completed here. I know it can't.'

'One other thing,' Chris said. 'What do you know about this revolution on the island?'

'Ha! That! It's just a cheat. I hear the radio; I talk to Goliath. They create a takeover using local people. They say it is religious. Goliath tells me that means there will not be any interference from other countries and that the revolution has already driven the Chinese navy away.'

Em was shaking her head in bewilderment. She looked at her watch. 'Chris. Time!'

'I know. I need to photograph these folders and send them up the line.'

'Photograph? No need,' Zhou said. 'You can have these folders.'

'And if we are caught with them on the way back?'

'Oh, of course!' said Zhou. 'Ahhh, but I also have everything on a micro!' He pushed his hand under the top edge of his sleeping mat and retrieved an envelope containing a thumbnail-sized memory card. 'I must keep that card here. The Colonel gave it to me to make a copy of everything for him, but I think you can copy it in your radio machine.'

Chris nodded, took the tiny card from Zhou and slid it into an aperture on the side of his radio. He pressed the transmit button.

'You getting this, out there?'

'*DG… yes. Two files, a longish one… looks like sixty pages, and a short one… seven. Looks good. Get out of there now.*'

'Before you go,' Zhou said, as he returned the micro to the envelope, 'can you tell me what the arrangements will be to get us out of North Korea?'

Chris looked across at Em. She shrugged her shoulders and jerked her head upwards, eyes to the heavens. 'Anyone out there with clarification?' Chris asked.

There was a moment or two of silence. Then a voice, low and metallic, started up. Chris pushed his radio towards Zhou, and they all listened to a statement. It said everything – and nothing at all.

'Dr Zhou, your brother will arrange the travel for you and your family across the river as soon as possible after you are back in Pyongyang. Once in China, you will be put in a safe house while arrangements are made for you all to leave the country. One other thing; we require you to bring all the other data from your research base relating to your weapons work. That has to be part of this agreement.'

Zhou was not surprised by this new condition. In any event, he'd gone too far to turn back. He nodded.

'I'm sorry, Dr Zhou. I wasn't aware of this new demand,' Chris said softly.

'I suppose I understand. Who was that?'

Em intervened, her creative instincts rising to the fore. If Chris Jamieson could do it, so could she. 'That, Dr Zhou, was the Director of America's National Security Agency. He speaks for the US Secretary of State and he, in turn, for the President.'

'And you confirm,' said Zhou, turning to look at Chris, 'that you will do your best to ensure that everything works as agreed?'

'Yes. That is correct. And now, we really have got to go.' He took a small plastic bag from his safari jacket pocket.

'Take this. It's a radio chip. Keep it on your person, or nearby. It will help us locate you day and night. It should remain active for the next six months or so.'

'Thank you,' said Zhou. 'Oh, and you can bang the door on the way out! They'll feel comfortable with that. They'll just turn over and resume their snoring!'

Zhou's attempt at a joke concealed a real truth. As they crept out and across the site towards the excavation area, they realised they could have banged their way in and out, and ambled across the site, chatting, in complete safety.

•

'I didn't know we were supposed to steal the scientist as well as his data!' Em said ruefully, as they made their way along the beach back to the boat, Danny leading the way with his torch.

'Nor me,' Chris replied. 'I doubt it started off that way. Someone obviously decided it was too good a side benefit to miss.'

'What's his new research thing... in the second folder?'

'I don't think you're going to like this, but it looks to me like he's working on a thermal lensing laser device for use as an anti-personnel weapon. It's a sort of laser that can blind a segment of a person's sight for up to five minutes or so. The thing is that the person affected doesn't know it's happening, and they can't see what's actually there – well, until it's too late.'

'Good Lord. Sounds like science fiction.'

'Yes, but it's all very real. So far, there's only been proof-of-concept stuff with laboratory models. He's now working on a life-size working job, and it looks like the military – theirs and now ours – have got their claws into it. They'll all be drooling over it in anticipation.'

'Lord help us! And the China thing?'

'He can't go back, of course, but it's more than that. China's got over ninety percent of the world's known rare-earth resources. They're crucial minerals vital to all modern technology – communications, space, nuclear, green energy, defence. The numbers I saw in Zhou's file indicate that deposits on this little island here dwarf China's. It's a guarantee that if the Chinese knew that stuff was here, their Indian Ocean flotilla would miraculously recover mid-ocean, do a U-turn and head back this way at full speed, followed closely by an aircraft carrier or two.'

•

The UAV pilot turned to the Djibouti commander, who was standing behind him. 'Back on the beach, sir – all five, and one of those radio chips seems to have changed hands. There's one in the hanger now. That Jamieson character still has the other. He's switched off his radio, by the way.'

'Mmmm! You know something, Jimmy. That man's either a genius or a madman, or maybe just plain ignorant!'

'Or all three, sir!'

'Yes, indeed… all three. Anyway, follow them. Get them back in one piece. They deserve at least that. If anything crops up, call me.'

DIPLOMATIC MALT

'One hundred percent certain. No gold!' the Russian Ambassador declared in a pompous tone. 'I, myself, have been to island, criss-crossed three times, and checked, double-checked, treble-checked! Asked people. Poked here, poked there. Nothing! To keep such secret on that small place is not possible. Everyone knows everything and, if they don't, they invent. They rumour. Nothing there. This trouble is just religious extremist thing.'

Lee Kwong Wei looked up from his papers, nodding. 'And I agree with Ambassador Smolski, and while I, personally, would like to help Mzinga get his rock back, my government is adamant. China cannot get involved. I have informed the President.' He smiled. 'And I very much regret I will not be welcome at State House anymore. Please feel free to use my visit slots, any of you.'

Sir William Bailey, the British Ambassador, looked over the top of his glasses at his American counterpart. 'The US, Peter?'

'The same, really. Our geology people see no reason to suppose the island would have significant gold deposits. The place just isn't right for that sort of thing. However, the US is, of course, concerned about the extremist thing, and particularly the possibility that the island might end up as a terrorist base hidden from the eyes of the world, and where they can train and cook up any plot they feel like.'

The Russian looked up. He'd been admiring his fingernails; they were impeccably clean and neatly trimmed, very much as his secretary liked them. 'If I might interject here, I think we would also agree on that. That Colonel man was in Ingushetia recently, and in Dagestan and Chechnya regions. We already have clandestine terrorist route through to Yemen. What is Great Britain's position, Sir William? Your country controlled here for long time.'

'I think we agree – no gold,' said Bill Bailey. 'We certainly feel very strongly about the terrorist implications. And you're right, Igor, we do have a colonial hang-up thing, a residual obligation, you might say. Even so, we are nervous about using force to sort this matter out. We've had enough trouble in the UN and the Security Council over recent years on such matters.'

He stopped for a moment and looked around the assembled group. 'And to be honest, gentlemen,' he sounded almost apologetic, 'the main reason I requested this meeting was to sound you out on the military option.' He laughed. 'And of course, to sample my latest malt. It's a fine 25-year Macallan. Do please help yourselves.

'And, yes, the military option. Now, I appreciate none of us can be certain exactly which way our governments will move on this one, but perhaps you have a view?' He looked at each of his diplomatic colleagues in turn.

'Well, Beijing has made its decision,' said Lee. 'We have too many other interests on the continent. But I believe my government would not shout too loudly if Britain decided to help get the place back, provided a formal invitation from the Ziaŵala Government requesting assistance was made. I think that is perhaps essential. In those circumstances I believe we would abstain from heavy critical comment.'

The Russian nodded. 'That is very well said, and I have already checked with home. Russian Federation would not get involved. We would consider behind-scenes support, though, if such was requested.'

Bill Bailey turned to the American. 'Peter?'

'Don't know. Not checked. I'll get a note off as soon as I get back in the office. My *personal* view, though, is that Washington is likely to be supportive of direct UK military support for Ziaŵala, though I *do* take Ambassador Lee's point about the importance of a formal request from the Mzinga government. If that was forthcoming, the US might even go along with you Brits. We'd probably have to, wouldn't we?' he laughed. 'Otherwise, we'd end up with you Brits throwing us out of DG!'

CORNERED

'Your people did a fine job on these gardens,' Peter Shaw observed, as the British Embassy limousine swept up the drive towards State House. 'A bit ragged here-and-there now, but, by God, in this early morning light they're still glorious.'

'They *are* quite something, aren't they?' Bill Bailey replied, looking up from his notes. 'One of the governor's wives back whenever was a keen gardener. She had a bit of an artist's eye. By the way, we OK with our strategy? Can't afford to get this one wrong.'

'Yep,' said the American. 'Just remember, though, you lead. He hates you just a little bit less than he hates me. Gets more aid from your lot.'

'Yes, but we also put him in detention, *and* we threw this place out of the Commonwealth.'

'But he loves that detention thing. I hear he goes on about it all the time. It made him a hero. He wouldn't be where he is today without a good stretch in a British slammer. One of the best stories I've heard was about how he learnt to cook the books while he was in clink: locked up with a couple of wayward accountants, or something, was what I heard?'

The British Ambassador laughed. 'Oh, that one! Just a story, a load of old cobblers, my friend. That was a disinformation thing. He was never in a jail or a prison. I know he claims he was. He regularly trots out this story about standing with his head pressed up against the bars of his cell staring at the wasteland of Dartmoor in the depths of winter dreaming of the sunny uplands of home and the freedom of his people. Actually he was exiled to Ascension for a couple of years – not a lot of accountants there! He spent his time eating, fishing and chasing anything in a skirt. Training in fiddling the books came much later. We seconded one of our Treasury people here to help develop financial monitoring systems for the National Bank just after Independence. The Old Man sucked him into his coterie of advisers, and our accountant then spent his time showing them all the tricks of the trade. Anyway, the accountant guy was put out to graze. He's now living a comfortable golfing existence somewhere on the south coast.'

The car came to halt by the flagpole. A burly, head-shaven character sporting an *I Love Bermuda* T-shirt, khaki shorts and flip-flops and with a Kalashnikov slung loosely across his right shoulder meandered over. He peered at the miniature Union Jack fluttering in the light morning breeze on the front of the bonnet. He caught hold of it by the top corner and rubbed it between his fingers. He checked his fingertips, shrugged and walked round to the passenger door. 'Who are you?'

'I'm the British Ambassador and this gentleman is the Ambassador of the United States. The President *is* expecting us.'

'Follow.'

They were led up the dozen or so wide marble steps, in through the main door, and into a small reception room on the left.

'Wait here. I will tell His Excellency you are here.'

'Not exactly a promising start,' muttered Peter Shaw, as the man left the room. 'You'd think he'd be here to greet us. Maybe he's forgotten we're coming.'

'Nah, he knows. He's just giving us the treatment! He'll warm up when he sees us. At least, I hope so; we need his compliance.'

'Good morning, gentlemen!'

They turned, startled; they'd not heard him come in. For a man of his girth, he moved remarkably lightly.

'Welcome to State House,' the President continued. 'It's Sir William Bailey and Mr Peter Shaw, is it not? It is some time since I met either of you. Please, sit at this very fine oak table. It was brought here from England by one of my illustrious predecessors. Excuse me but a moment while I order some tea.'

'Warming up,' muttered Bill Bailey to his colleague. 'At least he knows our names!'

Shaw nodded. 'Doesn't look cheerful, though.'

The President was back almost immediately. He joined them at the table. 'I believe I know why you are here, gentlemen – it's our little island problem. The business is a great nuisance, but I can assure you everything is being done to recover the island and to ensure the safety of your nationals.'

'That's very good to hear, sir,' said Bill Bailey. 'Our governments will appreciate that very much. Of course, as I'm sure you are aware, both Ambassador Shaw and I also represent a number of other countries with nationals on the island. In my case, there are the British citizens and also citizens from New Zealand, France, Sweden, Norway, Zimbabwe and Portugal. I believe, Ambassador Shaw, your Embassy also looks after the interests of a number of other countries.'

'Yes. We've at least three US citizens on the island, but there are also aid agency people from Peru, Brazil, and various other places.'

The President's eyes began to widen. What were they telling him? 'Yes! Yes, gentlemen. I am well aware of the position and at this very moment my P.S. establishment is drawing up a full list of foreign nationals on the island.'

Bill Bailey continued, 'What *would* help, sir, is a definite time scale for bringing this matter to a conclusion. Our governments would like to give reassurance on this to relatives of the expatriate workers and resident foreigners on the island. I should add that when we heard that China was going to assist your government, we were very pleased. We support that. The Chinese are efficient and move quickly. With their fleet on its way here, we assume it won't be long before the matter is dealt with.'

The President's head jerked forward. 'The Chinese! When? Where did you hear that?' He began breathing heavily.

'I believe one of your central committee officials mentioned it to my First Secretary at the monthly liaison meeting,' said Peter Shaw. 'I assume it is correct?'

'Yes… No. It's true, of course!' said Mzinga. 'The Chinese Government want to help so much. However, their Indian Ocean fleet has very serious technical problems, so, we, here, are going to use our own military forces to retake the island.'

There was silence. The two ambassadors sat looking at each other with that slightly astonished look that only great actors or highly accomplished diplomats can affect.

'Ahhh, Mr President, sir,' said Bill Bailey. 'You'll forgive me saying this, but that is *not* at all good news. Both our governments will be very concerned. He turned to the US Ambassador. 'Peter, I know we weren't going to reveal the information we have, but in these new circumstances, what do you think?'

The American shrugged. 'It's *very* regrettable. I don't see we have a choice in the matter.'

'The thing is, Mr President,' Bill Bailey continued, 'we have detailed evidence of the position on the island. What we know has to be in the strictest confidence, of course, but we have satellite evidence that there are upwards of three hundred heavily armed men there and they are led by experienced international terrorists. One of them, in fact – a Colonel Mahil – went to Ivundé with your government's approval to oversee the Madrassas Project. We also know that the local rebels there have the most modern M4 and AK47 assault rifles, and that the foreigners with them have numerous land-to-sea missile batteries, anti-helicopter shoulder-held rocket launchers and land mines.'

He waited a second or two, and then slid a number of A4 size satellite photographs out from the thick folder he was carrying. 'Perhaps you should see these,' he continued. 'In this first one, there are nine or ten armed men about to get into a truck. That's on the main road to the north coast – you may recognise the place. The others show various other groups of men, and we have, here, many photographs obtained by an unmanned aerial vehicle which flew over parts of the island just yesterday.' He passed over assorted photographs, including one showing the centre of the town and what looked like three men sitting behind a heavy machine gun outside Frankie's coffee shop. Mzinga recognised the place immediately.

Bill Bailey looked across at Peter Shaw, who had been listening attentively, admiring the smooth slide back-and-forth across a mix of truth and deception that only a master diplomat could achieve. Now it was his turn.

'Here's the problem, sir. Without intensive air cover, targeted munitions and the off-shore softening-up of the enemy, any military task force that Ziawala can send against the men on the island – and I must apologise deeply for saying this – well, it would be decimated. Any remnants able to make it to shore would get no further than the tops of the beaches, which will certainly all be mined.'

By this point, it was impossible to tell whether Mzinga was actually still listening, asleep, or dead. His head had fallen forward, his chin on his chest and his forehead held in his hand. A glistening line of sweat was oozing out from between his fingers and trickling down the back of his hand onto the photographs on the table in front of him.

'What am I to do?' he muttered – very much as though in a séance and seeking ancestral guidance. 'I am lost! Lost! I have promised my people. I have spoken on the radio. I have declared that I, myself, will lead our forces onto the island. There are people in the Party who will not let this pass. They will mutter and conspire against me. The People's Army... they will also not let this pass. They will come for me. Those Chinese could easily stop this! They think only of their own concerns! They are not true socialists!'

Not in his most reflective and empathetic moments could Bill Bailey have ever imagined that a time would come when he might feel even marginally sorry for this man. The corruption of the country's one-party regime was boundless, and the President was like some monstrous spider at the very centre of it all, raiding the treasury whenever he felt inclined, and appointing ill-educated kinsmen to lucrative senior positions. How could anyone feel sorry for the man? He looked across at Peter Shaw and could see an almost identical emotion in his eyes. It was time to row back a little, to light a candle at the end of the tunnel. He shrugged and nodded to the American. 'Your go.' He mouthed the words.

'Mr President, sir,' Peter Shaw said, slowly and gently, 'we have the greatest sympathy for your position, and perhaps there is something we can do to help.'

The President's head came up and his eyes began to open slowly, as though the tiniest spark of hope had begun levering itself into his brain. 'Help? How? You have an idea? What idea?'

'Well, it occurred to me just now that one or other of our governments – maybe even both – *might* be prepared to help. I stress the *might*. In these situations, Washington much prefers to be hands-off. They say it's the country's own business. In this case, though, there are those nationals we are responsible for, and it's very possible they'll end up as hostages. Sir William, what do you think?'

'I'm far from sure Britain would be able to help, though I do take the point about our people trapped on Ivundé. That might *just* sway my government in favour of doing something. I'm certainly prepared to send a note for the attention of the UK PM and the Cabinet about the situation.'

The President was now looking directly at them, from one to the other. 'Do you or your governments need money? Would that help, or perhaps guaranteed trade opportunities?'

'No. I doubt whether anything of that sort would help,' Bill Bailey continued. 'Nonetheless, you'll understand that we would be asking our governments to consider direct military assistance of some kind. That's not a request they would entertain lightly. Even if they *were* prepared go down that route, they would certainly insist on conditions. The least they would expect is an arrangement so that this situation could never arise again.'

'I concur with that entirely,' added Peter Shaw.

Mzinga was no longer listening. He was almost smiling. 'Yes! Yes! Of course. I understand. I am sure we can find an agreement. My country has much to offer. I *must* have those rebels driven into the sea! Please – and soon! Consult your leaders urgently. Demand a favourable response. By tomorrow!'

'Tomorrow! Goodness, that's tight. Sir William?'

'We *could* give it a go overnight, I suppose, but I'm far from sure our systems can react that fast. We might get a preliminary, holding response. Either way, Mr President, there is one thing I know my government would insist on. It relates to the issue of collective responsibility. Specifically, if we *did* manage to get some sort of positive-leaning answer by tomorrow, there would need to be discussion with your good self and also with others in senior positions of responsibility in your government.'

'Yes. Yes. Corroboration, I think you call it. I understand that is how your systems work. You require witnesses. That is good. How many?'

'Well, if we *were* to proceed to further discussion, it'd be wise to have one or two highly placed and internationally respected people present who could be signatories to any interim or final agreement we might come to. I don't know what Ambassador Shaw feels, but I'm thinking of such people at the level of, say, your Head of the Armed Forces, or the Head of the Youth Wing, perhaps even the Chairman of your National Bank. We, on our part, would have to bring our First Secretaries. They are highly respected and competent people, of course.'

Mzinga hesitated. This was all too neat. The people they'd suggested for his side made sense – even more than sense. He didn't understand, but then what choice did he have, and anyway couldn't he, Mzinga, even finesse the Devil out of Hell?

'Yes! Yes! I agree, entirely.' He was smiling broadly. 'Yes. We will do that. We will bring in the very people you suggest – all three. And please, press your governments very hard. I will expect the positive. Together, we can make this work. We will all benefit, and we can raise the relationship between our great countries to a new, elevated plane.'

Bill Bailey was totally unsurprised at the man's reaction. They'd been onto the ultimate safe bet when he'd named the President's closest cronies. They were the three highest rewarded and most corrupt members of the government and each of them, in turn, had numerous relatives and friends in influential positions down the line that they rewarded handsomely. If the President got pushed over, they'd all go with him – unless they were doing the pushing.

•

That evening in London – morning in Washington – there were meetings at the highest level. Faced with the overwhelming evidence, photographs, Zhou's files and the reports from their agents in the field – as Stryker, Freemont and Jamieson were referred to – agreement was quickly reached. In Washington, the Secretary of State had simply said, "A no-brainer. Get on with it." In Brussels, where she was arguing some arcane point with European leaders, the Prime Minister of Great Britain gave the go-ahead, subject to all members of the Cabinet emergency consultative group agreeing, or, if not, resigning.

38

ZERO CHOICE

Megan Prytherch burst out laughing. 'What a sight!' From the back seat of the limo, she was watching the President charging down the steps of State House, two at a time, right arm in his jacket, the left bent back at an impossible angle trying to find the other armhole.

Sir William Bailey looked up from his papers. 'He's keen! Desperate to get to the flagpole before we do. I don't think I've ever seen him so lively; didn't know he had it in him.'

'He's got a lot more than that in him, Ambassador,' said his PA over her shoulder. She was up front with the driver. 'Alfie, here, will happily give you the lurid, no-holds-barred low-down of all the women who've had to flee for their, well – whatevers – and sometimes got caught.'

'Can do, anytime, and for free,' Alfie confirmed, 'but it's a long story; there's been a lot of chasing, though, I think, not a lot of catching.' He brought the car to a gentle stop.

And there Mzinga was, jacket on, immaculate, beaming, arms outstretched in welcome.

'He's looking pleased, as well,' Megan muttered.

'That's because we're here,' the ambassador said out of the corner of his mouth, 'and more to the point, you and Sybil are here as well. He's counting his chickens. He thinks he's got more than he has. Explain later...'

'Good afternoon, President Mzinga, sir.'

'Good afternoon, my British friend, and you have a delegation – two fine ladies. Wonderful to see... Our American friend?'

'He'll be along just now. In the meantime, may I introduce my colleagues? This lady, Megan Prytherch, is the Embassy First Secretary and this is Sybil Thornbridge, my Personal Assistant.'

'Welcome, ladies, to my humble home. Ahhh! Ambassador, how do you manage to get such fine ladies to assist you? If only I could do likewise. You must tell me the secret. But please, come in... Ah! No. We'll wait a mo, as you wonderful British say. Here comes our good friend, Peter Shaw, and I can see he, too, has his First Secretary with him – another fine lady. I believe her name is Janie. Such an interesting name. Yes... and I have met her on many occasions. First, I greet them. Then we will all go in together for afternoon tea.'

•

Mzinga led them into a large meeting room overlooking the gardens. 'This,' he declared, 'is my Number One reception. Please do admire the fine views while I summon up some tea, and some fruit from my very own orchard.'

'That'd be very welcome, sir,' said Bill Bailey, 'but, first, might I ask about the people who will sit with you? I think we agreed yesterday that each side would have four people. As you see, there are five of us. Our additional member, Sybil, is here to keep a full record of the proceedings. She will not take part in the discussion, except, of course, to seek clarification, as she quite often does back at the office. She can be very persistent and has a very precise mind. She doesn't like untidiness.' He laughed. 'My apologies, Sybil. But, *your* people, Mr President?'

'Yes. Yes. Of course. That is very excellent! Be assured, my men are only a few moments away. First, though, I would like to ask if you have a solution which will lead to the expulsion of those evil dogs from my island.'

'Yes and no, Mr President. We have a *proposal*, but certainly *not* a solution yet. You will recall that yesterday we anticipated there would be conditions that we would *all* have to agree to in order for us to assist. We all need to consider those conditions.'

Mzinga hesitated, marvelling at the great deviousness he was convinced was hidden away in those words somewhere, though where precisely he couldn't fathom. He smiled broadly. 'Excellent! I will now send for my boys and order tea and fine fruit at the same time. You Americans call that multi-tasking, Eh! And I will order papaya. It is so good for the complexion, ladies, but then, your complexions are already so perfect! One moment, please. The refreshments will arrive, and I will return shortly with my boys.'

Five minutes elapsed and Mzinga was back with his men. He settled into a capacious, revolving, black leather rocking-chair at one end of the oval conference table. His back was towards the large garden window, the afternoon sun streaming in rendering his face a slightly ovoid, featureless disc.

'Ladies, gentlemen, everyone, welcome. First, I will have a brief word with my men. Then, we will proceed.' He swung, creaking, around to his right to look at the three men sitting silently, lined up along the table, each looking quite bemused.

'Dear compatriots, we are here to make arrangements for our allies, Great Britain and the United States of America, to support our forces in driving those evil terrorists from our precious Ivundé into the Indian Ocean.'

Both ambassadors sighed inwardly. The game had begun. They had fully expected this hijack manoeuvre early on. Now it was their turn. They smiled politely as they each methodically withdrew an identical pile of papers from their briefcases and arranged them neatly on the table.

There was a slight hiatus. Bill Bailey moved in quickly. 'Perhaps I can start the ball rolling? You will all know that, as ambassadors, we are merely humble messengers. We do the bidding of our governments. We have no power to change the instructions we receive from home.'

Everyone around the table nodded in a contrived gesture of mutual understanding.

'I make this obvious point,' he continued, 'because we have proposals of two kinds. There are matters which are open for some limited discussion, and others – three to be exact – which are not, and I stress the *not*. They are written in stone, you might say, even in blood. Now, before I ask my colleague, Ambassador Shaw, to take us through the proposals and conditions, are there any initial queries?'

There was silence, broken only by the crackle of leather and the rhythmic squeak of a chair as the President rocked slowly back and forth. Peter Shaw passed out two pages of text to each person around the table.

'Right. On the first page are three statements which we will all need to sign up to. That is, if you wish to proceed, of course.' He stopped to allow everyone to focus on the document.

'Statement One, and if I may, I will read it out aloud.' He proceeded, articulating each word very precisely:

'One. The government of Ziaŵala invites the United States and Great Britain to take any steps necessary, including the use of force, to restore order to Ivundé. If formally requested by the United States and Great Britain, this may include assistance from Ziaŵala's armed forces.'

As Peter Shaw picked up his second sheet of paper, the urge to look at the faces of the Ziaŵalans opposite proved irresistible. The Head of the National Bank was staring, expressionless, at the paper. That was expected. The Head of the Youth Wing and the Head of the Armed Forces, however, were looking at each other, eyebrows raised.

Peter Shaw refocussed. 'The second sheet contains *exactly* that same statement but worded as a communiqué addressed to the governments of the United States and Great Britain, all embassies and consulates based in Ziaŵala, the Secretary-General of the United Nations and the Chair of the UN Security Committee. At the bottom there is a space for the signatures and official positions of those of us here, along with the presidential seal.'

The President leant forward, silently concentrating on the text, his head and face now partly emerging from the dark shadow and catching the sun on one side. 'This is very good. I and my men understand the reason for the words in this statement,' he said slowly, 'but we would like a small change.'

'We can note your wishes, Mr President,' Bill Bailey said, 'but regretfully, we have no leeway in this matter. I'm afraid that *is* the public announcement we *all* have to sign up to. We understand its inflexibility and apologise for that, but shall we let Ambassador Shaw continue? Then we can see all three conditions. Ambassador Shaw?'

'Thank you, Sir William. Can we now go back to the first sheet? You will see, there, two other statements. I'll read:

Two. In the event of a decision to take direct action (e.g. military action) the people of Ivundé will be given formal advisory warning of at least twenty-four hours before such action.

You'll see in the footnote that two methods of warning are specified: a leaflet drop across the island, and an announcement on Ziawala National Radio.' He looked around the table. 'I'm sure we all appreciate the reason for this. Casualties – civilian or military – *must* be kept to an absolute minimum. Of course, President Mzinga, if you, yourself, were prepared to present the message on the radio and sign the leaflet text on behalf of your team here, and the National People's Assembly, it would demonstrate great humanity and statesmanship.'

'Yes. Yes. I think we are very happy with that.' No-one could see his face, but his voice was smiling.

'Now, point three,' the American continued, 'and I'll personally add that this is a really excellent condition for the country:

Three. The government of Ziaŵala requests Great Britain and the United States to assist directly in the development of Ivundé in such areas as communications, education, agriculture, natural resources, training for governance etc.

We have here a separate protocol on this for all our signatures. You all understand the importance of this particular condition,' he added. 'None of us wants a situation like this to arise again. A development plan will bring the island into the twenty-first century and will prevent that happening.'

'President Mzinga,' Bill Bailey said, 'there's a great deal here to take in all at once. We wonder whether you'd like time to consider these documents with your team. We can arrange to meet again towards the end of the week.'

'Yes. Indeed, and thank you, but we *must* deal with this *now*. My boys and I will go to my office for a few minutes to consider the documents. Then we can proceed.'

•

'What d'you think, Bill?' Peter Shaw asked softly as the President and his men trooped out of the room.

'Not sure. That furious-looking youth leader probably doesn't matter a lot. The bank man didn't move a muscle – an excellent imitation of a frozen zombie. Our good General is a different kettle of fish. He twitched and sneered silently at everything. What did you make of him, Meg?'

'Well, if there's a fly in the ointment, he's it. I was watching him. He looked quite outraged and angry at times... kept shaking his head.'

'You know,' Janie added, 'Mzinga sounded almost reasonable, but that stupid sun trick! You'd think he'd be past that sort of thing.'

'Yep,' said Peter Shaw, 'I'm with all that, and I'm sure the General is a danger point. I hear he's quite a problem for Mazinga.'

'*Mzinga*, Peter,' said his First Secretary, grimacing.

'Sorry, Janie! I know! But it sounds OK to me! Anyway, Mazinga,' – he grinned at his First Secretary – 'isn't so bad really. Quite balanced in some ways. We hear, though, he has to dance to the tune of that military character all the time. We may have to do something to tie the guy down.'

'Any ideas?' asked Bill Bailey.

'Well, we could always offer him an all-expenses familiarisation tour – first over to your place, then to the States. We could give him the works: roll out a few generals, get him into the clubs and onto the golf course. As things develop, we may need to let him have one of our armoured Humvees. I'm sure he'd love to be seen in one of those around town. It'd improve his credentials hugely for when he pushes the old man under a bus.'

'Yes, I like it,' said Bill Bailey, 'and I'm sure GB would go along with that.'

•

It was as their discussion turned to the fine rosewood furniture in the room, imported from Europe and the Far East by various previous colonial governors, that Mzinga and his team returned.

'Ladies, gentlemen, thank you for your patience,' the President said, smiling broadly as he settled back into his armchair. 'We have had very fruitful discussions and there is one very small thing we wish to raise, and two small questions; then we can all agree. First, Statement One. We very much appreciate what is said there, but we must ask for a small change of wording. We want it to say – in the middle there – that your countries... one moment, I have it here... yes... *will assist the armed forces of Ziawala to* and then the rest as there. You will understand, our people need to feel our forces are leading this – and the Chinese Government may be very offended if they believe their training of our army is not being put to good use.'

The British Ambassador nodded. He was ready. He'd reiterate and develop the theme he'd agreed with the American. 'Perhaps we should clarify Condition One, which as we indicated *cannot* be changed. Ambassador Shaw and I indicated yesterday that any landing on the island will be extremely hazardous. Our side, however, would deploy drones, UAVs, targeted munitions. These, of course, are things your armed forces do not have nor know how to use. Their deployment requires great skill. It is obvious our military *must* control their use.'

'Oh!' Mzinga sounded suitably disappointed. 'Right. And we understand and completely agree. It's just the *words* we'd like changed. I'm sure you understand our position. We just need to explain it to the people in a different way, in a way that makes sense to them.'

It was Peter Shaw's turn. 'President Mzinga, here's the thing. We *cannot* change the wording, and I can absolutely assure you the Chinese Government will be supportive. It is only on the basis of the statement, as it is written there, that we can go ahead.' He softened his voice. 'However, sir, it does occur to me that knowledge of the sort of modern weaponry that Sir William was talking about just now would be helpful for the leaders of your armed forces, and I am sure we can add into the agreement a training package including familiarisation tours overseas – in the UK and the US – plus some matching equipment.' He hurried on. 'Now, you said you had two questions, Excellency.'

'Yes! Yes! Very good! Familiarisation tours would be excellent! We agree to them… and now our two questions.' Mzinga felt great admiration for the exquisite deviousness of these foreigners. In one fell swoop, they had achieved their own aims – though he was quite uncertain what they were – and at the same time they had opened up a solution to the problem of his troublesome general, who was far too thick ever to understand what was happening or appreciate the finer points of this diplomatic game-playing. He smiled and went back to his notes. 'Our first question is, and I, too, will read: *When will you be able to take action*?'

'Janie… Megan,' said Peter Shaw. 'You two have seen the latest exchanges from Washington and London. What's it look like?'

'No-one's predicting anything, Peter. All the references are to the need for agreement to be reached *before* anything can be set in motion,' said Megan. 'Amongst ourselves, we were speculating on allocation, deployment and so on earlier today and *we* thought it might all take perhaps a week, subject to the signed document being received in London and Washington. That's a very rough guess, of course.'

'A week? Ahhh! That would be very excellent!' said the President. 'And now, our second question: *How will we draft a Development Plan?* You understand my people would like to see this. It will help to resolve our other problem… you understand?'

'We do. Sir William, you want to elaborate?' the American said.

'Certainly. I speculate here a little, Mr President, but once the island is secure, the UK and the US would send a development team to work with you and your central committee on the broad plan. Following that, there'd be a signed protocol and a fully worked project agreed within, say, five or six months. We would then attach technical aid people – experts – to work with your government, and on the island, getting things into place locally.'

It was as he was saying this that the sun slid from behind a bank of distant rain clouds and the President's features emerged fully from the shadow. He was beaming.

'Thank you. Thank you. That sounds excellent, and I think that concludes our business. My team and I will sign the necessary documents here and now. I will get my state seal for them.'

•

'What happened back there, Bill?' Megan asked as their limousine sped through the streets back to the embassy. 'There were all sorts of things I expected them to query.'

'I know, but what choice do they have? And actually, they like the idea of development money washing around. That's real sugar on the pill – not for the Old Man, of course, he's got more than enough stashed away for half-a-dozen retirements. No, for him it's face and the power thing. It'll secure his position and it'll save his neck for a while longer. The others will see endless opportunities to extend their fortunes and those of their families and tribal mates. They can imagine that next Mercedes and that house in Mayfair or Manhattan. There are endless possibilities.'

PART FIVE
CONSTANT BEARING

ETHEREAL CONFETTI

Em's overdraft at the sleep bank was higher than it had ever been in her thirty-eight short years. Tuesday was a day of fitful dozing, perspiration and cold showers. Mid-afternoon, Madame had crept in, asked her how she felt, and had taken her temperature, and prescribed water, two paracetamol and slices of papaya from her gardens for what she declared was 'certain de'ydration' and a 'touch of the dengues'. She'd added, 'Oh, and by the way, my Mr Abdullah 'as reappeared, by magic, and is also on his bed looking like – 'ow you say it – death warming up! Our Chris is also not in circulation. "Later, Madame," he shouts out to me when I knock on 'is door just now. It's all very strange. Our Anna 'as a theory but I said that in these difficult times we should not 'ave theories. We should not concern ourselves with what we do not know. It is sometimes wise to be ignorant, as my 'ubby often says… Now rest, I will check on you again in a while.'

•

Later that evening the three had emerged from their rooms, scavenged what they could from a deserted kitchen and agreed to meet in reception early the next morning. They then retreated to get what each hoped would be an undisturbed night.

•

Chris was up before six and, as the light grew stronger, he wandered downstairs and out into the car park. The three men were still at the road junction. Further up the road he could see Madame Lemessurier heading down towards them. She had a hessian bag over each shoulder and a bamboo cane basket resting on her ample middle. He watched in astonishment as she stopped next to the men and thrust the basket out towards them. They each took something out of it.

'Lord help us!' he muttered, as she came wobbling and bouncing down into the car park towards him. She was smiling broadly. 'I told you, Dr Chris. I said I would go up into town to get supplies and would not let those men stop me. I did it and 'ere we all are, safe and well, and with those much needed supplies.'

'Astonishing! What bit of magic did you employ, Madame?'

'Easy! Easy! Those three are locals, from the north, p'raps. They are not foreigners. They're very gentle... little bunny rabbits. I took some 'ot coffee, papaya and some of those small bananas to them very early this morning, before light. Fast asleep they all were. I wake them up, gently, of course, and promise them fresh bread. When they 'ear I am only going to the top of the 'ill, they nod. Then I reward them when I come back, and now look, I 'ave fresh bread, croissants, veggie samosas and some 'ome-made shortbread. I've even got fresh supplies of tea, coffee and milk powder. And, when I whisper to them just now that I need fuel for my generator, and I point up to Valli's, one whispers, "One tin, and, please, not further," and so we are now OK.'

Em came out from reception.

'Oh, you look so well now, ma chérie,' Madame continued. 'That's my papaya for you – such 'ealth-giving fruit!' She leant forward in a conspiratorial manner. 'Look, before 'e comes down, can I ask about Mr Abdullah? Can we talk in front of 'im? You know... tricky things!'

Em nodded. 'Yes, Madame, I'm sure we can.'

'Good. And now I must tell you. I know strange things are 'appening, and my Mirabilé is part of them. I will explain this to Anna and tell her that there is no big problem... and we should not 'ave worries... or theories.'

•

Stryker joined them later that morning. 'I just passed Madame and Anna in the corridor,' he said. 'They didn't seem the slightest bit surprised to see me. It was a smile and a good morning. Nothing else. God knows where they were off to.'

'They're surprised all right,' Chris said. 'It's just that Madame has a strong sense of communal preservation. She loves a conspiracy, and that requires the poker-face technique, something at which she excels.'

Stryker nodded. 'Anyway, either of you any views on what the next bit of this game is? I think things have to unravel here soon. To misquote a fine book, you might say that when things don't make sense, they fall apart; the centre cannot hold.'

'That sounds almost like a bit of Chris's gobbledygook,' Em said. 'But, yes, that's got to be about right.'

Anthony Stryker smiled. 'Either way,' he said. 'I think maybe I've got to leave pretty soon. I've a few bits of business to deal with.'

•

Later in the evening Em was dropping off to sleep when a faint blue pulse woke her. 'Sodding radio!' she muttered. She rolled onto her right side and retrieved it from where it lay on the floor at the side of the bed.

'Dr Em, Teddy Bear here. Apologies for disturbing you. Meg has asked me to tell you that there'll be a public announcement on the radio late tomorrow or on Friday about direct action. It was a very brief call. What do you think it means?'

'Not sure, Bess,' Em replied, though she had a pretty good idea. 'You know,' she continued, 'it might be a good idea for Meera to get in a good supply of food… just in case. Oh, and don't worry about waking me up. I'm about to do that to Chris, although he's probably wide awake anyway, planning the future of the world. I'll pass the message on to him. Speak later.'

•

Madam was listening to her short-wave radio, focussed, concentrating, her muscly legs crossed at the ankles, heels up on the edge of a low table. Her skirt was up above her knees. She was staring vacantly out into the car park. It was only when he sat down next to her that she registered his presence.

She looked over at him. 'Shhh! Listen!' she hissed.

He raised his eyebrows. 'Who?' he mouthed.

'President!' She pressed her finger against her lips. It was at that moment the speaker switched to the national language. And, as though she'd become conscious of Chris Jamieson's presence for the first time, and looking slightly embarrassed, she quickly slid her legs off the table, smoothed down her skirt and turned the radio off.

'Mzinga?'

'Oui, the man 'imself!'

'What's he saying?'

'The government 'as asked Great Britain and America to 'elp remove the extremists and terrorists from Ivundé. They 'ave agreed. The people must wait for a further announcement. Good news, n'est-ce pas?'

'Sounds like it. Anything else?'

'Oui, one other thing. They can use any means necessary to do the job.'

Anna and Em, who had wandered in during the exchange, were leaning up against the reception counter.

'And I've got a bit more,' Anna said. 'I was listening to the BBC World Service earlier. It seems a short statement has been issued overnight by the British Prime Minister's office saying that a formal request for assistance had been received from the Ziawalan Government to help restore order here. The Cabinet will be meeting first thing in the morning to consider the request.'

'So, we do not know yet! It's still the middle of the night there,' said Madame. 'They *aven't* agreed yet! I always say that Mzinga is a liar!'

'I think, Madame, all those guys are liars,' Chris said. 'Lying, prevarication, stalling are the key qualifications required for such a prestigious job. They are leader survival skills and let's be fair, though, it's probably only a small lie. He's jumping the gun a little, being a bit premature. In essence, it's probably true. It's too big a claim not to be. Now, if you'll excuse me for a moment, I think I need to track down Mr Abdullah and let him know what's going on.'

•

The door to Stryker's room was open. The Major was sitting in the opening onto his balcony in a flower-patterned silk dressing gown. He was listening to the radio.

'You heard?' Chris called.

'Sure! Come in. Softening up stuff. They'll be gearing up in DG and Djib right now. It means I'm going to have to move sooner than I'd expected... the next couple of hours. Do me a favour, will you, and tell Madame I'm off, but only after I've gone? I don't want to give her extra stress. And could you give her this?' He passed Chris a wad of US currency. 'That's six or seven hundred plus dollars. It'll more than pay for my room and enable her to restock. Can you ask her to clear out my stuff? There's not a lot in there, but she can keep anything that's of any use.'

'Will do. How're you going to get around? It's difficult out there.'

'Sure. But I just need to get to the clinic and then up into the bush a bit. I can get Danny to pick me up.'

'Are you coming back?'

'Dunno. Depends. Anything's possible. Either way, I'll see you at the other end: wherever… whenever… if ever, that is.'

•

Two Mercury 4B-7 UAVs took off from Djibouti, climbed to 15,000 feet and headed south on a pre-programmed route.

Over to the west, in the operations room on Diego Garcia, two men were listening to country and western, occasionally checking the progress of the 4B-7s.

Later in the afternoon, a scattering of small islands gradually appeared on their screens followed by the high central ridge of Ivundé swathed in a light mist.

The clipped voice of the Djibouti controller came in. 'You lot awake down there? Here you go; we're about there. Take over control when you're ready and look after them. They're our favourites. We want them back in one piece.'

One of the DG controllers turned to his fellow operator. 'OK, buddy boy, our turn to drive! We'll begin our run at 17.20 hours. I'm told they may have ground-to-air down there somewhere, but the Commander says they'll never get their act together in time. We'll be in and out of there before they even hear us coming.'

'Gotya!' his colleague said. '17.20 it is.'

Both men slipped on their headphones and mikes, took over full manual and voice control from Djibouti and began taking the UAVs down in a gradual descent, one heading out across the ocean to the east of the island, the other to the west in a great arc. At 3,000 feet, the UAVs levelled off. The men checked positions and turned their aircraft towards the island.

'17.19. Sixty ticks.'

'Yip.'

•

The 4B-7 from the east headed towards the northern madrassa site and dropped to five hundred feet. Immediately above the site, it released one of its two container bombs. At two hundred feet, a small explosion peeled open the container as though it was a ripe banana, releasing as it did a confetti-like cloud of leaflets, which floated gently down across the site in the still evening air. The UAV then turned north, rose to two thousand feet, and flew over the north-east coast township where it dropped another container of leaflets. The plane rapidly climbed to 10,000 and headed north towards Djibouti.

The second UAV swept in from the south-west and released a leaflet bomb on the southern madrassa site and a second on the town. It, too, then turned northwards and headed towards home.

Both controllers switched the planes to automatic and took off the headsets. 'I don't mind dropping bombs that are harmless,' one said.

'Yeh. I know what you mean. I had to send a couple of Hellfires down over Somalia recently. Not nice, I can tell you. Mind you, in some ways it's like it isn't real. You just have to pretend it's a video game, just like those things we practise on.'

'I've heard that before, but that's a bit worrying when you think about it.'

'I guess so. I suppose you've just not gotta think about it at all.'

•

The low, rapid traverse of the UAV across the town and over the top of the Mirabilé in conjunction with a single, high-pitched explosion took the beleaguered residents of the hotel by surprise. They rushed out into the car park. Above the town, in the evening sky, they could see endless bits of paper twisting and turning down to the ground.

'Mon Dieu!' said Madame Lemessurier. 'Confetti! What's 'appening?'

'Leaflets,' said Em. 'We're being sent a message.'

'And look!' continued Madame. 'We 'ave our own confetti coming down into my car park.'

They watched as four pieces of paper settled gently around the Mirabilé van.

'A miracle!' Madame said. 'A Mirabilé miracle, and they like my Mimi! Look. Four bits of paper and we 'ave four people – a good omen, is it not? It's my 'ubby at work!' Her face dropped. 'Oh! No! I forget – 'ole in the 'ead! There's Mr Abdullah. That's five!'

'No, Madame,' Chris said, 'you were right first time. It's still magic. There *are* only four of us. Mr Abdullah left a while ago on his travels again. He asked me to apologise and thank you for your hospitality and patience. He left some money for you. I think he may not be coming back.'

Madame nodded slowly. 'Right.' She turned to Anna. 'What we 'ear, my dear, is very strange… but no theories! And now, I will gather our four papers.' She scurried across to the hotel van and with a proprietary air picked up the four leaflets. She came back over and handed one to each of them.

The leaflet was in English on one side, and the national language on the other. It contained five short statements:

TO THE PEOPLE OF THE ISLAND OF IVUNDÉ

1. GREAT BRITAIN AND THE UNITED STATES OF AMERICA HAVE AGREED TO HELP RETURN IVUNDÉ TO THE SOVEREIGNTY OF ZIAŴALA. ALL MEANS NECESSARY CAN BE USED, INCLUDING FORCE.

2. YOU ARE ADVISED THAT ACTION WILL BEGIN 24 HOURS TO 48 HOURS FROM MIDNIGHT, TODAY (THURSDAY).

3. ALL CITIZENS MUST REMAIN IN THEIR HOUSES. ANYONE IN THE OPEN WILL BE REGARDED AS AN ENEMY COMBATANT.

4. WHEN THE EMERGENCY IS OVER, IT WILL BE ANNOUNCED ON NATIONAL RADIO AND BY LOUDSPEAKER FROM A VEHICLE WHICH WILL GO ROUND THE TOWN. ANOTHER VEHICLE WILL GO ALONG THE NORTH COAST. AT THAT TIME, YOU CAN LEAVE YOUR HOUSE SAFELY, BUT DO NOT GATHER IN GROUPS OF MORE THAN THREE.

5. ALL WEAPONS AND AMMUNITION HELD OR OWNED BY ANYONE MUST BE LEFT ON THE GROUND AT THE FRONT OF BUILDINGS.

Felix Q. Mzinga: President of the Republic of Ziaŵala
Gen. Frank Carter: Commander, USA/UK Ivundé
Task Force.

They read and reread the statements.

'Oh, dear!' said Anna. 'I wonder how those fellows up there are taking this. They're sure to have copies.'

'Mmmm. I think they are going to be *very* sensible,' said Madame, peering up the road at the trio. 'I know them. They will melt away, and we will sit tight, n'est-ce pas?'

WRITING ON THE WALL

Bluster, empty rhetoric, the screams of a condemned man: these thoughts coursed through the Colonel's head as he sat in the shade of the hangar building reflecting on the President's pronouncements on National Radio that morning. The Colonel felt quite relaxed about it, even amused. No-one would ever come to the fool's aid. The British and the Americans would never contemplate it. They'd use warm words and then would look away. Indeed, how could there be anyone so foolish as to support a corrupt dictator in his attempt to suppress a home-grown religion-based uprising on a tiny island? Even China – the country's most loyal ally – had turned its ships around mid-ocean and headed back towards India. They'd wanted nothing to do with it.

So assured was the Colonel of his analysis that he'd told his team, the back-up men and, over their radios, the local militia manning the roadblocks, that there was absolutely nothing to worry about. What they'd heard from Mzinga was all hot air, bravado, a complete load of nonsense.

And so, when, in the dying light, a UAV, appearing seemingly from nowhere, came sweeping low over the hangar and then on across the town, it came as a great shock to Mohd Reza Mahil. He looked up into the evening sky and winced in disbelief as a snowstorm of leaflets descended onto his base and, a little to the west, another onto the town.

A leaflet fluttered past his face, twisting this way and that way, scarcely an arm's length away. Instinctively, he flung out his hand and caught it mid-air. So easily was it done that it seemed to him that this had to be his personal copy from the Almighty. It was something committed to paper; it had a permanence; it had to be taken seriously. Manic histrionics from a corrupt dictator on the radio were one thing, something arriving in this almost magical, theological way was another thing altogether.

He read the five statements quickly and closed his eyes. He *couldn't* have got it all wrong. He read them again; the answer was the same. What he was looking at wasn't from a deranged man: it was far too rational, too precise, too unemotional. In any event, it was quite beyond the capabilities of Ziawala's tiny, ill-equipped air force to deliver anything using any sort of aerial vehicle.

He propped himself up against the hangar wall to draw what support he could from the cooling metal. He needed to think. The calculations of his backers had also gone awry. They had dismissed out of hand the possibility of any external intervention. They'd counted on the world viewing the Ivundé affair as a simple extremist takeover, a religious squabble on a benighted bit of rock in the Indian Ocean, and one which pragmatism dictated was best ignored. Yet why was it that the Chinese, with their network of spies across the country, had fallen for the story, while those pariahs, the British and the Americans, hadn't? And why had they chosen to drop their leaflets right on *his* base? They knew something. But how was that possible? The precautions he and his team had taken to ensure secrecy had been watertight.

At no time had he ever doubted that taking on the government of Ziaŵala with its ill-disciplined forces would be an easy matter. Victory was assured. Now, however, it seemed he and his men would have to face a trained international expeditionary force. The rag-tag of a local Ivundéan militia he'd inherited would melt away even before the first shot, and the North Koreans – Infidels all – he didn't trust. They'd certainly fight if Pyongyang instructed them to, and they'd cause mayhem with any invading force, but would North Korea ever issue such instructions. To do so would be an admission they were on the island and, worse still, that Zhou was in their hands and was helping them.

As for his own men, they would also stand and fight, but ultimately it would be futile. Many of them would be killed to no purpose. No. It was pointless wasting *them*, or his personal team, himself even, on a lost cause. He needed to get out, and onto the Qaaem, and take his people with him. At least he'd get credit for saving them. He'd also have Zhou's data and actual samples, so something of value might yet be salvaged from this whole business.

As he headed into the hangar with leaflets for his men the sudden realisation struck home that Goliath, his trusted lieutenant and friend, was now trapped in that hangar in the north with those DPRK thugs. He thrust a bunch of leaflets into Abdel's hands for distribution and hurried to the radio room.

Goliath's response was immediate. 'Colonel, sir, I am being required to using only English.' The Colonel could hear the tension in his voice and the deliberate mistakes in what he knew was Goliath's almost perfect command of the language. Someone was in the radio room with him, listening.

'Are you on loudspeaker?' he asked.

Goliath's reply was terse. 'That's right. No. Everything is calm here. We have all heard the radio broadcast and have received leaflets. I am being told we are ready for whatever happens.'

The Colonel could hear whispered voices in the background.

'What's happening, Goliath? Can you talk?'

'I must end now. We are waiting for other messages.'

'Leave,' hissed the Colonel in Farsi. 'Get out!'

The link was cut. Goliath would try to get away, he knew that, but those people were hardly likely to let that happen. They'd kill him and dump his body in the bush for the hyenas and jackals or feed him to the sharks. He knew too much. His very presence would put the DPRK into an impossible position.

The Colonel's next move was to contact the Qaaem, which at that moment was hovering just below the surface five nautical miles off the east coast. The captain confirmed he'd heard the President's speech on the radio and had informed his link in Socotra he had registered a low flying aircraft of some kind heading south-west.

The Colonel read the contents of the leaflet to the captain, switching into Farsi at key points to ensure all the modalities and implications were understood. Then, when he began to explain why it was impossible to hold the island against a disciplined military force, the captain cut him off impatiently and ordered him to get all his men back to the madrassa site and await further instructions.

41

SLICED TWICE

The two C17 Globemaster transports were lined up on the runway. The base commanders spoke briefly to the two squadron leaders and handed each a copy of the revised instructions that moments before had come in from London and Washington. They wished both leaders luck and retreated to their Mini Moke, where they sat in silence, watching as the giant planes roared into life and rumbled down the runway, with scarcely fifty yards between them. At the point of no return, the first, then the second, lifted off. At five hundred feet, already well out over the Indian Ocean, and looking like gigantic flying whales, they tipped to the left and, swinging around, headed westwards.

'That's it,' said the American commander. 'I think, my friend, it's time to say our prayers. Some support from the Almighty at this time would not go amiss.'

•

At 2100 hours, the UAV controllers in the Djibouti operations room picked up the signal from the Globemasters as they approached the island. They powered their Predators up to sixteen thousand and switched into the Globemasters' communications channel to eavesdrop on the chat amongst the unsuspecting aircrew. What their compatriots and the Brits got up to down on Diego Garcia was always good entertainment. It had trade value, and made for great gossip when they were in the bar or relaxing by the pool.

As the C17s reached the twelve nautical mile mark out from the island, Duane Womble called the Djibouti base commander on the intercom. 'Globemasters arriving ten thousand, three-five-zero, sir… dropping to a thousand and 220 knots… sending a visual to you right now.'

•

The captain of the submarine was climbing down from the conning tower onto the deck when the C17 arrived. At first, he thought it merely a rumble of distant thunder, which was quite common at that time of year. Instantly, though, it was above him, a lumbering, roaring monster. His panic was momentary only. He looked up as the Globemaster's black shape, stark against the blanket of stars, headed westwards. He recognised it immediately. While it was no threat to his vessel, it certainly *was* to the endeavour he was a part of. It was confirmation they had all misjudged the situation. He clambered back up the ladder and down into the submarine.

Had he stayed on deck tracking the dark shape a mere second or two more, he would have heard the engines of the plane throttling back as it dropped even lower. In the light from a crescent moon, he might even have made out over to the west the dark shapes of men, boxes and bags floating down towards the land.

•

The captain's message to Socotra, in Farsi, was short, simple, direct:

22.10. Transporter – Globemaster – passed. 1,000. Heading west. Island. Instructions? Highest Priority.

He then ordered his crew to take the vessel down to thirty feet; they would have to forgo their sustaining nightly dose of the fine, fresh, salt-soaked Indian Ocean air.

•

'My boys and their gear on the way down. Beat your lot!' Bobby said, sitting at his screen in Djibouti as he refocused his Predator's forward cameras on the west coast beach area about a third of the way up the island.

'Thirty ticks and mine'll be in place, too. Anyway, it's a cheat! Mine got further to go,' his fellow controller said plaintively, as the second Globemaster, which he was monitoring, swooped low over the northern madrassa site and on out over the ocean. 'Hey! Would you look at that?' he continued. 'That put the fear of God into that lot down there. All the lights on the site have gone out!'

'Yup. All scrambling to get under their beds right now,' Bobby replied. 'Don't blame them; I'd do the same. Those things make one hell of a row, ear-drum-bursting at that height!'

Now over the ocean, the northern C17 began a long sweeping 180 degree turn and headed back towards the island, aiming for an area of level ground three miles south of the northern madrassa site. As it approached the drop point, it slowed, and one-by-one, men fell from the back of the plane in a tight disciplined line. With all sixty-one floating safely down, the Globemaster turned to the south-east, where it joined up with its fellow C17.

Both planes climbed to 36,000 feet and headed east, back towards Diego Garcia.

•

And thus it was that, by midnight, seventeen hours after President Mzinga's announcement on Ziaŵala National Radio, and just seven hours after the arrival of the leaflets, the island of Ivundé had been quarantined into three parts: the northern third of the island, including the madrassa site and the north-east coast communities; the southern third of the island, including the southern building site and the town; and, the middle, containing the mass of the island between; an area, effectively, of no-man's-land.

42
BIG BANG

Duane called in the Djibouti Base commander. 'You gotta see this, sir.'

'OK. What am I looking at?'

'Northern site, sir. Twenty-odd individuals. Two large trucks – there, top left – then something smaller over here. They're all being loaded up.'

'What're they loading?'

'Can't tell.' Duane looked across to his fellow controller. 'Bobby?'

'Dunno. Boxes of some kind, looks like.'

'OK. That's promising,' said the commander.

'There *is* something odd, though,' Duane added. 'We've got an electronic twitch... there, just behind the small truck. Oops! It's on the move... into the truck.'

'Got it. Interesting. I think I know what it might be. Keep tracking it.'

'Site lights out,' Duane added. 'Aaaaaaand away they go! We have a mini-convoy.'

They watched the three vehicles leave the site and slowly head along the track westwards towards the north-south road, the smaller one sandwiched between the larger trucks.

Two hundred yards or so before the junction with the main road, the vehicles came to a halt.

'What're they up to now?' the commander asked.

'Stopped. Now some guys – seven, eight – running up the track towards the junction. One sec. I'll just refocus forward… nope, nothing there.'

'Where are the nearest Brits right now?'

'About three miles south, sir. Static. I can probably get a visual angle on them.'

'Don't bother. That's fine. That lot won't know about them. How about that radio pulse?'

'Still in the smaller vehicle.'

Five minutes later, the ghostly figures were back and the vehicles on the move again.

'OK. Crisis moment coming,' said the commander as he watched the progress of the vehicles. 'Duane, I confirm our earlier discussion. If the convoy turns south at the junction towards the Brits, we are authorised to hit the vehicles. We'll have ten minutes' leeway. I'll talk to the DG commanders and we'll all jointly confirm those instructions. If they turn north, we smile, relax, get ourselves some coffee, and let them get on with it.'

'Understood, sir… well, sort of,' Duane replied. He activated the Predator's firing protocol and brought up the laser crosshairs. 'But if I might ask, sir, what's it all about? We've heard a rumour they're North Korean military and they've been backing up terrorists. They'll only end up somewhere else doing the same thing again. Why not zap them and take them all out?'

The commander hesitated; he always liked the men under his command to know why things were as they were. 'Well, here's the thing,' he said slowly, searching for a way of expressing it, 'the US and UK Governments have decided there are *no* North Koreans on the island, and there never were any. I know! Don't say it! That *is* the position. We may think differently. The truth is that we want whoever it is we are looking at down there to escape, and—'

'North!' It was Bobby who saw it first.

'Thank God for that!' said the commander, visibly relieved. 'Crisis over. I figured they'd do that. It's just I had a niggling fear they might have been inclined to be macho and head south. Good. Anyway, they'll now head up to the coast. That NK sub we saw yesterday should reappear close in – about the same place – and those guys should disappear onto it. We expect that radio bleeper will go with them. Right, it's time to contact our people and give them the good news.'

As he turned to leave the room, Duane yelled out, 'Wait, sir! Ai yai yai! Gotta see this... talk about July Fourth!'

The commander turned in time to see a series of white and green flashes filling the screen. 'Bloody hell! What the eff is that? Where?' There was panic in his voice.

'Construction site, sir. Looks like it's been blown sky high. Bobby... you think?'

'Yep. Certain.'

The commander's panic subsided. 'Sorry guys, my apologies for the language. For one dreadful moment I thought it was the convoy. OK. In fact, that could be very convenient.'

'How come, sir?'

'Well, they've destroyed all the evidence. Here's the thing: we don't want to know they were there at all or, more accurately, we don't want them to know that we know they were there.'

The two operators smiled wanly at each other, and turned back to their screens, shaking their heads. It wasn't only politicians that came out with such abstruse, tongue-tying, sense-defying statements.

•

At 0100 hours, the instructions relayed through Sanaa to Socotra and on to the captain of the Qaaem were precise and definitive: they invited no response, no querying. The Colonel and his three lieutenants, Goliath, Idrissa and Abdel, were to leave immediately and get to the submarine, bringing with them paper and electronic versions of Zhou's reports, along with rock samples used by Zhou during his work. All other electronic and paper documentation relating to their stay on the island was to be destroyed beyond recovery. They had until 0530 hours to get to the beach. After that, the Qaaem would leave without them.

The twenty-strong detachment was to remain and do whatever was necessary to create a twenty-four-hour diversion while the submarine with the Colonel and his lieutenants on board got well clear of the island and was out into the deep ocean.

The final instruction was ominous and chilling. Under no circumstances were the Colonel, or any of his immediate lieutenants, to be captured alive, or the material they had fall into enemy hands.

Colonel Mahil listened in silence as the captain relayed the instructions. He grunted assent. There was no point in arguing or telling him that Goliath was certainly already dead. His political masters would shrug and simply see that as a problem out of the way. They wouldn't be concerned that the foot soldiers who would be left behind might end up shackled in some foul-smelling prison and subject to all sorts of degrading treatment. The men weren't a problem: they knew nothing.

The information that enemy paratroops had almost certainly landed on the island, with some possibly moving north and others south, added great urgency. The Colonel ordered his men into the hangar and instructed the radio operator to repeat the message from the submarine. He neither expected, nor got, any objections. He ordered Idrissa and Abdel to destroy all electronic and paper documentation while he, himself, sat with the men who were to remain, planning their diversionary strategy and tactics.

At 0200 hrs exactly, the Colonel, Idrissa and Abdel left the madrassa building site in their Land Rover. They headed into town at high speed, past the road junction to the Mirabilé, and north on the main road.

An hour later, a truck left the hanger building and headed into the town, leaving the building site deserted, and a much-perplexed night watchman sitting in his hut outside the gate, wondering when, or even if, he was going to get paid.

RETRIBUTION

Each man gathered his parachute up, slipped silently through scattered coconut palms and casuarina trees, and across a belt of deep Christ's-thorn up onto the murram-surfaced road.

Major Foley counted everyone in. He then sent five men back down onto the beach and into the water to retrieve the gear and supplies, while the others he led down the road to a point where the bush was impenetrable to the left and there was a clear view to the water on the right.

He selected and despatched three teams of four: one to conceal itself two hundred yards to the fore, the second back up the road to the junction to the east coast, the third across to the trees and beach area to the right. Two men were then sent seventy yards down the road to lay two heavy-duty stingers across it.

The rest of the men cut thorn bush and laid it across the road to create a crude barrier. The stingers would ensure any vehicle would lose stability and speed as the tyres shredded. The thorn bush would then bring it to a halt.

Thus prepared, they all settled in for what the Major fully expected would be a long and uneventful wait. He was mistaken. Thirty-seven minutes later, the forward team sent through a red alert. 'Soft-top Land Rover passing, doing about twenty. At least two. No obvious weapons. Seems to be nothing following.'

'Everyone!' the Major shouted. 'Land Rover. Two! May be armed.' He turned to his captains. 'Here, with me. Now!'

His men rapidly slotted into their agreed places either side of the road, some lying, some kneeling. The Major moved to the middle behind the thorn barricade, flanked by his captains. They stood, in complete silence, their M203 assault rifles raised, watching and tense as the headlights of the Land Rover, flicking up and down, slid around the bend and came into the straight.

•

Idrissa was on vehicle duty that night. The Colonel was sitting next to him, a light sub-machine gun across his knees, Abdel was hunched up in the back, clutching his AK47; each of them, in his own way, praying there would be no-one out there waiting for them in the dark, in that God-forsaken place. If there was, the Colonel knew it could only be where the east coast road branched off towards the bay. Only a singularly incompetent military strategist would choose anywhere else. And the idea that there might be soldiers marching down the road towards the town in the middle of the night was fanciful in the extreme.

And so, when the Land Rover bounced round the bend and jolted across the stingers, the Colonel was totally unprepared. Any danger point had to be at least four or five hundred yards further on. And yet, there, in the headlights immediately ahead, was a thorn barricade across the road and, behind it, five men with weapons pointing directly towards them. Idrissa instinctively slammed on the brakes. The Land Rover skidded and slid sideways, coming to a halt in a shallow ditch at the side of the road, the engine still running.

'Turn around! Go back!' screamed the Colonel. Idrissa was already in reverse. He took the vehicle backwards up onto the hump in the middle of the road and began heaving at the steering wheel to force it south.

Abdel, wedged in the back of the Land Rover, had caught sight of the roadblock over the Colonel's right shoulder, and now, as Idrissa wrestled to turn the vehicle round, he was ready. He could see nothing in the blackness out of the back of the vehicle, but he would deter pursuit. He raised his AK and fired into the dark.

'No! You idiot! Don't!' It was too late. The Colonel's husky scream was lost in the noise and the flash of the returning fire from behind the thorn barricade. Abdel was struck instantly and flung backwards up against the Colonel. The vehicle went bouncing and sliding towards the bend. Idrissa had finally lost control. 'Tyres gone, Colonel!' he yelled.

'Keep going! Off the road. Left! East!'

Idrissa had little choice in the matter, however. The vehicle was now in the grasp of forces he could not control. It was sliding sideways. He braked fiercely and then accelerated and forced it into the ditch on the left-hand side of the road and up over a small rise into the thorn bush.

'No control, Colonel!'

'Keep going! Keep going!'

The vehicle finally came to a shuddering stop scarcely off the road, wedged between a rock and a thorn tree. It was a misshapen wreck; the windscreen had gone and the soft top was in shreds, its frame a twisted, flattened metal skeleton, with a few tattered remnants of canvas. Miraculously, the vehicle was still upright.

'Idrissa, out! I will check on Abdel.' The Colonel knew exactly what he would find. He'd heard the soft tearing sound as the bullet passed through Abdel; it was a sound he knew well, and then there was the hiss as the projectile flew between Idrissa and himself and out through the windscreen.

'Dead!' he called out from the mangled rear of the vehicle. There was no emotion in his voice. He had to remain calm and controlled. 'We must move,' he continued.

'But Abdel?' said Idrissa, dazed, unable to grasp the enormity of their situation. 'We need to bury him… a small ceremony at least.'

The Colonel already had his compass out and his backpack on. 'No! They will find him and make proper arrangements; they are like that. Get two bottles of water out of the front. Quickly! They may not risk coming in here until it's light, but we must hurry. We do not have much time left to get to the beach.'

With only the Colonel's small torch to guide them, they moved off, threading their way through thick thorn bush and over foot-bruising patches of raised sharp-edged rocky scree. They'd gone no more than about twenty yards when they were flung violently forward as the vehicle exploded behind them, flames shooting up into the sky, carrying with them streams of multi-coloured sparks.

'Colonel!'

'The Land Rover. Come. We must move faster!'

•

Their progress slowed as the thorn bush grew denser. It tugged at their clothes and held them back; it punctured and scratched their arms and legs. The Colonel knew the road across to the bay had to be close and so, when they stumbled into the open onto the forestry track, relief flooded over him. He checked his compass. 'I don't understand what this track is, but we should follow it north. The road must be very near.'

Half-marching, half-running, they now made rapid progress. The Colonel, his torch pointing down at his feet, didn't see the Land Rover until they were right up to it. He froze and put one hand behind to hold back Idrissa. He moved his torch up. 'No-one,' he whispered. He shone the light over the vehicle. It looked modern and in excellent condition. This wasn't something someone had abandoned.

'This is another surprise, Idrissa, and this time a blessing. It may be an omen from on high. If we can get into it, can you make it go?'

Idrissa tried the doors and climbed up onto the step on the driver's side and peered in through the window. Using the Colonel's torch, he looked at the dashboard.

'It's very modern, Colonel, with computers. I think I may not be able to start it, but I can try. We will need to break in.'

The Colonel looked down at his watch. 'No. Leave it,' he said firmly. 'The road *has* to be very near. We can manage.'

•

Just before five, as a faint glow suffused the sky to the east, the two men made their way over the sandy rise and down onto the firm sand of the bay. The Colonel stopped. 'Here. This will serve our purpose.' He faced the ocean and began waving his torch with a circular motion to the right for five seconds, and then to the left. He repeated the movements, and again. 'That will be sufficient. The sea is calm. They are expecting us and will come to pick us up.'

They stood in silence waiting, straining to hear the sound of an outboard engine.

'I think I hear something, Colonel.'

'Yes. That'll be them, and it is now time for me to tell you something in case things do not work out well for us when we return home. I do not understand why we have not succeeded here, but you are not at fault. You have done well – and so did Abdel and Goliath, God rest their souls. One day, I pray that you and I will work together again and achieve great things.'

'Thank you, Colonel.' But the words hadn't registered; his brain was locked into the darkness ahead and to the rattle of the outboard motor as it grew louder. How desperate he was to get off this dreadful island, this place where everything had gone so well, and then so badly.

The Colonel continued, 'We must wait until there is a returning signal from the water's edge. We cannot be too careful in—'

Idrissa felt the Colonel brush very gently against him as he collapsed onto the ground at his side, his torch, still lit, falling with him and jamming up against his face.

'Colonel? Colonel!'

Idrissa knelt down. The Colonel's nostrils were translucent in the torchlight. Above them, between the staring eyes, he could see a large hole. Blood was oozing out. Idrissa's panic was overwhelming, uncontrollable. He rose and ran, zigzagging down to the water. He'd swim out; he could swim well; they'd meet him out there.

A bullet struck him in the left shoulder and flung him forwards, and a second in his side just below his shoulder blade. He was pushed violently face down into the calm ocean water. He tasted the salt on his tongue, and he was still.

The shadowy figure of a man, wearing night goggles and carrying a suppressed, sighted, bolt-action rifle emerged from the sand dunes above the beach and walked down to the Colonel's body. He bent down, checked the contents of the Colonel's backpack and put it to one side. He straightened out the body and methodically went through his flak jacket pockets until he found a small plastic box.

And, as the tinny rattle of the two-stroke motor came to a stop at the water's edge, the man picked up the Colonel's backpack, straightened up and walked casually up the beach into the empty darkness of no-man's-land. Swinging loosely by its strap in his right hand was his rifle.

Once over the rise at the top of the beach, he made his way along a pre-planned route through a scattering of low thorn bush to an area of impenetrable, tangled undergrowth, which dropped steeply away into the darkness. He stopped and opened the backpack. One-by-one, he threw each of the fist-sized rocks it contained down the slope. He dropped the empty backpack into a dense patch of bush over to his right. He then took the plastic container from his pocket, opened it and took out a micro-card, its miniscule terminals glinting in the starlight. He dropped the empty box onto the ground and crushed it with his foot. He held the micro-card for a moment or two and stood staring ahead into the blackness. He grunted, and then carefully placed the card in the sleeve pocket of his jacket.

THE AMERICAN

In the early hours, a plane had thundered overhead, rattling all the doors and windows of the house. They had retreated to the inflatable, climbed in and settled entwined for warmth and mutual security under the light canvas cover. Scarcely an hour later, there were two short bursts of what Danny declared was certainly automatic gunfire. This was followed by an explosion. The doors and windows rattled again, and it was at that point they decided they should get away from the house and boat altogether.

'Down the garden, Danny?'

'Yep, but dawn's on its way. Let me have a quick scout round first. I'll be ultra-careful… promise. God knows what's going on out there.'

Stifling her inevitable protest, he eased back the side of the boat cover and peered out. There was a faint smell of wood smoke in the still air mixed in with a strong, acrid smell of burning rubber. Everywhere there was silence, utter silence. Even the early morning song of the cardinals and weavers at the far end of the garden, rejoicing the arrival of a new day, was missing.

He pulled himself up onto the side of the inflatable, rolled, and dropped to the ground in a crouching position alongside the trailer. He edged around the twin outboards and in through the back door of the house. Once inside, he relaxed, straightened up and retrieved his binoculars from the bookshelf. He went to the front door, opened it slowly and, down on his knees, crawled out onto the gravel.

He was almost at the top of the driveway when he heard voices, low and hushed. They were coming from somewhere to his left down towards the road junction. He turned and crawled across Rosalie's flowerbed to the far corner of the garden. The voices were now much more distinct. He listened; something didn't make sense. While the individual words were inaudible, he was quite certain they were men's voices and that they were using English. More remarkably, one of the voices, he was certain, had a distinct British south-west accent, something he'd become well-acquainted with during their many visits to Rosie's father in his retirement cottage in Dorset, down on the south coast, and during the many evenings they'd all spent together in local hostelries.

He lay flat and parted the minyara hedge gingerly stem by stem to avoid breaking any of them and getting the white, sticky, stinging sap on his hands. He now had an unimpeded view down the road. Sitting at the side of the road, bathed in the early morning light streaming up the east-coast road he could see four men. They wore multi-terrain camouflage clothing. One had a greeny-brown beret, the others green caps with ear flaps. Lying by their sides were what looked like assault rifles. The man in the beret was talking into a small field radio.

After a moment or two, and not believing his own eyes, Danny crawled back across the garden and down the driveway to the house. He propped himself up against the front wall. Before he did anything else, he needed to think. 'When you have a problem, start at the start,' Rosie would say, or sometimes it would be 'if something's a puzzle, then unpuzzle it, forwards and backwards' Now, he had both a problem *and* a puzzle. '

First, the men weren't locals – he could see and hear that. Nor were they Arabs; he could see and hear that, too. Second, they spoke the Queen's English – well, some reasonable version of it. He still needed a clincher, though, and the plane in the night held the answer. It had come in so low, it sounded as though it might rip off the roof of the house. There also had to be corroboration and that was the gunfire and the explosion. The answer *seemed* obvious, yet he still needed to be cautious. Rosalie often said that when he was certain things were obvious, he'd still often end up with five as the answer. In this case a five could be a deadly mistake, and so he ran through the facts a second time, and a third. The answer came out the same. There was no getting away from it; nothing else fitted.

He closed his eyes, whispered the Lord's Prayer and stood up. And, with the day getting brighter by the moment, he walked up the driveway and out onto the dusty road. He looked back at the house, hoping desperately that she was still safely hidden away in the inflatable. Then he began making his way down the middle of the road towards the men, his hands visible by his sides, sweat running down his forehead, obscuring his vision.

•

'Major, code orange message. Watch. North,' one of his captains called from the side of the road. 'No panic.'

'Something coming?'

'Some*one*. Seems they've got an American, for God's sake!'

'American? Ridiculous! Can't be. What're those guys on?' He walked over to the radio man. 'Let me speak to Richey.'

He listened for a moment 'You sure – *and* a woman, you say? What do you mean?

'OK! Of course, both! No. You stay where you are. I'll send someone up.'

Ten minutes later, a man and a woman came into sight walking down the middle of the road, followed closely by one of the captains. When they were twenty yards or so out, the Major signalled the party to stop. He waved his hand over his shoulder. The captain nodded, and the three continued down to where the Major was waiting.

As he listened to their experiences of the previous twenty-four hours, the Major's natural wariness fell away. This pair – although nutty – were obviously genuine. He'd make a final check, though. 'Theo,' he called over to his radio man, 'you heard all that stuff. Get me a COMSAT profile, pdq.'

He turned back to Danny and Rosalie. 'You say you have a contact in the town and can talk to them using some sort of walkie-talkie?'

'Yes! No! Not really a walkie-talkie, sir,' Rosalie said. 'It's *much* better than that! It's not ours, and we can contact

323

three people. One is Teddy Bear – not their real name, you understand. We don't know who that is. The other two we *do* know. We went to a building site in the north with them. Twice! They're staying in the hotel.'

'Do you mean Jamieson and Freemont? You know their first names?'

Danny nodded vigorously. 'Yep. That's them: Dr Chris and Dr Em.'

'And that's *Emmeline*, you understand,' Rosalie added.

'And this equipment you've got?'

Danny pulled the radio out of his backpack.

Theo, who'd been watching, was quite fascinated by the exchange. He'd never seen anyone run circles around the Major before. But now – involuntarily – he was sucked into the drama. 'Bloody hell! Where did that come from?'

'Theo!' the Major said sharply. 'You know the rules! *And* a woman present! Remember the slippery slope: mild ones begat the heavy stuff. More importantly, communication suffers.'

'Sorry, Major. Apologies, madam. It slipped out. I'm just surprised to see one of those here.'

The Major looked over at Danny. 'Where *did* you get it?'

'Dr Jamieson – that's Dr Chris – gave it to us to use in emergencies. I think he got it in Djibouti.'

'Theo?'

'Make sense. They'll certainly have them there.'

'But there is a problem,' Rosalie added quickly. 'Only Danny and me can use it. If anyone else even touches it, it'll… *fry!*'

'Fingerprint coded, Major,' Theo added.

The Major nodded and turned to his captains. 'Right, chaps, the miracle we hoped for may be at hand… perhaps…

possibly. We might just have got ourselves access to on-site Intel. Theo, COMSAT?'

'Yep. Coming through right now. Not a lot: *US Marines, Lejeune, Jacksonville, three years' service, honourable discharge with meritorious service medal. Married.*'

'Visual?'

'Yep. Spot on.'

'OK. Enough!' The Major turned to Rosalie and Danny. 'Our apologies for the overkill. We can't be too careful.'

THE OCCUPATION

'**D**r Chris! Wake up! Wake up! It's me! We 'ave one big, big problem. Très mauvais!'

He forced one eye open and reached out for his travel clock. He missed, and sent the clock skittering off the bedside cupboard towards the balcony doors. 'Lord help me!' he muttered. 'It's got to be the middle of the night. What in God's name does she want?'

'Hang on, Madame,' he shouted, as he rolled sideways off the bed. 'One second… need to make myself decent.'

'Yes. Yes. But decent doesn't matter. 'Urry, 'urry fast!'

He slipped on shorts and a T-shirt and unlocked the door. Madame Lemessurier was hunched down – squatting almost – fully dressed and visibly shaking.

'Come in. Over here. Sit on the bed. Lots of deep breathing. Don't say anything yet – not *one* word. There's nothing that can't wait a few seconds this early in the morning.' He sat down on a chair facing her. She was rocking back and forth, hands on knees, head down and shoulders hunched up. She was breathing deeply.

'OK. That'll do. Head up. Now, tell me.'

'There are men, so many men, and with guns, out in my car park! I can see them, and I can 'ear them. Foreigners!'

'Right, and what are they doing?'

'Walking around, and some sitting by Mimi, talking!'

'Could you hear what they were saying?'

'No. A strange language.'

'And have they come into the hotel at all?'

'No, but they are peeping into my reception.'

'OK. Then I'm sure we can relax. Nothing dramatic is going to happen. What we do first is go and wake Dr Em.'

'But they'll see us!'

'Not if we go out through the emergency exit into the garden, and round. It'll be OK. We can knock on Dr Em's window; she won't mind.'

•

Par for the course, Em thought, as she pulled back the curtains to find them standing there, stretching up and peering in. She swung the window up on its side hinges. 'Good morning, you two. What you up to out there in the dark?'

'We have a situation in the car park, Em,' Chris replied. Madame will explain. Better still, perhaps she can show us.'

'A situation in the car park? Right. Let me get something on. I'll come out this way; I've been practising.'

Madame took them back along the path and around the end of B Wing to the front corner of the building. She thrust out her arm to hold them back. 'Stop!' she hissed. 'Look! You see, there, through the bushes. Why are they here, Dr Chris?'

'No idea.' But even as he said it, he realised he knew exactly why. 'Of course,' he continued, 'we can go and ask them.'

'Good idea, and it's my turn to do that,' Em said, sounding more confident that she felt. 'You'll remember, Chris, what you said about women in situations like this. I'm sure you're right. I'll give it five minutes, though. We need a bit more light. I don't want to emerge from the gloom like some ghostly apparition. They mightn't react too well to that. In the meantime, Madame, what about Anna?'

'Oh, mon Dieu! Anna! I forget; I can do that. I know a way round the front over the rocks.'

'And remember,' Chris said, 'when you wake her up, make her do some deep breathing. Two minutes. No panic.'

'Oui, and also no theories! I shall go now.'

'Good idea, and can I suggest we meet up in the kitchen in about half an hour?'

'But they'll see us go in there!' Madame said.

'True, but they know we're here. They'll expect us to appear at some point. It would be very strange if we didn't. We don't want them coming to look for us.'

'I think the light's a bit better now,' Em said, as she watched Madame scurrying off into the gloom.

'It'll be OK. Just remember, rule one, smile; rule two, do what they tell you, rule three, smile again.'

Em went through the emergency exit door and along the corridor into reception. She paused a moment and whispered a prayer. Then, taking a deep breath, she walked out into the car park. The low-key chatter amongst the men ceased instantly.

A man in military uniform came over towards her.

She smiled at him.

He pushed his open right hand up towards her face. 'Stop! Key!' He pointed over his shoulder towards the hotel van.

There was tension in his voice – whether from apprehension, or ill-intent towards her, she couldn't be sure. It was certain, though, that he wasn't in the mood for conversation.

She smiled. 'The van? One moment – I will get it. It's in the office.' She walked back into the reception area, round the back of the counter and into Madame's office, praying the key was in there somewhere.

Running along the wall under the window were two wooden battens from which hung a line of room keys attached to small circular, numbered brass tags. At one end, and standing out from the others, were two keys on a ring with a white plastic tag. She leant across and unhooked them. On the tag was the word *MIMI* written in small spidery capitals.

Out in the car park, the man was waiting. He took the keys from her and gestured her back in.

Chris was waiting for her. 'Not a happy meeting, I think,' he said.

She grimaced. 'You can say that again! He certainly wasn't up for chit-chat. He just wanted the key to the van.'

'Odd they should want that. They've got their truck.'

•

'Breakfast?' Anna asked with a wilful cheerfulness when they walked into the kitchen. Well, just about. 'I was going to have yours, Em… if you didn't come back.'

'Anna!' Madame said reproachfully. 'Not a good time to make a joke like that.'

'It's all right, Madame,' Em said. 'I was always quite safe, and you know, in times of stress, it helps to be cheerful.'

'Oui, and my 'ubby says that all the time. But it is so difficult. Anyway, what do those men say? Did they tell you why they are 'ere?'

'No, and I really don't think they're concerned about us at all. My guess is they just want us not to bother them.'

Madame Lemessurier sat staring at the back of her hands and nodded slowly. 'Mmmm. I understand,' she said softly. Her head came up. 'You three,' she said, her voice steady and clear, 'I 'ave been thinking. I will 'ide my bread rolls and some other things. We may need them. Those men, they'll get very 'ungry. Yes. They can 'ave my bananas – and water! 'Ubby is telling me just that... and 'e's also saying I must thank you all. But now, please excuse me.'

She stood up and strode off behind the free-standing cupboards towards the back of the kitchens.

'Odd,' Anna said, 'or am I just imagining things?'

As she said it, two men came into the kitchen from the restaurant. One went off around the cupboards to the back of the kitchen. The other stood silently, waiting for his return. The first man was back almost immediately. He shook his head and took a heavy revolver from a holster under his arm. He waved it at the three of them sitting at the table.

'Out!' He pushed round behind Chris Jamieson and jammed the barrel of the gun into his neck, grabbed the collar of his safari jacket and yanked at it, heaving Chris up. The two women jumped to their feet, and all three were bundled into the restaurant and pushed over to the far corner, where the man in military uniform was sitting on the low wall.

He looked directly at Em. 'This all your guests?'

She was alarmed and looked over at Chris. He simply smiled and gave a slight nod.

'Yes. All of them.'

'Good. Others are now coming to join you.' He jabbed his finger at Jamieson. 'You will sleep in this room with the new people. These two women will stay in the kitchen. Now, all of you, get your personal requirements from your rooms and bring them here.' He gestured to the two men standing guard in the doorway to the restaurant to let them out.

'You realise he thinks I'm the proprietor; I'm Madame!' she said, as they made their way along the ground floor.

'That's right. God knows where she's hidden herself away. She obviously managed to squeeze down behind something in time. We need to get back quickly, find her and sit on her. If we can keep her out-of-sight, she might just be a useful card to have up our sleeves.'

'You serious? Not much of a card, poor woman!'

'I'm not so sure. I think that may be underestimating her. We've another card, of course... our radios, and that reminds me, you'd better take them into the kitchen with you and put them somewhere safe, out of earshot of those guys.'

•

Ten minutes later Chris was back in the restaurant. Em and Anna were in the kitchen. He'd wait a few minutes before attempting to join them. Meanwhile, the aid agency people had arrived in the hotel van and were being manhandled in one-by-one. Each, in turn, had the plastic tie snipped off his bound hands.

When Thierry came in, Chris gestured him over.

'It's critical no-one mentions Madame. These guys don't know she exists. They think my colleague, Em – in the kitchen with Anna – is the proprietor. Could you warn your colleagues?'

Thierry nodded. 'Of course, but where's Madame?'

'God knows! Hiding somewhere. She disappeared about half an hour ago.'

As they were talking, Chris could see over Thierry's shoulder a line of men bringing heavy weapons and ammunition boxes in through reception and piling them up next to the reception desk.

'Something going on?' Thierry asked, without turning around.

'Not a lot. They're just bringing stuff in. They're settling in for a longish stay, I'm guessing.'

But he knew exactly what was happening: the hotel was about to be turned into a fortress.

46 EXIT

Chris was ordered into the kitchen to help the women bring mats, mattresses and crates of bottled water from the storeroom and into the restaurant for the newly arrived occupants. He found the women talking quietly outside the storeroom doorway.

'Is it safe for you to be here?' Em asked.

'Sure. Officially sanctioned! Been sent to help. Did you find Madame?'

'Yes. She was at the back of the storeroom. She was very calm and said she had somewhere safe to go and would now do her Houdini act! She asked us to leave some water and a few rolls out for her for later. Then, off she went. You can see for yourself. Go on in, between the mattresses to the far end.'

He squeezed himself sideways along a waist-high stack of single, polythene-covered mattresses, and was in touching distance of the back wall when he saw the low metal door. He stretched forward and pushed the handle down. The door swung outwards into the middle of a stand of long-established plantains. He stepped out and moved to the outer rim of the plantains. Between the fronds, up to his right he could just see the outer edge of the restaurant wall, and to his left, over towards the ocean, the baobab tree. Immediately ahead was a section of garden path, emerging at one end from dense tangled bougainvillea and disappearing at the other into thorny undergrowth.

Both women were smiling broadly when he emerged from the storeroom. 'Good, eh!' Anna said.

'Amazing. And I know *where* she's gone. I suggest we do some thinking. In the meantime, we'd better get started on these mattresses and water.'

As Em and Chris were carrying a mattress through the doorway into the restaurant area they heard a low-pitched buzz. 'Lord! Radio!' she hissed. 'Hold on.' She dropped her end of the mattress, grabbed at her shoulder bag and disappeared round the back of the free-standing cupboards. She reappeared almost immediately. 'It's both of them at it, Chris. Mine's Bess, yours is Danny and Rosalie. Yours is on top of the mattresses, left-hand side.'

Chris edged alongside the mattress, recovered his radio, and switched it on.

'Chris, where you been?' asked Danny. 'You had us worried.'

'Apologies. Somewhat occupied. Something happening up there?'

'Yes. So much! We need your help. Me and Rosie are with some British soldiers up near the house. They want to speak to you.'

Chris burst out laughing. 'Nice joke, Danny!' But even as he said it, he knew he'd made a mistake. It made sense – and besides, Danny didn't really make jokes. 'Sorry, Danny,' he added hastily. 'I didn't mean that the way it came out. Just surprised.'

'It's OK, Chris. Hang on. Here's the commanding officer.'

'Who am I talking to and where are you?' The voice came through sharp and authoritative.

Chris recognised the clipped abruptness of tone he'd always associated with the military. 'My name's Christopher Jamieson and right now, to be precise, I'm in a hotel storeroom on the edge of the town.'

'And the hotel would be?'

'The Mirabilé.'

'You have a diplomat there with you. Name?'

'Dr Emmeline Freemont.'

'Good. Right. My name's Foley. I'm the Major in charge of a Sabre B SAS group. I have an R and D here. They live nearby. They say you'll know where we are. We have UAV data and we can see that the building you are in has been occupied by a group of armed men. Is there anything you can tell us about the situation… numbers, disposition, weaponry, civilians?'

Chris Jamieson ran through the events of the morning.

'And my best guess is that, right now, there are twenty-five professional Middle East military in here, along with thirteen aid people, and four others. The place has been fortified, with heavyish weapons – machine guns I'm guessing – along the first floor, both wings, overlooking the car park and facing up towards the town. They've posted two men, one either side of the ground-level restaurant, looking out over the gardens towards the ocean.'

'Anything else that might help?'

'Well, this may be something or nothing, but there's an old fire exit from the kitchen storeroom into the gardens on the east side. It comes out into the middle of a large clump of plantains, just next to where the kitchen meets an accommodation wing. Only four of us know about it.'

'Certain?

'Yes.'

'OK. Sounds useful. Hold a moment. Theo, you see it?'

There was a brief silence.

'Yep, Major, got it.'

'Good. Thank you, Dr Jamieson. We need to do some planning. We'll speak later. Out.'

Chris pushed his radio between two mattresses and edged back to the storeroom entrance, where Em was waiting for him.

'What did Bess want?' he asked.

'She says she's been listening to communications back and forth and British soldiers have landed somewhere. It sounds fanciful to me, a bit of wishful thinking.'

'It's not. She's right. I've just been speaking to the Major in charge. They're up near Rosalie and Danny's place, and I'm guessing those two will have enlisted!'

47

ROSIE'S HEIST

'Excuse me, Major, sir,' Rosalie said. 'Soon, no shade. We'll melt. Our house is just up that way a teeny bit. You can do your business there. It's cool, and I've lots of Darjeeling, and even a good supply of home-made you-know-what.'

The Major looked over towards his second-in-command, eyebrows raised. 'Shade and Darjeeling sound good. Not sure about the you-know-what, though. Let's get an update, first. Theo, anything?'

'Stuff coming right now. Brig wants a word with you.'

The Major went over to the side of the road and put on the headset.

'Foley. Right. Understood. Twenty-four hours. Heavy, but we'll find a way. Out.' He waved his captains over. 'Let's get out of this infernal heat.'

•

Rosalie's living room was festooned with men, some snoozing, some on their backs staring blankly at the ceiling, others polishing their assault rifles, a glazed look in their eyes. There were more of them in the bedrooms, up the hallway, out on the veranda, and even some under the boat.

Rosie nudged Danny. 'Bet you're jealous! So many young, strong men in my house, and all so handsome, eh!'

He laughed. 'And *so* tired, Rosie! They couldn't get up to any hanky-panky, even if they wanted to!'

At the kitchen table, fortified with a never-ending supply of tea, the Major and his captains were considering their options. The message from the Brigadier had been unequivocal. *North done. Move south. No hostage negotiations. No civilian casualties. Twenty-four hours max.*

'As usual, he doesn't want a lot,' said the Major. 'It's a walking-on-water job, and it's got to be tonight.'

'Twenty-five miles at speed would be crippling,' said one of the captains. 'If we went at a more leisurely pace overnight and rested up in the morning—'

He got no further. Rosalie had been listening. 'Excuse me, sirs, *we* have transport.'

The Major looked up. 'Transport? You mean the inflatable back there?'

'Yes… no… we've also got a Land Rover. It's hidden on a forestry track in the bush just across the side road.'

The Major shook his head.

'I know. It's not big enough,' she continued. 'My idea is different. Hang on.' She waved impatiently at Danny. 'Danny, come over here. They need transport. Can we help them get to town?'

'How many? When?'

'About fifty… before dark,' said the Major.'

Danny pursed his lips. He glanced up at the kitchen clock. 'Rosie?'

'You know what *I* think, Danny. Can we *do* it?'

'Sure, if we move right now.' He turned to the five men around the table. 'You say the town's deserted. Does that mean safe? Can we just drive in?'

'Yes, except for the immediate area round the hotel place. Why? What're you thinking?'

Rosalie was developing her agitated look.

'OK, Rosie,' Danny said. '*You* tell 'em!'

'Excuse me.' She pushed an upright chair in between the Major and his second. 'I need paper and pencil, Danny.'

'Right,' she continued, 'what we do is drive through the forest in the Land Rover – half-hour max. We need to take two really good drivers with us – dirt road drivers, not crap tarmac ones!' She drew a line down the paper. 'Then, we come onto a big road here at the edge of the town and we go past the clinic, like this.' She added a rough arc-shaped line. 'Your guys then break into the Public Works Department yard – here. You'll need our big wire cutter thingies for that.' A final large square with a cross at one side was added. 'And we just heist a couple of the big PWD trucks… easily hold thirty each.'

'And don't forget gas. We'll need to get gas,' Danny added.

'He means *petrol!*' she continued. 'Anyway, we bring 'em back; we load up with your men; we go off back through the forest into the town. We'd be there about five. Gotta move now, though.'

The Major sat shaking his head, staring at the diagram. He was trying desperately not to laugh.

'You think it can't work, Major?' Rosalie asked, plaintively. 'It's easy. Honest. Two and bit hours max for the whole deal.'

'No. Don't get me wrong. It really *does* sound possible. It's just we're being taught a lesson here and these lads love that. There is *one* thing: we have these photographs of the central area of the town – scarcely an hour old – and, apart from a lorry in the hotel car park, bottom edge – here – we can't see anything resembling a large vehicle.'

Danny leaned over Rosalie and peered at the photos.

'That's OK,' he said. 'See that black patch, there? That's the PWD workshop roof. The lorries are under there, six or seven, maybe. They always put them under cover just before the rains.'

'And there's a drivable track running through the jungle stuff?'

'Through the *bush*. Sure is,' Rosalie said. 'It's from the old days. Danny keeps it clear. You think it'd be OK for the trucks, Danny?'

'A squeeze here and there is about it. We might have to take off the odd branch or two. We can take our chainsaw.'

Major Foley turned to his second. 'Seb?'

'Sounds to me like it's the only show in town.'

The Major nodded. 'OK. Agreed. Heist team, it is.'

'And we'll have to come!' said Rosie. 'You need *me* as the adviser on the way back with the trucks – I know where it'll be an especially tight squeeze – and my Danny will drive the Land Rover.'

The Major smiled. It was an irony he was well-acquainted with, and often to his embarrassment. For all the fancy technology at his disposal it was, as always, trumped by local knowledge.

48

STAND-OFF

The two PWD trucks rolled off the forestry track, banged across the ditch and bounced and slid in clouds of dust down towards the clinic. The jacaranda trees were just coming into red and purple bloom on either side of the road. They were quite magnificent, though the men in the trucks were too conscious of their own mortality to notice, or even care.

The vehicles made a final juddering slide into the clinic compound, one to the right, the other to the left. Six men leapt out of the back of each and dropped to their knees facing the building, weapons at the ready. Three from each group then moved cautiously into the building.

Seb Hursley emerged two minutes later. 'Nobody, Major – well, not alive. There's a body in the fridge with the medical supplies… a male, two holes in the right shoulder.'

'OK. We'll need to deal with that pdq. It's going to be a problem in this heat.'

'Not at the moment, Major. The fridge's a paraffin job. We can deal with it later.'

'Old tech. Good one! OK. Planning.'

They gathered round a small table in the clinic treatment room. On it was an aerial map of the town held down at the corners with weights from the clinic's stand-on scales.

'Right. One more time,' Foley said. 'Bob, you'll take your group down to the ferry area and hold the main road north and south and the jetty. We're going to need that. There's a route down between the houses. Try not to damage any property on the way. The rest of us will take up positions across the road running down to the Mirabilé place. We'll try a simple show of force thing, first. We know they're outnumbered. We'll make sure they know it, too. If that doesn't winkle them out, it's retreat and Plan B.'

•

And so it was. At 1805 hrs exactly, five, ten, twenty, then forty men moved cautiously to the brow of the hill in clear view of the Mirabilé down the slope. They slipped into their pre-planned positions – some kneeling, some lying. And, in the centre of the line, the Major and his second stood, looking down at the hotel through binoculars. There was a collective holding of nerve and breath, each man in the line ready to react at the slightest sign of movement.

The Major called along the line to either side, 'Gordon, Jones, Binks – left. Fredericks, Posey, Wells – right, the first-floor machine gun fellows. If one of them as much as blinks, you know what to do.'

'Main entrance!' his second called out. 'Hold! Three civilians. No! Careful, you lot. They've got AKs, and the guy in the middle is in some sort of uniform.'

'You all hear that?' the Major called out. He looked down at the hotel through his binoculars. 'Uniform is the bossman. We'll have to be super careful. Peters, Smiggles, Gibson, cover those guys.'

'Hold again!' his second called out. 'More. It's civilians this time, hands on heads, and including a couple of women.'

They watched in silence as two armed men shepherded the hostages out by of the front entrance of the hotel and into the car park. There, they were manhandled into a line facing up towards the town. The gunmen stood close up behind them.

'Jones… Wells,' the Major called. 'I'm nervous. You see those two guys?'

'Negative here,' Jones replied, almost instantly.

'A shoulder, sir.' Wells added. 'Light's not good. Risky-plus.'

The Major grunted. It didn't matter. He could now see what was happening. 'OK, all of you, relax. It's poker time. They're playing their first hand. They're showing us they've got hostages.'

And, as if to confirm this, the two gunmen began pushing the civilians back into the hotel.

The Major stood staring down at the hotel and pulling at his unshaven chin. In the still, heavy evening air, it sounded like sandpaper being rubbed against wood. His men had heard it more times than they cared to remember. They knew what it meant: he was thinking… scheming… working out how to do the job. It was time for silence.

The man in the uniform had now reappeared. He was standing to attention in the main entrance to the Mirabilé almost enveloped in dark shadow. He was looking up the road towards them.

'Seb,' Foley said quietly to his second, 'Plan B it is. They're not going do anything dramatic tonight. They'll want to negotiate a safe exit and my bet is they'll open negotiations first light tomorrow. We're not going to let them get into that. Ask Theo to route us through to that Teddy Bear character and onto our American friend. We need his boat down at the ferry terminal asap. Warn Bob that he'll be towing it down the main road.' He burst out laughing and shook his head. '*Teddy Bear*! Lord, would you credit it? Everyone in this place is bonkers.'

•

'That was nervous-making,' Em said, as she sat down at the table in the kitchen.

'*Nervous-making*? Jeepers! I'd call it terrifying!' Anna replied. 'There was a moment when I felt certain they were going to do us all in! What on earth were they playing at?'

'You didn't see what was up the road?'

'You must be joking! I had my eyes closed. Why? What was it?'

Em hesitated for a moment. 'There was a whole gaggle of armed British soldiers – I mean dozens of them, armed to the teeth – strung out across the road just this side of Valli's place. It's my guess this lot are going to use us as a bargaining chip to negotiate a way out.'

'Lord help us! But that's a good thing, isn't it?'

'Possibly, except the British don't normally negotiate in hostage situations. With all these aid agency people here, it'll probably be different, though,' she added hastily. 'Let's hope so, anyway… shhh! Someone coming.'

'What do you make of that then,' Chris said, as he came through to the back of the kitchen. 'A bit nasty really, but there is a bright side. Our guards have now disappeared. It seems we've been left to our own devices... oops! There goes my radio again. Excuse me a moment.'

'Radio?' Anna said. 'What's he talking about?'

'Well, it's a bit complicated. I'll explain later. Give me a moment, I need to check something out with Chris.'

•

He pulled his radio out from between the mattresses. He pressed 4. It was a man's voice: 'Got him, Major.'

'Foley here. Jamieson?'

'Yes.'

'Good. Midnight. Sea. Baobab by the sea wall. We're told we'll need a guide to get through the gardens. Can you help?'

'Not sure. Possibly.'

'Well, we don't have a Plan C. Do your best. Out.'

Chris met Em as she came into the storeroom. 'Tonight,' he said quietly. 'Midnight, by sea, and we've got to provide a guide to get them through the gardens. That *has* to be Madame. Let's hope she comes for supplies. We'll leave a message in a container in the plantains with her rolls and water.'

'And if she doesn't pick it up?'

'Then, it's me, and I've only the roughest idea. Just pray she feels hungry.'

BENEATH THE MARBLE

Madame Lemessurier's long-departed, much-loved husband had spoken to her from his resting place below the white-topped square metre of granite hidden in the bougainvillea, a yard to the fore of the great baobab. From there, he had watched over her and their joint creation, the Mirabilé, for twenty-three years. Under his guiding spirit, she'd been safe and secure.

His message had been clear: '*You are coming to a crossroads, my dear. A time of great challenge is upon you; strength and courage are now needed for a grand endeavour. You must win through.*'

And so, a few minutes before midnight, she had emerged from the security of the baobab and climbed onto the sea wall.

And she now sits there sideways on, her arms enclosing her legs, her head resting sideways on her raised knees. She is looking out into the dark across the still water. She sees the surface of the ocean reflecting in exquisite detail the magnificence of the universe and begins counting the stars. Her view wavers, becomes unstable; her eyelids flicker. She'll rest her eyes for a moment or two. And now her focus is lost. The reflections of the stars grow faint and are replaced by the figure of her husband standing next to her. He's smiling; his arm reaches out around her shoulders.

'Tin-tin. Strength!' she mutters. 'My time of trial' as come; I 'ave to get the show on the road, n'est-ce pas?'

'Yes, my dear, and I think soon. Listen. Listen carefully to the sounds of the ocean. That is what you must do.'

A faint splash cuts into her dream.

The apparition fades, and she is alert. She sits immobile, listening. She is rewarded by another splash. It might have been a lone sardine breaking the surface as it desperately tried to evade a predatory tuna, but there's another, and then more. They are repetitive, regular, and getting ever closer. She fumbles in her brassiere and extracts a small torch, which she points out to sea. She begins waving it back and forth.

'Cap. Light! Forty, left.'

Hursley peered through the darkness. His eyes were no longer as acute as those of the younger men in his team. He put his hand on Danny's shoulder. 'Shhh. Hold.' The message was passed back to the man paddling at the stern. The inflatable began slowly drifting sideways on the light current.

Danny was the first to pick up the light again. 'Ahead, over to your left… a torch.'

'They can't possibly see us out here,' whispered the captain.

'But they can *hear* us,' Danny whispered. 'There's no breeze. The surface is so flat that every little sound just bounces off and skitters on for ever.'

'Hang on.' The captain raised his assault rifle and looked through the night scope. 'Got it. Oh, my God! There's a woman sitting on a wall waving a torch around.'

'What's she look like?'

'Roundish, firm-featured, middle-aged… sort of strong legs.'

'Madame,' said Danny. 'It's safe. She's your guide, and right now, we need to get paddling again. We're beginning to drift too far. It'll be murder if we don't turn the boat right now.'

Hursley wasn't an instant decision man; he liked a second or two to run things through his head. Sometimes, though, that just wasn't an option. 'OK. Do it. You lot, get your headgear organised,' he hissed back to his team. 'Remember, at the slightest sign of anything, into the water, down, south twenty, and in up against the wall to regroup.'

Danny and the stern-man slowly forced the inflatable round and angled it in towards the torchlight, its movement getting ever more frenetic.

They were a mere twenty yards out when they heard Madame Lemessurier's hoarse whisper. ''Ere! This way. Not down there. You'll 'ave a puncture!'

'She's right,' said Danny. 'We've got to get right next to where she's sitting.'

As the inflatable bumped up against the wall, Madame shone her light down on the eight men in the boat, their faces a patchy black and white. 'Mon Dieu!' she whispered. 'Ubby, can you see this?'

'Madame. It's me, Danny. Don't shine the torch in our faces. We're going to throw a rope up. We've got this end.

Can you find a small tree or a really strong root to tie it to? Do a double-double knot.'

•

Five minutes later, the men were grouped around the baobab. Danny meanwhile had pushed the boat off from the wall, paying out the rope as it went. Fifteen yards out he let down a stern anchor.

Madame was addressing the group. 'My two doctors and my 'ubby – he lives just behind me here – 'ave asked me to take you on the fast lane to my 'otel and to bring people back. I can do that, but no torches. There are bad men in my restaurant watching. You must stay close behind me. You must say nothing. I know the way like the back of the 'and… and don't clink-clank those nasty guns!'

TERMINATORS

One would need to stumble into them to know they were there: eight men, silent, squatting in a tight semi-circle at the back of the darkened kitchen....

Sensing the time was right, Seb detached himself from the group. He crept to the entrance to the restaurant and lay flat on the smooth, cold concrete. He slid forward inch by inch until he had a clear view. To his right, in the faint, reflected glow from the low-power emergency lighting in reception, he could make out along the walls of the restaurant the recumbent forms of the hostages. At the far end, silhouetted against the starlit sky, were the backs of two gunmen, each sitting behind a small table, one either end of the low outside wall. The man on the left was slumped forward, head down, seemingly oblivious to the world, the other, on the right, was leaning forward, chin resting on his hands.

To his left, just inside reception, Seb could see the backs of two other men squatting behind a machine gun mounted on a tripod. It was pointing out into the car park through the open hotel doorway. The ammunition belt was draped over a box and out across the marble floor.

Back with his team, Seb allocated each man a number and a task. He chose carefully. One and Two were to do the primary job, while Three and Four were to deal with the men at the entrance.

The four were then to rouse the hostages one at a time and instruct them to move silently to the kitchen where Five and Six would lead them out to Madame and take up positions at the back while she took them through the gardens to the baobab and boat. Two short trips would then be required to take them across to the ferry stage.

Seb Hursley himself would remain just inside the doorway into the restaurant as the back-up. He would stay there until the Major's diversion had started and would then fall back and wait for Madame to return. If things fell apart, everyone was to improvise, a process they were all well-acquainted with, as very little ever went to plan.

•

At 0058, the men moved forward and formed a semi-circle around the entrance into the restaurant. At 0059, Seb tapped the first two on the shoulder. They moved out into the restaurant and up the central area towards the two men at the corner tables. Three and Four then felt a light touch and they, too, moved out and silently took up kneeling positions, each with a silenced Sauer pointing at the head of its designated target. Five and Six waited behind their captain.

At 0100, the men at the tables facing out into the Mirabilé gardens, one asleep, the other half-asleep, felt one last twitch of existence as the life was snapped out of them. An AK47 slid across a table. The men in reception, behind the machine gun, instinctively turned to look, and their heads were side on as each was struck by a bullet from a silenced pistol. They were both flung forward, one onto the machine gun, the other onto the ammunition feed. There was a metallic clatter. The Captain and his men froze. One... two... five seconds. There were no voices and no movement out along the corridors. All they could hear was the growing panic-stricken whispering of the hostages as they were woken one by one, and then pushed and pulled towards the kitchen.

As the final man left the restaurant, the captain switched on his radio. 'Done, Major,' he whispered. 'Your turn. We're off!'

'In ten.'

A volley of shots rang out from just beyond the car park randomly peppering the front of the hotel, followed by volleys from the left and the right. Seb Hursley calmly made his way through the storeroom to the exit door. He closed it quietly behind him and felt his way through the stand of plantains where he joined Five and Six to await Madame's return.

•

It was around 0200 when the men along the first-floor corridor, hunched behind their various weaponry, were visited by their leader. In a calm, matter-of-fact way, he informed them that four of their comrades were dead – executed silently in the night – and that the hostages had disappeared. He was at a loss to explain the bursts of automatic fire in the dead of night, which, as far as he could tell, served no purpose.

His men knew at once that their opponents were certainly infidels, possessed of evil spirits, and had practised their black arts. How could it be otherwise? Their leader knew differently. There had to be a logical explanation. And, as he stood in the half-darkness looking at the lines of deserted mats arranged along the walls of the restaurant, and then over at his two men lying forward across their tables, as though asleep, he knew he'd been outsmarted, and a high price had been paid. Final victory, though, was yet his. The submarine with the Colonel would surely now be well on its way out into the deep ocean, heading north. He and his men had done what was required of them. Their mission was complete and successful. Prayer and wisdom were now needed.

As dawn broke, the leader gathered his men together in the reception area. He talked to them quietly. They said a brief prayer, laid their personal weapons neatly on the low tables and then, one-by-one, walked out into the car park with their hands on their heads.

Outside, they organised themselves into two rows and watched in silence as two men, one unarmed, the other with a holstered side-arm, appeared from behind the mango tree and walked down the slope towards them.

PART SIX
HEAVING TO

SILVER LININGS AND CLOUDS

A beaming Meera came swirling out of the customs shed and onto the landing stage, her fine, black hair flickering and dancing in the morning sunlight. 'Good morning, everyone, and it is so good a morning, is it not?' She stood, hands on hips, surveying the gathering. 'Ahhh! You are all tired and all hungry. I know it. But fret not, there is a tasty solution. Behind me, my Mina is in the customs shed laying out a dazzling white, Irish linen tablecloth on the chief customs officer's table. In baskets, she has the finest of rolls and the best samosas ever produced on this island... made by you-know-who. There is yet more. My Wallimohamed is in the car park with the good Bess. In the back of our Toyota are two giant urns, one dispensing tea – fine Darjeeling – and the other somewhere-in-the-middle coffee. Oh, yes, and we even have some of our soldier friends out there for good measure. They say they are here to protect us. But me, *I* think they just want to be fed and watered. I jest, of course! Please, come.'

Chris was sitting propped up against the shed next to Em. 'She's cheerful,' he muttered, 'and she's right. You know, some of that somewhere-in-the-middle coffee sounds about right to me. Coming?'

Em nodded. 'Darjeeling for me. I've got a migraine starting up. Coffee would be a disaster.'

As they emerged into the morning sunlight from the side of the customs shed, Bess called them over. 'Dr Chris, Dr Em, come, meet one of my soldier friends.'

'Drs Jamieson and Freemont, I believe,' the Major said. 'I'm Foley. Thank you for your help; it was a game-changer.'

Em smiled. 'I guess it's what we're paid for. Anyway, Major, can you tell us what's going to happen now?'

He shrugged his shoulders. 'I know what *we've* got to do; anything else is speculation. We're keeping the non-residents here while some of my men are going off with the aid people to collect their belongings. Others are winkling out the ferry crew with the assistance of the Immigration Officer; he claims he knows where everyone is. We then send you people off to the mainland, and the residents home. At midday an island-wide curfew begins. And that's it. Look, could you do one last thing for us?'

Em nodded. 'Of course.'

'We need the hotel woman kept here for about an hour. There's military stuff lying around her place... and one or two other things we wouldn't want her to see. My people are on the clear-up right now. If you and the New Zealand girl could then bring her up, and pick up your own stuff, that would be very helpful.'

'I'm sure we can manage that,' said Em. 'Chris?'

'Certainly. In any event, we need to discuss something with the locals before they go off.'

'We do?' She looked at him askance. 'What?'

'You'll see. Come on.'

•

'I think you're owed an explanation,' Chris said quietly to the small group of local residents huddled together in the shade at the front of the customs shed.

'Hang on, Chris,' Em said. 'We don't really need to go into this… I mean, does it matter? Anyway, we can't be sure.'

'Sorry, Em. I think it *does* matter and I *am* sure. Life's too short. Just tell Burnett I wouldn't shut up. He'll understand. He knows the cost of taking me on.'

He turned back to the others. 'A brief digression, if I may. There's an island in the South Pacific. The first westerner to visit the place a couple of hundred years ago called it Pleasant Island, and that's exactly what it was. But now, perhaps two-thirds of the place resembles a moonscape. The place has been torn apart by the mining of guano, phosphate used as fertiliser. Once blessed by nature, that island is now cursed by mankind…'

'Guano's bird do-do, isn't it, Danny?' Rosalie whispered.

'Shhh.' He nodded.

'The island's financial reserves, once huge, from the guano, have been eaten away. Ninety percent of the population are squeezed into a coastal strip… and many of the island's young people have left for new lives in New Zealand, Australia, and elsewhere.'

He hesitated for a moment. He needed to link things in

and neither underplay nor overplay the position. 'What you need to know,' he continued, 'is that perhaps a fifth of your island along the upper east coast, and in the seabed there, consists of rock and sediment containing deposits of rare-earth minerals. They are the raw materials of the new age, critical in communications, space exploration, weapons technology, mobile phones, medical equipment, aircraft engines, clean energy. You name it! What you've seen on the island is the struggle to control those minerals. You can forget the religious thing.'

'Are you saying this place may end up like that guano island, Chris?' asked Danny.

'Not exactly. The mountain slopes along the upper east coast will be mined along with the adjacent coastal seabed. There may be patches of radioactive slurry affecting the seas there. But your island is much, much bigger than the guano place, and most of it will remain largely untouched. I'm guessing there'll be other changes, though: a new tarred road running up to the north, perhaps an airstrip somewhere on the north-east coast, a deepwater port somewhere near here. The town will become bigger, with foreign mining companies and their workers running around the place. There'll have to be new schools and a hospital here to replace the Clinic, with another in the north. To put it bluntly, the modern world is about to descend on the island.'

Em felt the urge to intervene, but she knew it would be a waste of time. He was right; he was even underplaying the situation. She'd seen herself what had happened in the Amazon basin and in the Congo.

Chris continued, 'I'm sure this will still be an attractive place to live. It just won't be the same attractive place... In any event, I'd like to apologise for the part I've played in this matter, not that it could have been stopped, and at least we *can* say that these developments will be in the hands of more principled organisations and people, than might otherwise have been the case... Well, we can hope that.'

Rosalie was nodding and looking at Danny.

Meera looked remarkably cheerful. 'Hey-ho,' she said brightly. 'Thank you for that oration, Dr Chris, and please don't chastise yourself. We guessed something like this was afoot. And, after all, it will all be good for business.'

Madame joined in. '*I* don't want any more business, and I'm certain my 'ubby doesn't want more people photographing 'is fine, white piece of marble.'

Valli opened one eye. 'That son of mine, Johan... yes, I think we will open a shop in the north for him. He will become a great businessman, and Mina, my girl, you will have a big hospital to run! Bess, you will be her commander-in-chief!'

'Yes, indeed,' said Meera. 'Every silver lining has a cloud.'

Em smiled. Meera was being smart – or foolish. She wasn't sure which. 'I think, Meera, perhaps you mean the other way around?' she said gently.

'Yes. Yes. You are so right. But Valli likes it that way round. He's a half-glass-full man, you see.'

PART SEVEN
SCUPPERED

TRAPPED

It's an early Friday morning. A light dusting of snow lies frozen on the ground; the air is crisp, clear. The moors will be perfect. Martha will come. It'll be good for her to get out a bit. He'll take his camera, with its fine new lens. There are sure to be endless animal tracks.

'Telephone, dear,' she calls, disturbing his train of thought. 'Some man; he didn't say… way back voice; I sense I may have heard it somewhere before. I dread to think.'

He picks up the phone. 'Good morning. Christopher Jamieson. Can I help you?'

'Hello, Dr Jamieson. It's George.'

'*Lord protect me!*' Chris whispers under his breath.

'You'll remember,' George continues, 'we met at Marlborough house – that island business. Marvellous job. We knew the moment we saw you that you were just the man for that one. Yes, indeed, quite excellent. Anyway, did you know that Dr Freemont – our lovely Mavis – has been moved on, well, *up*, I suppose? She's been transferred to Cheltenham. I'm not sure it's her favourite posting, though… misses her judo pals, and it's further from her mother's place. Anyway, I'm sort of doing her job here and I'm—'

He'll cut in, just in case.

'Yes. Hello, George. It's nice to hear from you, and I'm sure Dr Freemont will adjust. Promotion is a great thing for one's psyche. Give her my congratulations and thank you for calling to let me know.'

'Doctor, no! Wait! There's something I need to ask you. There's a little job we have in China. I think you may have been there before. Just up your street.'

'Look. George, I don't wish to sound impolite, but before you go any further you need to know I'm just *not* interested. I've family commitments, and I need some R and R. That island thing took it out of me. Please, find someone else, and do give my regards to Dr Freemont. Thank you for calling.'

'No… no… Dr Jamieson! Please! Please don't hang up! It was the Director himself, who told me I must contact you. It's three-line-whip stuff. You must listen. Please!'

'George, the chances of me changing my mind are less than absolute-zero… and that's a state of affairs that doesn't exist. Anyway, my wife would murder me. I'd be no use to anyone, dead!'

'Absolutely! And that's right. I really *do* understand. My wife's the same. It'd be mayhem. But, if you could *just* listen, that would definitely be enough. I promise.'

'OK… China?' He makes his exasperation obvious.

'Well, yes. That's it. There's a problem. Oh! One second – my other phone. I have to answer it. Please, please, don't go away.'

'My apologies, Dr Jamieson. That was the Director's PA on the line. The Director would like to invite you down to lunch with Dr Freemont to talk something over.'

'George, I think I've made myself clear. *Please* give him my sincere apologies. I really can't do anything else for you. That's all there is to it!'

'Please. Please. Hang on!'

In the background, he hears a hurried mutter of voices.

'My apologies, again, Dr Jamieson. I've now been informed that I can tell you that there's a package up near the North Korean border and someone has to go there and collect it. Simply that. Oh! Apologies again, Dr Jamieson, someone's now whispering in my ear... yes... I'm now told it's three packages – two big, one small – and I have a note here from Dr Freemont saying you'll understand and she just *knows* you'll want to help. She is saying something about you agreeing one night in a hangar. I daren't ask what that means!'

Jamieson closes his eyes as the dreadful realisation hits him. 'When do they want to meet?' he asks tersely. 'Can it wait a week?'

'Dr Freemont says Monday, 1100, lunch at the Director's club, the Triple C – off the Mall. She says it's already booked. Hands are tied!'

He swears silently under his breath. 'So be it, George,' he says wearily. 'Thank you.'

He puts down the phone, takes a deep breath, turns and heads for the kitchen to face the wrath of his long-suffering Martha. She'd come round – always did – but he needed to roll out a good story, one she might actually believe.